12:07

THE SLEEPING

Movies of the coast and the burning cross
Hold tight as your fingers glow
Give another place another time
Watch the traveller, see things you didn't know

Other Books
by
L. Sydney Abel

Gruvel the Great
Ish-ish Ishbochernay
Keypya and the Pirates
Kingsley and the Spider
Marge and the Wobbly Onkey
Mr. Runkin's Secret
Patrick Duck
Smelly Nelly Welly
The Evergreen Wolf

12:07

THE SLEEPING

L. Sydney Abel

SPEAKING VOLUMES, LLC
NAPLES, FL
2015

12:07 THE SLEEPING

ISBN 978-1-62815-267-8

This book is for

the souls that made it back into the light and for those that didn't

My acknowledgements are, as always, to Karen

Five, look at me as one who is indebted and sad at the same time

PREFACE

You know when they're here... you can feel them.

Remember; stay awake, because when they come for you and take you, there is no coming back. If you give up fighting then you might as well give up living.

To James — come sit next to me.

We are who we are and not who we wish to be.

Table of Contents

CHAPTER ONE

1974

Recipient's eyes were clamped open. Electric filament burnt 12:07. The number had been given. Many have the number. But only one is for this Messenger.

2013

James would fight for his life many times—always winning and yet always fearing, that anytime soon, it might be his last.

James' hands rushed to what felt like a mouth full of grit, as he began spitting out splinters of white. His fingers felt for his teeth which weren't there. A coughing that tasted of blood shook him awake.

Sitting up and feeling disorientated, James again felt for his teeth. He only needed to know they were there; his fingers and tongue satisfied his doubts.

There was heard a snap of a latch from the closing of a front door.

James groaned as he slumped back into the warmth of his mattress. He cocooned his ears with the sheets. *Mr. Green has probably entrapped a lonely female OAP*, he thought. *What a sly old dog. He might be a nice old man, but even a nice old man can have a devious mind. No doubt he's plied her with drinks, got her sloshed and is now about to...*

The stairs creaked as only his stairs did. *Was that my front door?* The thought assaulted him loudly, sending the hairs on the back of his neck to bristling attention. *Is someone coming up my stairs?* That thought was no less attacking. Doubt terrified his mind; *no-one could be. Besides, the door alarm is on.* That thought didn't give the reassurance it deserved. He felt insistence to panic, to want to go and see… but he couldn't. His body was held rigid with a ridiculous fear.

The door handle to his bedroom turned, making hardly any sound. But he heard it. The door gently swung open, squeaking, as only his door did. He tried hard to turn and face his intruder. Sweat began to cover his body, as the corner of the bed sank when something sat down. He wished and wished for his limbs to move, but they didn't. It was in those moments that all became still. Nothing could be heard apart from his own rapid breathing, which was loud enough to wake the dead.

It's nothing; it's nothing, his mind kept blurting aloud. Yet the bed still had a weight to the bottom corner. *Why wasn't it moving? What was it waiting for?*

James felt defeated. He was dying in his own claustrophobia. A crushing dread pressed upon his entire spirit. Then there was movement—a crawling up over the body movement—and whatever moved was now rested on top of him, lifelessly heavy.

Haunting visions of every kind entered his mind until he could stand it no longer. He gave everything he had, somehow managing to pull all his energies into vocal brute strength.

James yelled. At first there was nothing, as his face contorted into Quasimodo ugliness. But the scream that eventually came out was so torrid—as if it had erupted from the fires of hell—that it burnt the oppressive air.

"AAARGGGGGGGGH," spat gutturally violent, shaking the very foundations of his soul.

In fact, the scream was a mere whimper. But to whatever was laying lifelessly heavy, that scream tore through its presence like a slashing blade, sending whatever heard it back to wherever it came.

James now lay in a cold sweat. He was drenched from head to foot. Groping for the light switch he clicked the bedside light on—its burn was trying so hard, but such a small thing could not beat such a great force.

Whatever came only withdrew into shadows, waiting to attack, hiding, and gathering its strength for another try. But as long as this small bulb shone in this large room, keeping up its fight, James felt safe—safe for the time being.

James sat up and wiped his face with the sheets. All his senses were on high alert. Blood pounded a fast drum beat within his chest that resonated through his ears. A surge of adrenalin pulsed through his veins making him feel sexually aroused. He lowered the sheets to reveal a glistening-wet torso. He looked like he'd just spent the last three hours having wild, unadulterated sex—he was sweat-ridden and exhausted, but still ready.

God that felt so bloody real, he thought, looking at his side table—the light of the lamp silvered the title of a novel he'd been reading into gleaming glass shards, making his peripheral vision glitter jaggedly.

Feeling thirsty, he picked up the glass of water he always had there for night time sips. The glass felt unusually cold and wet—his fingers slightly slipping over the condensed surface—as he tried to take a drink. His nose recoiled at a foul smell and his hand responsively released its grip. With a crunch, the glass hit the floor, then in slow motion bounced gracefully, before sending splinters of itself and its sickly, putrid contents, to all directions of the compass, across the polished wooden floorboards.

James propped himself up; his arm supporting his upper body trembled. In complete shock he finally realised that someone or something had definitely come into his room. He had not imagined this. The clock by the bed, with its segmented LED display, flashed repeatedly 12:07:00. Its display should be red, but it wasn't. He looked around his room—everything was in monochrome. He leaned forward and frantically rubbed his eyes till they burned with the fire for living. Then the colour came back. On the floor was a broken glass, its shattered pieces lying in pools of ordinary drinking water. The red LED display now read 02:09:01… 02:09:02… 02:09:03… The stairs creaked, the latch snapped again as his front door closed. It had been another visit.

Half-closed early morning eyes tried hard to focus on the door alarm. Sleepy fingers pressed in the keypad's four digit code, rendering it unarmed.

The latch was held back, the door opened and James blearily looked about.

Mr. Green—from the downstairs flat—stood waiting outside his equally opened door. This bent-double and grey-haired old man craned his gaze upwards and commented: "You should get some sleep." His warm, blue-grey eyes smiled.

James wasn't in any mood to comment, so he nodded in agreement.

"I'm waiting for the post," Mr. Green said, unperturbed by James' standoffishness.

"Are you now," James remarked in a sarcastic tone. "You do know it's Sunday?"

"Yes," Mr. Green confirmed. "I'm expecting good news…" Mr. Green talked away as James tried to look interested, but James' mind was elsewhere.

A white-painted vestibule echoed Mr. Green's cheery voice. Hard ceramic floor-tiles seeped a cold emptiness into an eight foot by eight foot entrance hall. A table that had seen better days—along with a ladder-back chair that flanked it—rested against the only available wall space. A painting of Pollock similarity—which hung like it was upside-down—did nothing to cheer. It seemed to have been placed there for the sole purpose of confusing the day, which was fitting in many ways, as life always confused the true believers in repenting worthlessness. Like the painting, life was just merely dripping away. The entrance door to this stark room remained closed and closely watched by Mr. Green.

Suddenly a flapping letterbox vomited a single white envelope.

"That'll be for me," Mr. Green proclaimed.

Then without hesitation, James did the kindly gesture of picking up Mr. Green's mail and handing it to him. Mr. Green's shaking hands took the letter with care and with a radiating smile on his face, he turned and went.

A few minutes passed while the locks were tested, then a pulsing, piercing siren wail that lasted only seconds proved that nothing living came last night. Two logical questions to last night battled for supremacy. If James had dreamt it, then why was this nightmare slowly expanding? And if it wasn't a dream, then what was it that came? Until he knew these answers, it was pointless suffering more unanswerable questions.

CHAPTER TWO

Monday morning's sky was dark and threatening—rain was definitely coming. Lance hated the beginning of autumn. It wasn't the weather that depressed him, although that was enough to depress anyone; it was the simple fact that his birthday had come and gone—over a week ago to be precise, but he still felt the presence of its misgiving. He had real hatred for his birthday—he didn't know why, but it gave him the strangest feeling that the day didn't belong to him. It made him feel indifferent, so he passed it by without any form of celebration. His hopes were for it to rain today. It seemed fitting in a cleansing way. Today's clouds carried a silver lining.

Lance strode casually into his office. He was so early, he'd beaten his secretary to work, and that was something that very rarely happened. Sitting down he gave a satisfied look. Lance loved this room—his room—where he kept his toys, the things he craved for during his struggling years at college. Some thought the room sparse, and it may well have been, but to the man behind the burr walnut art deco desk, it had everything he required. Comfort things. The desk for instance, once belonged to a wealthy business man in Manhattan, New York, USA. During the great crash of 1929 and on the thirteenth floor of a building, where an office window looked pleadingly upon Trinity Church, a calm man with nothing left to lose, gently pulled open the right side desk drawer and took from it a Colt M1903 Pocket Hammerless. He then placed it into the roof of his mouth and unceremoniously blew his brains out—it was Black Tuesday, October 29th.

The other things Lance possessed hadn't such a dramatic history. But that varied depending on how you looked at them. Most people have stress things, a Newton's Cradle or a Pin Art for example. Lance had something better—a 1962 Fender Jazz Bass. This was not a copy or a reissue or even a Custom Shop special. It was a genuine Fender "pre CBS" (before the sale of Fender to CBS Broadcasting Company), and was very collectable. This baby had two stacked knob pots, giving volume and tone control for each pickup. Around '61 this configuration changed to three control knobs, where two were for the volume of each pickup and the remainder was for the overall tone. Some with the concentric arrangements were still made in '62, so this beauty was rare. It was looked at with Love—the love that had a capital L.

Beep... Beep... Beep... Lance looked at his watch and with a button push, cancelled his reminder. He pressed his desk intercom, sending a deeper toned beep to his secretary's desk. Miss Imogen Swan had just arrived; she was everything a man wanted in a secretary—brains as well as beauty.

She answered into the intercom: "Yes, Mr. Lewisham." It was said in a softly spoken, middle-class, perfect English accent.

"Would you come in please, Miss Swan?"

His office door opened and another beauty appeared.

"Yes," Miss Swan said, entering the office in her coat and still with her bag over her shoulder.

Lance looked into her eyes, she looked into his.

"Coming or going?" Lance joked.

Miss Swan smiled. Everything about her smouldered sexuality, the simple way she said 'Yes' seemed to have sexual connotations.

7

"Could you pop out of the office later for me and collect a small package from the florist's?" he said, with an appealing childish grin.

"Sure, when?"

"Any time before lunch will be fine, if it's not any trouble."

"For you, it's no trouble." She was doing it again, giving him the look she knew he loved. "Would you like me to put Friday's files away?" she said, rolling her eyes towards the filing cabinet.

He nodded and watched her strip-teasingly remove her bag and coat, put them on a chair, and then, with a slow sultry walk, take the files to the cabinet. The bend-over followed. It was the full touch your toes bend, where the legs remain straight and tight, when she pulled on the bottom drawer. It slid out easily; she placed the files at the very front and in no particular order.

Lance's office had two fantastic views. One overlooked the river with its stunning city sights and the other was literally right in front of him. This fantastically formed and curved human sculpture, with a behind that wanted caressing, even tenderly slapping, and most definitely taking, wore a pencil skirt so tight and short that in the position it beheld there was no upper body to be seen. At this moment why would you want to? That's an altogether different view. Pure tall legs in black high heels supported that wonderful display of womanly beauty. Painted nails on slender fingers, belonging to delicate hands, silently slid the drawer closed. Miss Swan stood up and turned to reveal her coveted figure. Her dark hair was tied back in a loose ponytail which left shorter strands to curl and caress around her forehead. She looked the secretarial dream.

She smiled before saying: "Is there anything else I can do for you?"

Oh, yes, there was—but he was a married man. "No. Not at this moment, Miss Swan, thank you," Lance said with regret in his voice. He knew that she knew she excited him. "Just let me know when my first patient's here, that'll be all for now."

She smiled again, turned, and left the room taking her coat and bag with her to hang up beside her desk.

Lance wiped his brow with the back of his hand and sighed deeply. He got up and crossed the room, picked up his bass off its stand and sat in a chair. He held her close to his chest, his heart beating wildly into her resonant wood. She might be getting on in years, but this old rock 'n' roll relic with her original Olympic-white finish that had yellowed with age and stained from gigging in more smokier bar rooms than he could ever imagine, was still a picture of beauty. The dints, chips and partially worn away finish only proved she'd had a truthful life. She looked a true Pastorius, a well-played musician's instrument that was now, sadly, in retirement.

He plucked her open A. It sent vibrations through him that he urgently needed. He didn't need to connect her to an amp. The resonance and sustain of her body was all he required right now. Like a junkie's need for substance—he needed to feel her. And he was doing just that. Her body connected with his, and it felt solid and proud. It felt good. She gave him no illusions.

The trick with Miss Swan happened every morning, albeit variations along the same theme. It was his early morning pleasure and she gave it so well. He knew she'd remove the files and put them correctly away the moment he left the office for some bodily reason. He knew she liked to give him pleasure, he saw it in her eyes. And he really did like that.

In the corner, next to a separated washing facility, Lance has his small private gym. Nothing much, just a few weights and a walking machine. Hanging alongside was a heavy bag. It wasn't just any heavy bag. It belonged to The Rock from Brockton—the great Rocky Marciano—the heavyweight champion of the world, from 1952 to 1956. Lance had a photograph of the man himself, working his hands upon its leather.

Rocky had died two days before Lance's birthday, on August 31st 1969, in a small private plane crash, at the age of only forty-five.

Lance loved to hit the leather, working his hands as Rocky did. It kept him fit and for someone approaching Rocky's age, he looked pretty good. He stood five foot ten and was not over muscular; a toned body to him was every woman's fantasy. He had dark-brown hair too; it all went with the supposedly tall and handsome look. The two things he didn't like about himself was his longish nose and French aristocratic chin. He was very proud of his physique in a quiet, modest way.

He would work his hands later—for given strength—into what promised this afternoon, to be an arduous few hours away from work.

CHAPTER THREE

It had started raining and puddles were forming on the dark grey tarmac paths that led between the rows of headstones. A sombre sky, darkly cruel, weighed heavy in the afternoon light. The mourners came in procession behind the heavy, carried coffin. Black umbrellas shielded them from the rain, protecting the men's suits and the women's dresses. The few gathered around the open grave, their polished shoes sinking slightly into the wet grass. The family of the deceased stood in solemn thought, dabbing at tears with paper tissues. The Vicar, in his dark robes, showed a sorrowful look as he glanced at his prayer book. But the words he spoke were of no comfort, as the casket was steadily lowered into the wet earth. The lips trembled on the faces of the son and daughters as they said farewell to a Mother they loved.

From underneath an old tree, in the far corner of the cemetery, the lonely figure of Lance stood—under his arm was the small package collected by Miss Swan. Staying hidden from view he watched the burial with absolutely no emotion showing on his face. Rain water dripped from the leaves above, onto his head and the shoulders of his black suit. His hair hung wet, clinging to his face.

The Vicar said his last words as the family in turn dropped small handfuls of wet earth into the gaping hole, onto the coffin lid, making dampened thuds upon landing. A solitary lily was softly dropped to land almost perfectly upon the brass plaque. The Vicar then shook the hands of the bereaved and silently left. His precious time was required all too soon back in the chapel for the next family service. After all, the church has to make a living even if it is out of the dead and the grieving.

From his distance, Lance could see the family huddled together—forming one black mass. A short time passed before the mass grew smaller as each family member, with their own thoughts, walked head down to the highly-polished, waiting, black cars. Rain gathered in growing droplets to slide off the car roofs and down the windows, like falling tears. Lance's thoughts were of the years of misery he'd known from the woman now lying deep within the damp earth. Some think that's where you wait sleeping, till you are called for on Judgement Day. Others think that when you die you go straight to God and are judged there and then. He would like to think, and hope that on this occasion, heaven would forget about this one and leave her buried there for all eternity.

The cars drove away passing look-alike others—humble mere reflections—coming to do exactly the same thing. Grief, pain and sadness were adding more grief, pain and sadness. To Lance, the serenity of a cemetery was like a safe haven. It was peace away from everyday toils, to be alone with one's own thoughts. And Lance was doing exactly that, safe for the time being on holy ground.

As he watched, he saw two grim-faced men arrive and quickly shovel the earth back into place, hopefully without being seen. It's not a sight for a distressed family to see. When finished, they left the place as tidy as possible, not an easy task with everything so wet—but they tried their best. The Sexton arrived with flowers and wreaths from the deceased's loved ones, he placed them upon the mounded grave, then left.

For the moment all was still—silent but for the patter of rain on the leaves above. Lance left his place of hiding and walked towards the grave. What he had just witnessed, he wanted to see up close. Standing there he looked down upon the wet brown earth. The cards on the flowers, protected from the rain in plastic envelopes, read goodbyes of love. He read them all; he didn't feel their pain, their loss. Any feelings he had, had turned to regret with the passing of time. Now nothing could be changed, ever. He said his 'goodbye' in an ambiguous tone that left him feeling uncertain of his true thoughts. It wasn't worth saying anything more, and besides, the dead couldn't hear. As he stood there the coldness of the ground seemed to push upward into his bones, leaving him feeling numb. His wet fingers opened the package, and from its damp insides he grasped at a small wreath of green. He tossed the foliage beside the flowers, turned and left. Feeling cold to the core he pushed his fingers through his hair, pushing lank strands up over his forehead to reveal an ashen face. With eyes that would never forgive, he made one last look back across God's acre. Finally she could never hurt him again.

He was sodden when he arrived at his car, a 1969 Morris Minor 1000 four door saloon, which was discreetly parked a few streets away. He opened the door and slid onto the back grey-leather seats, took a towel from a bag and covered his head like a prize-fighter entering the ring. In fact, he felt like he'd just left the ring and was too dazed to know whether he'd won or not. The towel's softness was like someone giving empathy, while rubbing his head and face dry. He slid his jacket, shirt, shoes and trousers off and placed them into a black bin bag. He then dried the rest of his body down, the hairs on his arms stuck on end upon his goose flesh. A sharp glance around to make sure he wasn't being watched, allowed him to remove his socks and boxer shorts. They followed into the abyss like his other discarded garments. Now naked and shivering and feeling freshly alive, he leaned over into the front passenger seat and pulled through to the back a sports bag containing freshly bought clothes. He slipped on new, grey tracksuit bottoms and over his head pulled a matching hoody. His body instantly began to warm up as the soft fleece lining soothed his cold limbs. With new trainers on his feet, he felt ready to face the rest of the day.

Between the front seats he climbed and started the engine—it grumbled slightly as it started. He could now get on with the rest of his life, knowing there was at least one person less in this world that had judged him wrongly. He drove away knowing he had to discard the bin bag. It wasn't long before he sighted a litter bin. He parked alongside, got out, and feeling good about what he was doing, threw away a hardened layer of himself. Now that was done, he felt even more removed from everything that had happened that afternoon. A feeling of shedding a skin, that could never remind him ever again, felt good.

CHAPTER FOUR

It was always lonely coming home to No. 113 Padstow Avenue.

This modest, four-bedroomed, terraced Victorian dwelling was nearly everything the Lewisham's ever wanted. They had a lovely home—comfortable and beautifully furnished. The only thing missing were children; they had wanted children, desperately. They had tried in their early years of marriage, but trying never happened again.

They met in their late twenties: Katherine was small, blonde, beautiful and intelligent, and starting to enjoy life; her years of study at university had provided her with exceptional qualifications in law. With a job in a large company accepted, all was well—she was going to move up the ladder of success. Within a few months the company offered promotion, she took it; her life was geared to a career. She was having a great time. It was work during the week, but at the weekends she would see friends and taste the night life.

Katherine met Lance—her gallant knight—at a friend's Christmas get-together. For the gallant knight it was love at first sight. For her, he was just another guy.

Lance had given her his favourite chat up line, on seeing eyes of a pale Bermuda blue: 'Your eyes are beautiful—let me swim in them for eternity.'

He received a distasteful look. But at least the ice was broken, and he, for once, was telling the truth. They chatted, listened to music and sat together all night. The next thing they knew, it was morning. He hadn't even kissed her, but he'd wanted to.

Half a year passed, and then one night she realised she loved him. It wasn't anything magical, just recognition. She hated being away from him, if she lost him it would be the end of her world.

Engagement and marriage was all within a year. They were so happy; their life was going to be wonderful. Then shortly after their marriage she became pregnant. Everything seemed fine, but life can be cruel and in the sixth month of her pregnancy something dreadful happened. One night she couldn't feel the baby moving, she became terrified something was wrong. She was rushed to hospital and was admitted for tests; the sad news was that the baby had died.

Their lives were torn apart. She had to go through with the delivery, only the end result was already known. A small, lifeless body was delivered and removed—Lance thought it best that Katherine had no visual image of their dead child. He couldn't even bring himself to look.

The baby girl's body was cremated and her ashes were interred somewhere unknown to them, it was what Lance had wanted. All arrangements were sympathetically made by the hospital's chapel priest.

The doctor told them that a tragedy like this can sometimes happen, that they were strong and nothing was physically wrong, so there would be plenty of time to have more children.

Lance, at that time, was a studying gender psychiatrist, he seemed to cope. It wasn't like he didn't care; he just removed himself from the situation. What choice did he have? He had to be strong—strong for her. She wasn't that strong, it took much longer for her to accept. Even now, fifteen years on, she hadn't really got over it. She never would. She used work as a tool—the more time she devoted to her job, the less pain she felt. Work seemed to absorb her grief. That was Katherine's form of therapy.

When it had become almost one year to the date of Katherine's suffering, she looked up the hospital chapel priest. He was a kind man, very young and very understanding. He listened to her plea. She had all the relevant paperwork and after checking his records, he took her to a corner of the church grounds, where he alone had knelt and put in the ground her daughter's ashes and prayed. This time they both knelt. It was something she needed to do, to accept what had happened. She would never forget, but she would try to forgive. Life with love was hard enough, without adding hate. She said a silent prayer to the daughter she wasn't meant to have—her name was Claire. She never told her husband. Every year, on the date of Claire's birthday; she visited and placed a single lily where a small brass plaque rested, simply saying 'Claire, your Mummy loves you'.

In the house everything was just how Katherine left it earlier that morning, feelings of sadness still hung oppressively in the air. She sat on a chair and sank into its deep softness, and burst into tears. She sobbed her heart out, as a week of loss and worry finally broke her. Grief had caused her mental distress and this morning's funeral had made her physically exhausted. She took sharp intakes of breath causing her lungs to ache and her chest to tighten. Tears streamed from her eyes. Salty, they painfully burned her sore lids, and with her hands clasped to her face, she tried to wipe them away. The more she wiped—the more she cried. The salted tears ran in reddened tracks over her lips and down her chin. She tried to control her breathing, but it hurt as she cried uncontrollably. For a long time she cried, until, finally, crying wore her out and knocked her into sleep.

Through the silence, a sound like furniture being moved vibrated through the ceiling. There followed a sudden, loud bang. Katherine jumped up and ran into the hall. Her eyes climbed every stair tread with unease, and met nothing but an empty landing. With a pounding fear she stepped onto the first tread. She didn't know whether to go up and see what had caused the noise or wait to hear if it happened again.

"Hello, Kath," the air whispered.

Katherine knew the voice—was her mind playing tricks? "Who's there?" she called. She didn't know what to expect. Her heart beat even faster—her breathing stopped.

"It's only me!" the air whispered.

"MUM?" shot loudly from Katherine's mouth. A pounding chest, gasping for air, was suddenly aware of what she had called.

Katherine's body jumped, every muscle tensed. She sat up shaking; she'd been asleep, slumped in the chair.

Oh my God, she thought, with her hands clasped to her face. She now began inhaling deep, slow breaths.

Feeling giddy and nauseous she tried to bring her mind into reality. She needed a drink of water. At the kitchen sink she turned on the tap, and splashed her face. Her mouth kissed the fresh, running water as she drank. The sound of water filled her ears as the coldness bit her mouth and throat, quickly removing the feeling of being sick. Grey faced and with trembling hands, she turned off the tap to bring the house into silence again. Time felt, for a few brief moments, like it was standing still.

Katherine went to the stairs again. There was nothing, all was quiet. Hesitantly she climbed the stairs, one tread after another. When she finally reached the top she was starting to feel foolish. She walked into her bedroom; it looked just the same as earlier that morning. The bed still not made, the covers kicked back airing. The indentation of her head remained on the pillow.

Suddenly there was a strong smell of perfume, so strong that it made her head reel. The wardrobe door creaked, then a crack so loud, just like the one she thought she heard before, shocked her backwards. She almost fell; carefully she opened the wardrobe door. The dressing mirror, which was fixed to the back, was cracked from top to bottom. No glass fell, but her heart was in her mouth. The smell of the perfume had gone, and as strong as it was, not a trace could be smelt. She knew that scent, it was her mother's favourite.

Katherine looked at herself in the broken mirror, her reflection distorted into two. "Mum," she said softly. "Thank you. Say hello to Claire for me... tell her I love her." In her mind, a vision of her Mum holding her daughter's hand seemed to give her comfort.

A soft, white feather appeared and gently floated down to rest tenderly in the indentation on Katherine's pillow, it was a simple gesture of her mother's watching love.

Katherine sat on the bed, she hadn't noticed. But she did know, without a doubt, that her mother had just been there.

Seventy-five per cent of Lance's patients had gender-related problems. The other twenty-five per cent were sent to him by their representing lawyers, prior to court appearances. Katherine's company valued his professional evaluation and work ethics.

'Do you remember when...?' was something Lance always asked his patients. It was an exercise for trying to look back through time, to recall anything no matter how odd it seemed, from when they thought their problems first began.

Some were receptive to this question, others stubbornly awkward, and one or two aggressive. It didn't matter to Lance, he was there to help. His time was their time. As much time as they needed.

Katherine and Lance didn't talk about their work to each other. Professional confidentiality they called it. That was not unless they wanted professional guidance, and then they would discuss it through a scenario situation.

Lance had a simple exercise that he set for his patients. If anything strange happened—write it down. 'To keep a record of unusual events' was how he explained it. So Katherine heeded that, everything she could remember she jotted down on paper. The date, time and place—she recorded every detail. Everything from the time she thought she fell asleep to when she was standing in front of the broken mirror. A record of what had happened written down so she couldn't forget, not to fabricate later, but to jog her brain in case she'd missed something.

It rained all day. Heavy drops beat against the window panes. A dark-clouded sky hid the sun from view, giving the rooms a strange character. It was difficult to tell whether the light had relinquished so that darkness could take over.

Katherine decided to soak her tired body; she ran a hot bath and added perfumed oils. Undressing in front of the bathroom mirror she saw her sore eyes, bloodshot and swollen. She stood there naked, feeling saggy. It seemed like the elasticity her bottom once had, had stretched itself out—it had succumbed to cellulite—and she didn't like it. However, her breasts had naturally enlarged from their girlish smallness to a rounded, womanly handful over the years—she liked that, but felt disappointed that they no longer passed the pencil test. She had, unfortunately, fallen to the chocolate craving that was starting to give her an overindulgent tummy. She turned sideways and breathed in. *That's better*, she thought.

Through the mirror she imagined seeing her husband, behind his desk, ogling his secretary—the twenty years his junior—Imogen, bending in front of the filing cabinet. The mirror rippled, allowing her body to look like Imogen's—tall and slim and firm. She now had the body she secretly desired to have, the one her husband lusted over and longed for.

Katherine blinked and the image faded, she was again her ageing self—she could tolerate Lance's toys, but a pretty thing like Imogen, he was not allowed to have. He could window shop to his heart's content. But touch was a definite NO. She had already joked to him that she would cut off his dangly-bits with a large, rusty blade, if he ever so much as laid a finger on such a pretty thing. All his toys were older than he was, so anything younger was out of the question.

Upon lowering herself into a deep, hot, scented bath, she let her green-eyed thoughts drift away as she lay listening to the rain hitting the steamed-up bathroom window.

When Lance came home at his usual time, he rushed by Katherine like a whirlwind. She was preparing their meal and hardly noticed him as he disappeared upstairs to wash and change. When he came down, his face was a picture of guilt. He didn't know how to broach the subject of that afternoon, how do you say sorry for all the hurt caused by two people who just couldn't see eye to eye?

Lance sat silently at the table swirling the contents of his drink with his finger. Ice cubes clinked against the sides of the glass making a venomous hiss. The fizz quickly went from his vodka and coke.

"I'm…" he tried to say something, but the right words weren't coming into his head. Everything he thought of saying sounded harsh and cruel. He watched as the most precious piece of stardust brought him his meal. She was his heaven sent, his morning star, his evening star, his leading light. Why couldn't he tell her this?

Katherine sat opposite and took a sip of wine. "Is it ok? I just did something quick," she said, half smiling.

"Yeah, fine... I love anything you make for me," he said, smiling back.

Bermuda blue eyes appeared grey inside lids that were red and slightly puffy—she'd put a little make-up on to try and hide the fact that she'd been crying.

Lance wasn't stupid, not this time. He knew this day would be hard for her, especially when he couldn't be by her side to support her.

"It's okay. I know it's been a tough day for you," he showed real concern in his voice and looked at her with genuine understanding. "I just want to say how sorry..."

"Oh, so you do know what I'm feeling."

"Of course I do," Lance said, getting ready for the onslaught. "I have been through all this, remember?"

"Oh, I do," she answered sarcastically. "Yes... I was there for you on both occasions... do you remember?"

"Yes, Love, I remember," Lance said, with a sinking heart that filled with remorse. He knew he couldn't have coped if it wasn't for her support; when he'd lost his parents, she was his rock. He should have been with her today, but how could he? He hadn't seen or spoken to her mother in eight years. "Do you remember how I told you 'I asked for you'?" he said, hopefully trying to change the subject, as he took a drink to wet his dry mouth.

"Yes," Katherine said, not giving the slightest care. "I've heard it so many times; I know you asked God for me—or so you say."

"I did... I asked him for you." He couldn't have said it with anymore truth.

"Or someone like me," Katherine responded with an aggressive tone and harsh expression.

Katherine was angry; her emotions were on high and ready to snap. She thought she could cope, but feelings have a way of surfacing. Standing, she picked up the wine bottle and threw it. Lance ducked; the bottle hit the wall and smashed, covering the wall with wine and the floor with glass. Just below where the bottle had hit, hung one of Lance's designer art prints, it dripped a delicate chardonnay off its lowest edge. The canvas's earthy, dark-brown background showed the cross of Christianity burning. A yellow printed verse that looked like it had been scraped into the very earth and filled with molten gold seemed to glisten in its new wet covering. A verse so intriguing, so confusing, made compelling thoughts. It read:

> Movies of the coast and the burning cross
> Hold tight as your fingers glow
> Give another place another time
> Watch the traveller, see things you didn't know

"At least it wasn't red," Lance joked, trying to humour the situation.

"You asked for me and got me," Katherine choked with tears, as she stared straight into his soul. "You never asked for Claire did you? If you did, we might have had her!"

Lance couldn't see through the welling of tears now stinging his eyes, this was a subject he would never talk about—he didn't know how to. He stood up and walked towards the storm, putting his arms out, reaching for any tenderness. Katherine responded by hitting his chest, pounding and pounding on it, over and over again.

"Let it out, darling, let it all come out," he said, with a burning throat of emotion that tried to remain strong.

She continued to hit him furiously—blow followed blow. Eventually all that pent-up energy ceased, and her head slumped down onto where those clenched fists had only recently inflicted pain. Lance slowly drew himself closer and gently closed his arms around her, encapsulating her sorrow, hoping he could devour it into his own body. He so much wanted to take away her pain. He hoped his love could still do that.

CHAPTER FIVE

Katherine was drained—if anything was needed now, it was sleep. Lance picked her up in his arms like the gallant knight he was supposed to be, only that's not how he felt. His tiny bundle helplessly clasped her hands around his neck. She needn't have, he was not going to drop her. Katherine closed her eyes, letting her head rest upon his shoulder, as sleep came and took her away.

Lance wished he could time travel; he would carry Katherine back to when he first saw her. He would only watch her beauty, catch her smile, take pleasure in her laughter, but never speak to her. If possible he would catch her fragrance—essence of Katherine—and keep it forever. Then he would disappear like breath in the wind—she could start her life again, free from his cursed soul.

He carried her upstairs, to lay his sleeping beauty onto her side of the bed. Carefully he removed her clothes and with the realisation of how fragile she really was, he silently let himself cry. *If ever a woman deserved more, then it was she,* was his thought. Slowly and tenderly, he placed the covers around her body and softly brushed her hair from her face. His hand was pricked by the calamus of a single white feather, whose down of the afterfeather gently stroked the side of a beautiful face.

Lance placed the feather onto the bedside table and said softly: "The angels have visited you, Darling, they're watching over you."

Lance walked over to the window. Looking out, he noticed that the rain had stopped and a fresh wind blew, hopefully to blow all the demons away. The street lamps with their white glare reflected distortedly on the wet road. Trees swayed in rhythm, their leaves seemed to have a deep, hypnotic rustling. He drew away from their calling and shut tight the curtains. He was about to leave the room, when the idea of *if it was out of sight it wasn't there* encroached his thoughts—he was thinking like an ostrich with its head in the sand.

Lance quietly closed the door, leaving Katherine to sleep.

Downstairs, in a dark living-room, Lance sat heavily onto a soft chair. He closed his mind from all thoughts, put his head back and relaxed. He began emptying the events of the day into his own mind's recycle bin. Coldness came over him as the air chilled; it seemed to stifle his breathing. Lance looked around as his heart thumped fast. It seemed to muffle itself against his chest wall in its bidding to conceal his fear that he wasn't alone.

Lance seemed to be wearing blinkers; darkness flooded his outer vision and was closing in. What small amount of grey-light this room had was diminishing fast. Soon all that he could see was a tunnel of sight, then nothing. He tried to stand up, but he couldn't move. He was helpless. Then he heard a sound, it was the turning of a door handle. The air moved over him as the door opened.

"Katherine, is that you?" he called.

His voice sounded dull and distant. There came no answer. There was a presence in the room; a deep impenetrable sadness filled him. Shuffling noises like the dragging of feet upon his stripped floorboards came slowly towards him; an almost inaudible whooshing of sound ran through his ears.

The sound compelled him to listen. The more he listened the more he could hear. There were distant voices calling for help, screams of terror and sobbing all intermingled, swam around the air. In that sound, Lance could hear himself crying as a child, screaming terrified as a teenager, and shouting panicky as an adult. There were others too; all lost in the darkness, crying, screaming and shouting. The writhing sound was held together by nightmare memories that were somehow growing bigger and bigger, as fragments of living souls were being knitted to the souls of the dead.

Lance screamed his wife's name till his throat ripped:

"KATHERINE! KATHERINE! KATHERINE!"

The darkness swallowed the screams; his voice was pulled towards the others in a mixing, whirling, endless spiral that tugged at him. He felt like elastic snapping as another small part of him left him voiceless. Then suddenly, silence fell like a ton weight crushing his lungs and every sound wave imaginable.

In the dark, Lance felt like he was only a pounding heart trapped within a lifeless shell. He needed to move, to see, to reach out. He wished his muscles to move so much, that they felt like they were tearing him apart in a bid to find some light. He sensed something close, the air tasted foul. In his pain, he wanted to scream his wife's name again. His lungs engulfed the decayed air until he had enough to finally let out her name:

"KATHERINE!"

Something was now towering over him. The assailing figure lowered itself on top of him; he felt he was being submerged into death. His only escape was to kick and punch. And he did—he drew energy from his love for Katherine. It was a fearless love that burned within his soul. He wasn't leaving her—ever.

The door opened and Katherine switched on the light. The darkness changed from a thick black-fog, to wispy grey-smoke, then to nothing, and all within the second it took for the electricity to burn the tungsten.

Katherine stood there rubbing her eyes in the yellow-white glow. Lance was asleep in the chair, twitching violently. She crossed the room and knelt down beside him. He was whimpering like a dog. She touched him ever so lightly on his shoulder, and he woke instantly.

"Katherine!"

"Shush…" Katherine said, taking her husband's hand, "you've been dreaming."

Lance's look of confusion quickly left, as a soft look of caring in his Katherine's eyes pulled him back into her world.

"What was the dream?"

"I don't know. I can't remember. Was I dreaming? Was I even asleep?"

"I hope so because you're soaking wet, and the only way you get like that is after sex." She smiled knowingly, giving a suspecting look. "Dreaming of your secretary were you?"

"Don't be stupid, you're all that I need," a hurt-looking face said.

"I better be," Katherine said, standing up. "Come on my gallant knight, it's time for bed."

Lance looked down at his white shirt; it was soaked through, to the point where he could see his skin through it.

"What time is it?" he said, wiping sweat from his face with the palm of his hands and then wiping them down his trousers. "Is it morning?"

"It's just after midnight."

Lance stared at the clock; its black marble case looked like it was part of the black marble fireplace, its soft ticking gently passing away time. Its small hand pointed to twelve and its larger was resting between the first and second marking.

He whispered the time: "Seven minutes past twelve."

Katherine was walking towards the door; she turned and asked: "Sorry… what's that you said?"

"It's just that number…"

"What number?"

"I don't know… I can't seem to remember." His mind was desperately trying to think. 1207 flashed involuntarily from his subconscious, giving him a strange, confused feeling.

He couldn't do it. Every time the realization of the numbers came to him, his thoughts would fog and the image would go. He stood up and joined Katherine at the door. As they left the room he flicked the light switch. The room became dark again as the door closed; keeping whatever may be there. An exhale of breath, from a pitiful sigh, hit the back of the door.

CHAPTER SIX

Five days passed. James lay on the bed. His eyes grew extremely heavy and started to close. At first he tried to fight it, but the more he relaxed the more drained he seemed to become.

He became aware that he could distantly hear the radio—it sounded like a local station, with some DJ talking in an overfriendly patter that didn't sound genuine. Then the frequency shifted, drifting out of one station and into the next, like the old radio sets when you turned the big control on the front. James focused hard on the sound; he felt drawn and needed to listen. The high pitched whooshing noise drew him in further. A station was found; now old-time music-hall songs were being sung. He seemed to recognise them but didn't understand how. A station shift again, and a church choir sang—

James found himself standing in a living-room. It was empty of all furniture—the rugs, curtains and pictures were long gone. He felt he knew this place as he walked around on the bare floorboards, his feet leaving footprints in the dust. The large bay windows flooded the room with rays of light which sparkled like glitter from the disturbed floor covering. He stood in front of a black marble fireplace, its grate empty. Once it would have burnt coal, throwing warmth and life into this now cold and damp room. Now only black sooty deposits remained. They peppered the rusting iron-grate like spent Christmas wishes.

He looked to the door; it was closed—shutting in memories of past times. He could hear laughter and happy voices faintly in the air, his senses heightened by the smell of spruce and orange—

James was no longer in the room. He was on the other side of the door, standing in the hall. His feet felt cold on the red and white diagonal tiles. A chill crept up through his feet and into his bones. It was darker, almost gloomy with all the doors closed. Coloured light illuminated the first few yards with criss-crossed patterns on the floor and wall, as sunlight penetrated the diamond-leaded panels within the front door. Looking back towards the dark he could see the stairs. White spindles with a dusty dark wood banister drew him. He walked slowly, half not wanting, half desperately seeking, up the stairs. At the top he stopped. All the bedroom doors were shut. The gloom seemed oppressive as he stood there in what little light there was—

James now found himself in a bedroom; it was much brighter as the light poured in through the window. It was another stark, empty room. The walls showed signs of damp in the corners. Richly patterned wallpaper displayed squares of how the paper once looked before the hanging of many pictures. Time had a way of decaying everything. This room felt even more cold and frightening in its brightness.

Now he was by the window, looking at his reflection in the glass—he looked ghostly white. He looked down onto the wooden boards; his bare feet had disturbed its dusty surface. Again the dust glittered.

He turned and walked—for reasons he didn't understand—towards the darkest corner. There he stood on the spot where something large was once situated, and felt a sudden sharp sting to his foot. Warmth crept along its entire sole. Looking, he saw a pool of blood that spread outwards from his foot like the flowing of a river upon the scorching summer earth after the rains come. Balancing on one leg, he lifted his pained foot backwards so he could see the source of the flow—blood spat from a sharp needle-like object embedded within his skin. He pulled it out, a severe pain shot up through his body. James fell to the floor in agony. A splinter of mirror, about two inches long, was held tightly between his fingers. Blood ran freely from the wound, not-stopping—

James was back on his bed, the radio stations were drifting in and out again. He instinctively sat up and examined his foot—it was fine. There was no blood—no cut—just flesh, and cold flesh at that. He stood up feeling unsure of his surroundings, almost as if he wasn't there. He looked down to the bed, only to see himself sleeping—

James was on the bed again; it felt so unreal that every time he got up he saw himself lying down. He struggled to shut out the sound of the radio, its whooshing fading, getting fainter the more he fought. Finally with great concentration, he ripped himself from his dream-like state and shakily stood up, then sat down again feeling weak and faint. His limbs ached, drained of all energy. He wondered what the time was; he looked at his clock displaying its red LED numbers of 12:07:00. They seemed to have stopped. *Funny,* he thought, as he shook his head trying to focus his mind to the last time this happened. *They're my birth numbers—the twelfth of July.* Then the red LED numbers changed and counted 02:09:01… 02:09:02… 02:09:03…

CHAPTER SEVEN

One week can pass quite quickly. But one week without sleep can seem like a living hell, and James was in hell.

When it's difficult to sleep it can be frustrating in itself. James wished he had insomnia, when the more you think about sleep the more you stay awake. He was finding his sleep deprivation increasingly difficult. The more he tried to keep awake the more his mind would shut down. His dilemma to keep awake created his difficulty with sleep. His 'Catch-22' was that if he slept, they—The Sleeping, as he was beginning to call them—might visit again.

James knew The Sleeping wouldn't always come. Sometimes he could sleep like a baby. But what he didn't know was in which sleep they would come.

A strange notion came into James' mind, and he had no idea why. It's not like he was thinking about the past, he was just trying to remain awake, but it seemed like a good idea at the time. He left his flat at 2.30 a.m. His journey would take a good hour of driving. The night air was fresh, a cool breeze circulated around the interior of his car as he drove with the windows down.

3.30 a.m. approached and those familiar streets became visible in his car's beamed headlights. A friendly glow from the street lights caressed the houses, where, as a mere lad of eleven, he'd delivered the evening papers. They looked just as they did all those years ago. He could imagine himself drudging around the corner with a shoulder that ached from a bag that was too heavy for his skinny frame.

James drove slowly down the road thinking of how wet he used to get when it rained, and how cold those bitter nights were when the winter wind bit into his knuckles and cheeks, turning them red. The Christmas tips he received made up for it. He depended on them. The help it gave him in buying presents for his parents was much appreciated, a debt he repaid every Christmas to his own paperboy. *The good days,* he thought.

He rounded the corner. There was the house of a girl he'd fancied who once told him what she'd like to do to him. She was older, blonde, very pretty, and extremely wicked. James was twelve and only a stupid and shy kid. If only he'd let her, but it was too late now. All water under the bridge of life. He wondered if she'd ever married, had children and whose; but what was the use in wondering?

A few more turns and he had reached his destination. He parked the car and turned off the engine. Silence and darkness of the early hours shrouded everything like a veil of protection, just like it used to. James looked up towards his old home. Thirty-two years his parents had lived there. Now another family resided there. It felt strange to know he could never again walk in those rooms. His bedroom where he'd slept was now occupied by another sleeping body. The living room where he'd watched television was silent and dark. Visions of that room graced his mind with years of fond memories. An ever-changing Christmas tree merged an old year into a new year. Now that room would display someone else's tree year after year. The kitchen where he'd eaten his meals—the stairs he'd fallen down—the toilet… he stopped thinking—he didn't want to go there anymore. *Quick! Think of something else,* he told himself. *Think of anything… think of friends.*

So he did.

Stepping out of the car felt strange. It had been many years since his feet had touched that pavement. The years had passed like yesterday, suddenly gone. James breathed in deeply through his nose, he could smell his youth. Everything smelled surprisingly, just the same. How? He didn't know how and he didn't care.

James took a stroll and walked along the road where he had played as a kid. Two doors down was once the house of a very dear friend. They'd met when they were both five. This extraordinary friend, extraordinary in the fact that he knew he was different, would totter down the path, dressed in his mother's frock and high heels, and call for him to play out. How people were truly different in their sexuality had never occurred to James, until pop music hit his ears. Sadly now, that long-ago friend was no longer in this realm of the living. Wherever he was, James wished him happiness.

Carrying on walking, James reached the end of the road; a whole new experience was remembered as a surge of adrenalin rushed through his veins and pounded on his heart like a ringside bell. The house opposite had a side passage, and this was the place he fought and won in one of those silly shows of male aggression, when defending the honour of a girl seemed the right thing to do. *Those foolish boyish days,* he thought.

And where was that girl now? He didn't know, let alone care any-more.

James turned and backtracked to his car. He remembered an old song explaining that you can never go home again; nothing will be as it used to be. Nothing remains the same. But he did have all those memories of his childhood home. Nothing could ever change that—a home where happiness and sorrow went hand in hand. Laughter and a few tears were all the right ingredients to make a wonderful home perfect for an up-bringing of fun—and James had spent lots of happy times there, a head full of times he could never forget…

James felt a slight shiver, he felt like he was walking with ghosts. Opening the car door, he quickly got in and sat there in the dark silence. He remembered that this house—the house he grew up in—was where it had first happened. One night, in the bedroom's darkness, the wardrobe door had opened and from it walked a shadow.

What he saw was taller and blacker than the very darkness it walked. Its face was white and without eyes. Hollows emitted an emptiness that held no sorrow. Its haunting slow walk, with an overpowering sadness that encapsulated your soul, drew you into its dark presence. Even now, his mind could still see it, so there was no doubt whatsoever. Young as he was back then, he definitely saw it. When he screamed, it retreated back across the room and back into the wardrobe. James was five and The Sleeping had been coming ever since.

James closed his eyes. He couldn't keep awake any longer. If they were coming to get him tonight, then he would fight them like he'd always done. He fell asleep in his car, and slept like a baby.

The Sunday morning sun glared through the windscreen of a silent, parked car. Inside, James' eyes opened from the warmth and then shuttered closed in response to white-light pain.

Gratitude of a few hours undisturbed sleep dissolved in his realisation that home was an hour away, and that hunger was calling. James stopped off at a supermarket for some fresh orange juice, a packet of streaky bacon and six free-range eggs. He even got a smile from the young and pretty, flirtatious cashier, free of charge. Sunday morning was looking good.

As James stumbled up the steps to his home, he noticed that the front door that led to his and Mr. Green's flat was slightly ajar. Caution and suspicion were quickly overtaken by the thoughts of sizzling bacon and sunny-side-up eggs. He pushed the door further open with his foot and then kicked it shut behind him. It was then that he noticed several cardboard boxes piled two high, outside Mr. Green's door.

James opened his door—an entry beeping greeted him. Alarm turned off and the shopping put down on his bottom stair, he returned to the cardboard boxes. Curiosity had beaten his hunger.

Something felt wrong. James nosily or good-neighbourly opened one of the boxes. Inside was nothing but old suits and shoes. He opened another, only to see shirts and ties and a wide, leather belt that had seen better days. He opened another; this one was full of photographs. On the top, facing up and looking right at him was Mr. Green. Albeit, this Mr. Green was a perfectly straight, standing man in his mid-fifties and in an army uniform, but there was no mistaking those warm, smiley blue-grey eyes.

James carefully rummaged deeper into the box and gently pulled out a handful of photos. He recoiled when his eyes met the rotting corpses of disembodied soldiers, the colour of the earth they merged into, and how harrowing the eyes of the dead looked into empty space. From other photographs, weary men looked straight at him with soulless eyes. Eyes that once saw the beauty of living, had now been tarnished by death's horror and looked hauntingly lost in the waiting for their turn to die.

Something told James to put the photograph of Mr. Green into the inside pocket of his leather jacket. He did as his thought instructed.

The doorbell rang, sending James' arm reflexively to jump from his leather jacket inside pocket and into the air, whereby he poked himself in the eye. Tears streamed down his cheek as he shakily put the other photographs back into the box. The doorbell rang again. James stood up and opened the door.

"Good morning," a man in brown overalls said.

James looked the man up and down. He hadn't asked for anyone to call, so he assumed it must be for Mr. Green. "Can I help you?" he said civilly.

"I've been sent to collect some boxes that have been left outside Mr. Green's apartment," the brown-overalled man said.

James hated the word 'apartment'. His face cringed at the Americanisation of the simple word Flat. His eye still shed tears; he wiped them away with his hand as he said: "Come in."

James opened the door wide and stepped to one side to allow this portly man past.

"If it's not a good time, I'll come back tomorrow?" the brown-overalled man said, wishing to do exactly that. He hated it when weeping friends hung around. It's not like he wasn't sympathetic to people's feelings, it's just that he'd rather not get involved.

"No. If you've come to take the boxes, then take the boxes," James said, dabbing at his smarting eye with a handkerchief to absorb the flow, rather than making it worse by using his fingers.

The brown-overalled man gave a sigh followed by a grunt, as he picked up one of the boxes and carried it off to his van, parked outside. He did this several times, and as he picked up the last box said: "My colleagues will empty the apartment as soon as possible."

A pregnant pause followed—a gormless expression slid onto James' face. "You mean the flat's going to be for let?"

"Yes, once it's empty and cleaned up."

"Has he gone?" James recalled his last meeting with Mr. Green and how happy he'd looked at receiving his mail.

"Yes," the brown-overalled man said. He wondered if he were talking to a dim-wit.

"When did he go?"

"He went on Thursday."

"Did he go alone?"

"Excuse me!" the brown-overalled man said. Confusion as to where this line of investigation was leading made him look as simple as the man he was talking to.

"Did he leave with someone?"

The brown-overalled man pondered about that, then said, "Well, that all depends on what you mean by 'someone'."

"I thought he might have told me he was going," James said, lowering his handkerchief to reveal a painful, bloodshot eye.

"Try not to reproach yourself," the brown-overalled man said with sincerity. "When that someone comes to take you, there's no time to let others know." And while balancing the box with one hand, he patted a numb-looking James on the shoulder with the other. His touch to James sent a shiver through him—just as if the Grim Reaper himself had suddenly stroked his skeletal fingers along his backbone.

The brown-overalled man turned and left, pulling the door closed behind him.

James was left feeling stupid and alone in a cold white painted vestibule. "Did God write to you, Mr. Green?" echoed ghostly from his lips. "If he did, I don't want to receive that sort of good news—not yet anyway."

James picked up his shopping and back-kicked his door. It snapped shut. As he climbed the stairs he thought about Mr. Green and his good news letter from God:

Dear Mr. Green,

I'm pleased to inform you that your life will now end. I hope you did with it as you wished and that you took every opportunity to enjoy your mortal existence. Looking forward to seeing you soon,

God x

39

P.S. Judgement will be at…

James stopped at the top of the stairs. Horrible thoughts struck him. *What if it wasn't God that took him? What if it was The Sleeping?*

A pan sizzled with bacon and eggs. A glass of orange juice was being swallowed, a gulp at a time. James, with nothing more on his mind than eating, seemed compliant to whatever may be in waiting.

CHAPTER EIGHT

The phone rang insistently as Miss Swan unlocked the door to the office. It continued to ring as she removed her coat and hung it in its usual place. It only stopped when the receiver was finally lifted from a seated position.

"Good morning... Mr. Lewisham's office, how may I help you?" said an unrushed Miss Swan.

The person on the other end of the phone said nothing.

"Good morning... Mr. Lewisham's office, how may I help you?" Miss Swan repeated.

Some grunts accompanied with a heavy breathing dispersed into her ear.

Miss Swan resisted from saying anything. Instead she listened to more heavy breathing. Then when she heard what sounded like her name being whispered, she felt extremely uncomfortable.

Distressed and fuming, she slammed the receiver down. "FILTHY BASTARD," she shouted, in a tone that spat disgust.

Miss Swan stood up and walked briskly up and down to remove the shakiness from her legs. Her hands trembled as her whispered name echoed around her frightened thoughts.

Several minutes later, the office door opened and in walked Lance, with a vacant expression that displayed a satisfied smile. "Morning, Miss

Swan," he said, as he passed her. "Coffee would be nice on this fine Monday morning," floated firmly from his cat-like grin.

Miss Swan said nothing. Her lips tightened to thinness as her eyes scowled at the telephone. *Come on, ring again. Ring, you pervert, ring!*

Lance picked up his bass and pressed her to his chest. He plucked the open A and felt her voice melt into his heart, and then adding a rhythmic blues riff, he drifted his thoughts away.

Feeling extremely relaxed, Lance again gently plucked the open A before setting his ageing beauty back on her stand. Her voice drifting in the floor beneath his feet, made him ready for the day.

He took his position behind his desk. Miss Swan's arrival brought a waft of fresh coffee with essence of pulse-racing scent. If anything was going to keep you up, then this aroma was better than any little blue pill.

The bend-over began. Miss Swan, the fantastically formed and curved human sculpture, performed her filing cabinet routine like a pro. Pleasing her boss was foremost on her mind. Long legs and a bottom that craved attention balanced magnificently on high heels. Then came the turn, that coveted figure had the desired effect. Lance's eyes rose to hand-full breasts. Miss Swan stood and waited and smiled. A slight flush to her cheeks seemed to make her lips redder. Lance returned the smile.

"Is there anything else I can do for you?" Miss Swan said. She was questionably wishing.

There came that unfortunate same reply.

"No. Not at this moment, Miss Swan, thank you," Lance said. Regret was a wilting feeling.

He thought deeply. *What would happen if I said yes? Would she respond favourably? I can't...*

As soon as Miss Swan left his office, Lance's day felt like it was going to last a week. No matter how many people sat in front of him—telling their anxieties about what or who they thought they were—he was in no way a help. He, to all intents and purposes, looked like he was paying attention, but, to be honest, he was surmising over the doodles he'd drawn on the notepad in front of him. To his patients, the ones who watched, it was like he was writing concentrated notes that would somehow help them come to terms with whatever problem it was they were having. It's a messed up, turned upside down world.

Lance had, over the last week, drawn 1207 in as many configurations as he could. He didn't understand why he had done this or what it meant. But apart from his ghostly visit at seven minutes past midnight last Monday night, he had no other association with that number. No divine enlightenment would give him the answer. He seemed to be alone in his thoughts. All he saw, on the paper in front of him, was the stupid stickman he'd just sketched hanging from the number seven. *Seven is supposed to be a magical number, so am I the stickman?* He was grasping at straws.

Four patients came and four patients went, and they would come and go again, until they were happy with the way they are. Lance often wondered what true happiness was, and if there was such a thing as a truly happy person—happiness is such a momentary thing.

Lance stood and walked over to the window. His reflection stared at him like a stranger. He turned away, and wanting love, reached again for his 62 Jazz Bass. He knew Kath didn't mind such an old lady giving her affections.

"Ahem!" cleared the silence.

Lance's fingers slipped from his beauty's neck.

A dark-haired man, with a strong athletic figure, was laid upon his conversational couch. "Oh! I'm sorry," Lance apologised, "I didn't hear you come in."

"I'm the one who should be apologising. I should have knocked and introduced myself—I'm James Walker, I made an appointment this morning and rudely coerced your lovely secretary into a lunch-time session... I hope I'm not intruding as I really need your help."

Lance felt something he'd not felt since his college days. He felt a real yearning to know more about this man. He took his place behind his burr walnut desk; there he pulled open the right side desk drawer... and hid away his doodling.

"I can't sleep!" James stated.

"Not a lot of us can," Lance responded. He understood his own bouts of insomnia.

"I should say..." James began with due hesitation, "what I'm trying to say is... is that I try not to sleep."

"And what do you think your reason is for that?" Lance said, leaning forward.

James closed his eyes, and looking like he was going to nod off there and then, said: "If I sleep they'll come for me. They've always come for me."

"Who comes for you?" Lance asked quietly.

"They do... The Sleeping... they come for me."

"Who are The Sleeping?"

"I don't know," James answered truthfully, "but they've been coming since I was five."

"Do you remember when and exactly how they first came?" Lance questioned, leaning back.

"Yes."

"Then relax, and in your own time, tell me about it."

James talked as Lance intently listened.

Lance pictured his patient's anxiety. It was as if he was seeing exactly what James had seen. He was also beginning to feel that same anxiety.

Miss Swan came into the office to put Friday's temporarily placed files into their correct alphabetical filing location. She crouched down, without any performance, and did the task in hand.

"You're the charming creature I spoke to on the telephone this morning," James said, from his prostrate position. He whispered her first name like he did earlier: "Imogen."

Miss Swan's head turned sharply, her face flushed.

James was on his feet and advancing towards a rather frightened and bewildered Miss Swan. He stopped inches away from her and cocked his head down to those shapely ankles. Higher his eyes roamed, and higher still they roamed, until they rested upon her breasts.

Miss Swan's breathing increased rapidly. Her breasts quaked with every breath she took. This was her time—she was ready.

CHAPTER NINE

An enquiry led to a lengthy, over the phone, form-filling exercise. Mr. Green felt comfier talking from his hotel room than having someone, whoever it may be, staring at him like he didn't exist. All the questions, which had to be answered, simply gave that impression. Besides, he had the money. And money spoke louder than any words.

The high street was busy. People bustled bumpily in their lunch hour. Traffic either crawled or waited at lights. Mr. Green waited patiently at an empty desk at the estate agents, in his request for a certain rental property.

He looked out of the window into the street. *So many unwanted people in this world,* he thought. Then his vision shifted to his reflection. His grey hair silvered in the incoming light. His bent-double frame wasn't any straighter even when sitting. His warm, blue-grey eyes were smiling again.

"Mr. Green, sorry to keep you," the young estate agent said, with a gestured shrugging of his shoulders, indicating he felt that he'd taken too long in his enquiries and was genuinely sorry for the time he'd taken. "Would you like a coffee?"

"No, thank you," Mr. Green said.

The young man sat and opened the file to property No. 111 Padstow Avenue.

"Is everything in order, Raymond?" Mr. Green asked, acknowledging the name on the badge pinned to the shirt opposite.

"Our client was a bit doubtful about you letting at first, Mr. Green," Raymond said.

"Was it that he thought I might drop dead at any moment?" quipped Mr. Green.

"Your age was questioned," Raymond said, joining in on the joke. "But, when I mentioned that you had instructed me to say you would like to pay one year's rental in advance, his opinion changed."

"I thought it would. Money docs have power."

"It does," Raymond confirmed.

Raymond read through the document in relation to Mr. Green's choice of property. He pointed out everything that a tenant needed to know about possible breakdown to fitted appliances, what tests had been carried out, and any other critical safety practice. Mr. Green looked uninterested. Raymond was just doing his job. Half an hour passed within a blinking of Mr. Green's eye.

"Well, Mr. Green," Raymond said, finally getting to the crux of the matter, "all I need is your signature and a cheque for the one year's advance rental. I see no need, on this occasion, for a deposit."

Mr. Green gave a contented smile and read the document he was putting his name to. All was in order, so he stylishly, and with great flourish, put his name on the line indicated. Raymond had never seen a signature so magnificent. He made a mental note to sign his name just as magnificently.

Mr. Green looked at the document again, and smiled at the figure of money required. His right arm twisted to reach his jacket's right hand pocket. His right hand delved in and pulled out a thick roll of money. The yellow elastic band around the notes was flicked with the thumb and twanged to rest upon the index finger. There it came to rest like a greatly-oversized gold ring. Note after note was counted out, until the exact sum lay curled upon the desk. Raymond smiled. He liked this old man's style.

The money was counted again, this time by Raymond, before being taken away.

Mr. Green looked out of the window. Less people now strolled. The road was virtually empty of traffic.

Raymond returned with a receipt, and sitting and smiling he looked over the paperwork one more time before handing it over.

Mr. Green waited a bit longer before asking, "When can I collect the keys and move into No. 111 Padstow Avenue?"

"As soon as the paperwork has been processed," Raymond said.

"Will that take long?"

"It can take up to a week."

"Oh! That long," Mr. Green said, twisting his left arm so his left hand could reach into his jacket's left pocket. Another thick roll of money was produced, this time bound by a red elastic band. "I hope it's no longer. I've got just enough to pay the hotel bill for another week."

Raymond's eyes widened. "Where are you staying?"

"At the Savoy—I always stay at the Savoy."

Raymond's eyes widened even more. "What happens when you're left holding just elastic bands?"

"I ask for more money."

"You just ask?"

"Yes."

"Who do you ask?"

"Are you sure you want to know?" Mr. Green said, with a darkness emitting from every part of his being.

"No," Raymond said.

"Good," Mr. Green said, "you wouldn't believe me anyway."

Raymond flinched as Mr. Green rose from his chair and extended his hand in gratitude and farewell.

"Take the hand, son, it's not going to bite."

Raymond reluctantly took the hand.

A tight grip, from someone so frail-looking, shook strongly. Raymond trembled. Mr. Green was someone he would never forget.

As Mr. Green walked away from the estate agents, a mother and child overtook him at speed.

"You can run—but you can't hide," Mr. Green said, in a way that only the child seemed to hear.

The small hand that gripped his mother's slipped from security. A boy of nearly five years of age turned and stood staring into warm, blue-grey eyes. Such a sweet little face radiated such blamelessness. After all, it wasn't his fault.

"Hello," the boy said.

A hand reached for the smaller and was soon on its way again. The mother not once looked at Mr. Green; she was in far too much a hurry. The free hand of the boy waved goodbye.

"The Sleeping will come and pay you a visit," Mr. Green called. "It'll be soon." But the boy was far, far, away. Only the blur of the mother could be seen weaving between passers-by.

Raymond looked again at the paperwork. He'd never seen a form with so many blanks. The estate agents' protocol would be to reject such a customer, but the client always had the last say. And as Mr. Green pointed out 'Money does have power'.

CHAPTER TEN

Miss Swan took the moment with precision. She pulled the man she wanted into her arms. She kissed him like she had done so many times in her dreams.

"My darling," she breathily whispered.

"Not quite the introduction I was expecting," James said, licking his lips.

"I don't understand," Miss Swan said. A faint redness flushed her cheeks.

"Well, Miss Swan, I would say 'Hello… I'm James Walker' and extend my hand in greeting. You would take it and say 'I'm very pleased to meet you'."

"Is this a game?" Miss Swan questioned excitedly.

"Do you want it to be?"

"Yes."

"Very well, if that's what you want, then it's a game."

Miss Swan, again, took the initiative and pulled the man she wanted into her arms. "I like this game… James." She advanced her kissing to touching. Her hands moved over a tight torso to below the belt line.

"Do you always behave like this in front of your boss?" James asked.

"I can, it seems, when my boss becomes… James," Miss Swan whispered, lowering herself into a kneeling position.

The belt became undone. The trousers and boxers lowered.

Imogen performed like she had done so many times in her head, whilst doing her morning routine of the bend-over.

James groaned to the point where he held Imogen's head and thrust forward. He released his pleasure.

Imogen took his pleasure with a swallow. She'd wanted to do this for so long.

Miss Swan stood and tidied herself. She stared into the eyes of the man she loved. The man she loved stared into hazel-brown elated pupils.

"You'd better pull up your pants," Miss Swan said. "You wouldn't want to be caught with your trousers down." A smile almost turned into a giggle.

Boxers and trousers were raised. Shirt got tucked in, and belt was fastened to as it was just minutes before.

"I understand the rules," Miss Swan said, in her comprehension of this new game. "Whenever you call me by my first name, I'll know that you're James—make it soon!" She then turned and walked away like a cat that had got her cream—literally.

Lance seated himself behind his desk. He looked around for his unexpected lunch-time patient. He was gone. A pen was reached for and notes quickly made:

Name: James Walker
DOB: 12/07/69

"Whoa! 1207," Lance said, with a ghostly shiver. "Now that's spooky."

Everything James had said was remembered and written down.

Lance was beginning to have empathy with this character James Walker.

Miss Swan began sending a text to her flatmate Stephanie:

Guess what just happened? :-)

A few seconds followed before her mobile vibrated. Her inbox showed 1 new message:

No games—just tell me :-)

Miss Swan's thumb quickly replied:

Gave Lance a B.J., tell you more tonight xx

The door to reception opened, and a rather heavily built man, wearing a dress and wig and make-up, with the appearance of an ageing movie star, approached the desk.

Miss Swan acknowledged with a smile. "Hello, Ms Drummond. Mr. Lewisham will see you shortly."

Ms Drummond smiled as sweetly as possible, and took a seat.

Miss Swan had seen many things for her age. Nothing perturbed her. She couldn't understand why a man, who obviously looked like a man, wanted to dress like a woman. She'd met many women that were actually men. True females could tell the difference, no matter how fabulously gorgeous these imposters looked. Some men can't see beyond the breasts and curves produced by feminising hormones.

The next patient buzzer sounded.

"Mr. Lewisham will see you now, Ms Drummond," Miss Swan announced.

Stephanie Duke lounged on the couch in ripped jeans and a t-shirt, watching the BBC News. She fidgeted with the remote. She'd deliberately left work early; she could as a freelance fashion designer who answered only to herself. Wanting to hear about Imogen's ground-breaking episode—with the forever talked about gender psychiatrist—was eating right into her.

Stephanie was elf, almost boyish, like. No matter what she ate, made no impact upon her appearance. She was naturally skinny, flat chested and willowy boned. Her hair was cropped by her own hand and bleached. She could add any food-colouring she liked to create the look she felt best suited her mood. This morning felt like a cool-blue relaxed sort of week, so her hair was coloured with butterfly pea. She was beginning to think she should have coloured it with cochineal instead. One glance at Stephanie's delicate face, told you she was definitely a she. Her make-up was all woman. She had pale-blue eyes.

Imogen opened the door to her flat in exuberant mood. Her flatmate was waiting.

"Well?" Stephanie ejaculated.

Imogen rushed to where Stephanie was laying and sat with such an explosion of energy that the old couch beneath them both creaked in upholstered-pain.

"How did it happen? Did he come onto you? Did he make you?" Stephanie asked with a scowling-eyed jealousy.

"He called me by my first name. He's never done that. We've always obeyed his rules of office protocol."

"That didn't answer my questions," Stephanie said, sitting upright.

"When he called me Imogen and walked towards me, with such a wanting look in his eyes, I took the initiative and kissed him."

"And then?"

"And then he suggested we played a game."

"I bet he did!"

"I had to play—I wanted to play—I longed to play."

"I get the idea. You played suck-suck. That's disgusting!"

"No, it's not."

"We never play suck-suck."

"That's because you have nothing sticking out from between your legs for me to suck."

"That's not the point, and besides, there are other parts you can suck." Stephanie looked dejectedly into the face she cared about the most.

"Don't spoil it for me, Stef; I've wanted this for so long. I can't help my feelings towards him."

"Feelings—you think I don't have feelings?"

Imogen held Stephanie's hand. "Please, Stef, the past is the past—we've had sex together, you know I'm not fully into women—you said you understood."

"I do, but do you understand that he'll never leave his wife?"

Imogen looked hurt. She looked into Stephanie's eyes and wept.

Stephanie put her arms around her friend and hugged that coveted frame. "He'll hurt you. I can't bear that, but if that's what going to happen, then it's going to happen no matter what I say. I hope I'm wrong." She then kissed Imogen upon the eyelids. "There… tears gone," she said, as if talking to a child.

CHAPTER ELEVEN

Raymond had put the paperwork through the system as quickly as he humanly could—something had told him to.

It wasn't long after, that several previously-collected boxes were being delivered to their new address.

A brown-overalled man said to the occupant: "Not long in storage this time, Mr. Green."

Mr. Green just smiled and signed the delivery note in his usual flamboyant way.

Tuesday through Friday passed, without any game-playing. Miss Swan performed her bend-over, every morning, with a girlish grin, and wished for James to return. Lance window shopped. The 62 jazz bass hadn't been lifted for four days—she was beginning to feel rejected. The heavy bag hung like a dead man—lifeless. The burr walnut desk, however, was being used to its full extent. The right side desk drawer was being pulled out, to reveal the notes on James Walker, and slid closed again, at half-hourly intervals. It was like the number 1207 was slowly being etched onto the back of Lance's eyes, as a tattooist gave breaks from the pain.

It was after six and Katherine was standing, with a shiver, at her open front door, studying the man before her with close scrutiny. She felt odd doing this, but for some reason it felt like this man projected no soul.

A bent-double and grey-haired old man craned his gaze upwards and said: "Hello, Mrs. Lewisham—I'm Mr. Green; I'm your new next-door neighbour."

Katherine smiled and thought: *How polite*.

"I hope I'm not intruding?" Mr. Green said, while flashing warm, blue-grey eyes that dissolved any thoughts Katherine might have been forming.

Katherine smiled again. "Of course not," she said, "please come in." She stepped aside allowing Mr. Green to give a courteous, even lower bend—which seemed impossible to do—before he stepped over the threshold. Intuitively he felt that The Sleeping had been. He could smell their deathly-odour trapped in every shadow.

Katherine closed the door and accompanied Mr. Green into the living room.

"Nice room," Mr. Green said, looking around.

"Thank you," Katherine said, accepting the compliment. "I like it."

Like most strangers, Mr. Green felt uncomfortable. There were lots of things he could say, but he wasn't with the person he'd come to see. He felt it better to remain silent until his host spoke.

"I was expecting a family to move in next door," Katherine said truthfully and without thinking. "Oh, I'm sorry—I didn't mean that I'm not..."

"No need to apologise, Mrs. Lewisham, I fully comprehend. If only one could touch the spirit of children then the void wouldn't feel so empty."

Katherine looked vague. She could feel her mind being searched by the soulless.

Mr. Green warmed his blue-grey eyes again, making Katherine's thoughts dissolve into the room's shadows. His assessment of Katherine was that she had become hollow of life—he knew she deserved better, but he couldn't feel sympathy anymore. It wasn't his job to feel sympa-thetic. His advice would be: You get what you get—lump it, or do something about it! But he wasn't there to give her any such advice.

Katherine, not really feeling one-hundred per cent about Mr. Green, suddenly and surprisingly decided to show him around her home. She had no understanding why she felt she had to do this, other than it might take her mind off the headache that was forming across her brow. It could have simply been because Mr. Green showed no sign of wanting to leave—asking him to go would be rude, to say the least. Also, it would kill time before Lance came home. This weekend he wasn't away on one of his seminars or whatever he liked to call them.

Mr. Green seemed to climb the stairs easily for a bent-double old man who had trouble raising his head more than four treads up at a time.

At the top, he stopped and said something that made Katherine warm to him. "I can feel that someone very close to you has recently visited."

Katherine looked across to the wardrobe. "The mirror broke," she said, not knowing why she should divulge such a thing to someone she had only just met.

"Wardrobes are a gateway..." Mr. Green said, and paused to see the expression on Katherine's face. Katherine looked interested. "A mirror is cracked to prevent something that is not wanted from entering your world. Your mother is protecting you."

"Tell me, Mr. Green; are you in any way psychic?"

Mr. Green, with all honesty, answered, "No."

"If you're trying to frighten me..."

"I'm not," Mr. Green said. "I have no reason to scare you. I'm only telling you why mirrors crack. As I understand it, the soulless can travel from one realm to another by the use of a looking glass, or mirror as it is called today. Do you believe that you have a soul?"

"Of course," Katherine replied.

"Next time you look into a mirror and see yourself, you will recognise that the person on the other side has no soul. It's like they only mimic your actions."

"It's only a reflection, Mr. Green. Are you an avid reader of horror fiction?"

"But is it only your reflection? How do you know it's not you without a soul? And no, I don't read any form of fiction. All my observations are from life itself. Living can teach you more than any amount of words strung together can. The eyes, Mrs. Lewisham, tell the living from the dead."

Katherine looked into Mr. Green's eyes.

Mr. Green smiled and averted her gaze. "I'm living, but only just," he said, looking at the wardrobe. "Now whether I have a soul... that's another matter."

Katherine's mouth felt dry. Changing the subject to refreshment steered the way to the kitchen. Mr. Green happily followed.

Lance's designer art print greeted Mr. Green.

"Do you like it?" Katherine said, noticing the look on Mr. Green's face. It lit up like he'd been given an unexpected gift.

"Very much," Mr. Green said.

"I've never understood it," Katherine confessed. "Do you?"

"Of course," Mr. Green admitted, and then blatantly added: "I wrote it."

He then read aloud the words: "Movies of the coast and the burning cross. Hold tight as your fingers glow. Give another place another time. Watch the traveller, see things you didn't know." He also added the words that weren't written there. "When there are no eyes watching over you, and the air is sparked in fear. No strength of pride and hope. One man and his dreams are broken."

Katherine stood in wonder. "When did you write it?" she asked.

Mr. Green reflected. "It was on the 29th October 1929. I was in my office, on the thirteenth floor of what you would term a sky-scraper, in Manhattan, New York. It was a terrible day—it became known as Black Tuesday. I wrote the words on a piece of yellow paper and taped it to the underside of my desk. I turned and looked out of the window at Trinity Church. Then I pulled open the right side desk drawer. What I did then... you don't need to know."

Lance was in a traffic jam. Tail-lights stretched as far as his eyes could see. He wasn't going anywhere fast. On the seat beside him were his notes on James Walker. He wanted to discuss that strange lunch-time meeting with Katherine. He knew he couldn't discuss a client's confidentiality, but technically James Walker wasn't a client. He'd secretly looked at his secretary's appointment register; no record showed that James Walker had made an appointment. There were also no future appointments. Discussion about him broke no professional conduct.

Traffic was starting to move again. Another forty-five minutes and he'd be home.

Katherine and Mr. Green had decided that a glass of red wine was the perfect way of getting to know each other. They sat next to each other at the kitchen table.

Mr. Green had such warm, blue-grey eyes that Katherine found it easy to tell her life story. Katherine gave as much warmth back as she listened to Mr. Green talk about his time as a photographer, and how as a photographer he'd been appointed to record the casualties of battle and the triumphs of victory during the First World War. He saw no victory in seeing men die. Even the ones that survived such horror looked like they'd died.

Katherine thought she understood why the man sat opposite her looked like he had no soul. There was no-one around to tell her otherwise, so she believed what she now thought and ignored her initial prognosis. Not once did she question his age.

Lance parked his Moggy 1000 on the drive. He picked up the file from the passenger seat and hauled his tired limbs out into a welcomed standing position. He stretched his back by arching his shoulders backwards and groaned in his discomfort.

The Lewisham's back door was on the side of the house. It was easier, after parking, to enter the house via this door, than to walk around to the door that everyone else used when either visiting or delivering.

Lance walked into the kitchen and was greeted by the sight of an old man drinking red wine with his wife. He gave Mr. Green a curious stare as he took off his coat and hung it over the back of an empty chair. He put the file down onto the table and watched Mr. Green's eyes.

Katherine stood up. Mr. Green glanced upon the file before doing the same.

"Lance, Darling," Katherine said with a twinkling eye, "this is Mr. Green, our new next-door neighbour."

Mr. Green smiled and extended his hand.

Lance's response was impolite. He looked at the old man with unease and left the room.

Katherine was only halfway through apologising, when Lance returned with a tumbler full of vodka and a little coke. He didn't sit down; instead he stood and surveyed the old man again.

Katherine didn't know what else to say. She looked embarrassed.

"Maybe if you left us alone," Mr. Green said, tenderly patting Katherine's upper-arm.

Katherine responded by leaving the room. She stood in the hallway feeling drained. She looked into the hall mirror and recognised the person on the other side as having no soul. She pushed her hair from her face and observed the mimicking.

A shaky feeling hit hard, making her lean against the wall. Silence cloaked all her movements as she slid down to the floor. She rested her head in her hands and listened.

Mr. Green sat down again and took hold of the situation.

"Is your head swimming in questions about James Walker?" he said, craning his head upwards to gaze into suffering eyes.

"It is," Lance said, taking the chair opposite and sitting with a heaviness that showed his tiredness. He didn't know how this old man could know anything about the file that was plainly in view. There was nothing written on the front, other than 1207.

Mr. Green smiled. He could just simply say what he was and what he was here for, but that wouldn't satisfy. A job that had taken years deserved a pleasurable ending. He reflected back to when Lance was almost five. He could still see a sweet little face that radiated such blamelessness, exactly the same as the little boy he saw only days before.

"Do I look familiar to you, Lance?" Mr. Green said, leaning his bent frame closer to the table.

Lance felt as if he did, but couldn't recall. "No," he said.

"Are you absolutely sure? Think about your parent's next door neighbour—the one you used to visit—the one that told you stories."

Lance thought hard. His recollection was of an old gentleman standing at his sink, washing pots. Lance inwardly laughed as his recall expanded to the old gentleman gently waving to him, through the open

61

window. His next memory wasn't that amusing. He remembered coming home from school and seeing boxes piled outside the old gentleman's back door. He'd been curious, so he'd climbed over the wire fence for a closer look. His eyes saw open boxes deep in old suits and shoes. He remembered his investigative fingers rummaging between newspapers and magazines; it was the shock he got at seeing hundreds of sepia coloured photographs of soldiers with missing limbs, laying in fields of mud, that had frightened him the most. The heads on those limbless bodies looked like they'd been sculptured out of brown papier-mâché, and their faces pressed into shape by someone who had no idea of what the human face looked like.

The picture of horror on that child's face was again being shown.

"You remember the photographs?"

"Yes." Lance looked deep into blue-grey eyes, and for a moment saw the face of the old gentleman.

"Do I look familiar now?" Mr. Green smiled.

"Yes. But you died!"

"Yes. I died."

Lance's expression changed to distrust. "You're not that old gentleman," he spat. He felt deceit. "You're playing with my thoughts—what are you? Are you a clairvoyant—a swindler—a cheat—what's your game? I've a good mind to throw you out, no matter how old you are."

"I'm not a clairvoyant or any such insult, and I don't play games. I'm Mr. Green; I've always been Mr. Green. I've lived and died many times—whether you believe that is up to you. My job is to tell you the truth and help you back to where you belong."

Lance looked puzzled and intrigued. *What the hell does he mean 'Where I belong'?*

CHAPTER TWELVE

Stephanie knew how bad it felt to love someone and not receive that love back.

This week had been hard for Miss Swan. She'd finally tasted the man she wanted. Every morning she saw his eyes hunger after her, but no matter how hard she fed his appetite—with her filing routine—there was no reciprocation towards her feelings. Flirting was the only thing on the menu. She wanted to play Lance's new game, but Lance wasn't letting James out to play.

The flat shared by Miss Swan and Miss Duke was once a warehouse; that's to say, theirs and several other flats now occupied the interior of the warehouse's Victorian façade. As red-brick warehouses go, this one was rather appealing. Steps led to a central entrance door which then led to four ground floor flats. A staircase climbed to four more above. Each of the upper flats had the added feature of a private roof garden that looked over a canal.

Miss Duke leaned over the railing of her roof garden. She was watching for Imogen. Droplet earrings of white-gold brushed her cheek. Stephanie was dressed to thrill. Her hair was white and delicately spiked. It touched her neck and didn't touch her neck, playfully. She'd spent time on her hair so it looked like she hadn't. The evening breeze dashed along the street and up the red-bricked warehouse, like Romeo to his Juliet, flutter-ing her 1940's purple-flowered tea dress. Small hands with slender fingers, displaying shimmering purple nails, gripped the black iron.

For a Friday evening, the route home was unusually empty of another living soul. Imogen trudged along, in no hurry whatsoever. She imagined its emptiness was due to her. She was a ghost in her own world. To her, ghosts didn't exist—which was a contradiction of terms.

"Up here!" Stephanie called, on seeing the lone figure.

Imogen, using only her eyes, looked up. *At least someone's pleased to see me*, she flippantly thought. She walked up the steps and slid her keycard into the mechanical lock. It clicked and opened.

The sight that greeted her at the top of the stairs was reminiscent of a WW2 spy movie—Stephanie's stance, clothes and make-up set the scene for an open door that led to shelter, aimed at all those with a wounded heart. The temptress leant against the door frame seductively.

Imogen, feeling like a spy coming in from the cold, slid between woman and door frame. She took off her coat and hung it over several others that cluttered the wall. Her bag was dropped to the floor. Her shoes were kicked off, and a much smaller woman stood.

The door closed.

Stephanie walked past Imogen and stopped. She turned and said, "Do I look OK?"

"You look beautiful," was the honest answer.

Stephanie looked into doe eyes. Her gaze then lowered to hand-full breasts that were softly covered and hidden by a tightly fitting, pale-blue cashmere jumper. "I wish I had a pair like that," she said, looking down at her own.

"You can have them."

"I'm not having plastic surgery; you know how I feel about things like that."

Imogen smiled and fluttered her eyes. "That's not what I meant."

Stephanie wasn't in the mood for words. She closed in, like a wild animal, on the thing she wanted. Shimmering purple-nailed fingers teased up the tight-fitting jumper. Small hands undid a lacy bra and raised it up. Lipstick-lips parted and played a tiny version of suck-suck.

Imogen slid her fingers through Stephanie's hair. "Take me to your bedroom," she said, panting. "Show me what else your mouth can do."

"Do you want me to behave like a man?"

"No. Be a woman."

"I'm glad you said that—if you had wanted me to be a man, I'd have left you standing there with your tits out. I don't like playing other people's games," Stephanie said, taking Imogen's hand and leading her to her bedroom. "I play the only game my womanly heart knows."

They both looked at each other with rainbow eyes. Nothing more needed to be said.

CHAPTER THIRTEEN

Mr. Green looked pleased—Lance was baited.

"Explain?" Lance said, now determined to listen rather than pick the old man up by the scruff of his neck and throw him out the door. "It better be good."

"Right, I'll begin by telling you how James Walker came to be upon this earth," Mr. Green said.

"Are you a relative?" Lance asked.

Mr. Green laughed. "No, Lance, I'm only a messenger."

"And who do you message for?"

"You know who," Mr. Green said, without feeling. "I'll refer to them as The Sleeping, but that is only one of their names—they have several. Don't be concerned about what others call them."

What others? Lance was caught and being drawn in. He wanted to know all there was to know about James Walker, and if that meant having to listen to Mr. Green's absurd delusions about himself, then so be it.

"James Walker," Mr. Green began, deterring his eyes from Lance, "has no birth certificate—it's as if he doesn't exist. But he does exist and I've been following him for most of his life. His mother's name is Margaret Walker; his father's name is unknown. Margaret Walker was married with two children when she was having out-of-marriage relations. The affair, as in many cases, ended due to her pregnancy. Her marriage also ended—well it would, wouldn't it?

"Margaret Walker gave birth to a boy on the 12 July 1969, she named him James. He wasn't created out of want—he is 'The Unwanted', and the unwanted have no place in this world." Mr. Green's eyes seemed to cloud to black. An expression of wasted time etched itself deeper into an already aged face. His skeletal frame creaked to an even lower posture. He groaned the pain of a living hell existence. "So, Margaret Walker," Mr. Green continued, "not wanting to keep this baby, took him to the Sisters of Hope Convent. It was in the hands of Sister Miriam that she left him.

"Sister Miriam did what she thought would be in the baby's best interest. Sister Miriam is a believer in all that is good—she is a fool…" Mr. Green paused. He glanced, for a second, into Lance's face. Lance was absorbed. "The only information she had been given was the baby's Christian name, date of birth and that the birth had not been recorded. Sister Miriam chose to keep that information to herself, and yet she knew that all information about abandoned children must be passed to the relevant authorities. She thought that if she hid his circumstances, she would be protecting him. She was wrong—I said she was a fool—there is no protection for those that are not meant to be.

"She acted upon her feelings—she knew of a woman that desperately wanted a baby. This woman was unable to bring her pregnancies to full term, for one reason or another. She had only recently gone into labour and lost her fifth child. Sister Miriam made the kind act of taking the abandoned baby to her. A bond was quickly made.

"Sister Miriam now made that delayed registration of birth—it is usual for an unknown date of birth, as the good Sister made this out to be, to be determined by guesswork based on how old the baby looked. A simple subtraction gave a rough estimation of the day and month. Sister Miriam intervened by requesting that the birth date be written down as the day that the child came into her care. Again, she thought this would protect him, and again she was wrong. The registrar did as requested. The child's name was documented as the name given by the child's new mother..." Mr. Green paused again. He gave an upward glance. There was almost delight in his face. "I see you're taking notes, Lance. Are you treating me as one of your patients?"

Lance didn't respond to such flippancy. He continued to scribble down everything he was being told.

Mr. Green looked away, and carried on: "The story of James Walker, Lance, is not fictional in any way. It is a story nonetheless, and still has some way to go. I'm pleased, so far, that you are not turning me away and grouping me with the crazies. The term 'insane' must surely be applied to someone who deems himself to have lived and died and lived again many times, in his pursuit of someone who should not have existed. I don't, in anyway, question my own sanity—I am what I am. I'm simply The Messenger."

"I'm not going to term you as anything, Mr. Green," Lance said calmly. "If you have delusions of being The Messenger for The Sleeping, then so be it. If it makes you happy in your belief, then who am I to judge?"

"I don't have delusions, Lance. And for the record, I'm not happy. I must finish my job and offer back The Unwanted. Only then will I be at peace."

Lance didn't say another word, but he thought many things. The one thought that lead all the others, was that Mr. Green had told him that he was there to help him back to where he belonged. For some strange reason, he was beginning to feel that the old man sitting opposite was here to do just that. Something was scratching its way out of the darkest part of his very existence and growing in its belief. He poised himself with pen.

Mr. Green, without a glance as to whether Lance was ready to listen to more, continued his story:

"What is termed 'The Room of Truth' is at the end of a brick tunnel, far beneath St. Thomas' Church. That part of the church dates back to the 11th century. The structure that rises above ground level began construction in 1571.

"Of those that are involved in the day-to-day running of St. Thomas', only a few are aware of the brick tunnel and the room that is at its end. Sister Miriam is one of those; she is the one that spends her time in 'The Room of Truth'. She is The Custodian of its sins. She enters this room by another way, by the tunnel that leads from the Sisters of Hope Convent.

"You will not find what I've just told you in any books. Secrets are often the most disturbing. It won't hurt me to tell you about this room. The dead can't hurt me, and there are many dead entombed in that room. They are there because they died there. Theistic Satanism was practiced there. Young Pretty Things, from both sides of those tunnels, were woken from their beds and taken to that room for what they thought was an initiation ceremony. And to all intents and purposes it was. Their souls were given to Satan by acts of sexual pleasure, with the final slitting of their throat. The altar would flow in blood, to be drunk.

"That practice is no longer carried out; you'll be pleased to hear. Records of events are historical facts. The church loves historical facts, and especially if they are secrets kept to themselves.

"Make a note of all that, Lance. You will need to recall 'The Room of Truth' when you visit Sister Miriam."

Mr. Green craned his gaze upwards towards the ceiling. It was as if he was looking through the upper floor and roof, towards the dark, star-lit sky. He lowered his gaze to Lance, who was busy scribbling away. He held that gaze, waiting for the inevitable question.

Lance paused his writing. The pen wanted to deposit more ink, but without any more words there was nothing more it could do. It waited ready in the hand that quivered.

"And?" Lance asked, itching to know.

"Do you want to know about the depravity?" Mr. Green said playfully.

"You know I don't," Lance said.

"I know you don't," Mr. Green smirked. "I'll tell you what you want to know tomorrow. At this moment in time I need to rest." He pushed his bent body up by the use of his arms, as hydraulic jacks, against the table top. "I recommend that you sleep before we meet again," he said, turning and leaving the room.

Lance remained seated. Nothing more was going to be written tonight. He lowered his pen and watched Mr. Green leave.

"Goodnight, Mrs. Lewisham," Mr. Green said, passing Katherine in the hall. She was still sat on the floor. "I hope you heard all there was to hear?"

The front door opened and Mr. Green stepped out into shadows. The door closed behind him, leaving The Sleeping's deathly odour to remain in every shadow for a little longer.

A few minutes passed before Katherine managed to pull herself up. She stumbled into the kitchen and sat shakily next to her husband.

The glass of vodka and coke, that Lance had poured earlier, was still on the table. Katherine grabbed it and drank it, in one gulp.

"I think I'll make a few more of those," she said in a hazy calm.

Lance followed Katherine into the living-room. Neither felt like eating an evening meal. The lap-top was brought out and surfing commenced, initiating a liquid supper. Katherine poured the drinks. Lance didn't object.

Mr. Green was right about St. Thomas' being built in the 11th century. He was also correct in its rebuild in 1571. And annoyingly, he was also truthful about there being nothing in regard to what lay beneath St.

Thomas'. A search into the nearby Sisters of Hope Convent also brought up nothing about secret passages or rooms. The only new thing to learn was that the original convent had suffered the same fate as the original St. Thomas', which was originally a monastery. Both had suffered from the fury of Henry VIII. After the pillage of their wealth, the monks and nuns protested conversion to the new religion. Many who were true to the Catholic faith died for their beliefs. Both buildings suffered the same fate of fire in 1538, with the dissolution of the monasteries. It wasn't until twenty-four years after the death of the King that building upon the monastery ruins had begun.

Lance thought about the worship that was performed far underground between these two buildings. *Did those followers of Satan destroy the houses of God above, in a bid to hide their secrets from those that chose to pry?*

About an inch of vodka remained in the bottle. Katherine was drunk and feeling sleepy.

"Mr. Green thinks my mother is watching over me," Katherine slurred.

"He's a crank."

"He hasn't a soul."

Lance picked up the bottle of vodka, looked at it, and put it down again. He swayed slightly.

"Beddy-bye's is calling," he said, pulling Katherine up. He turned off the lights and directed his wife towards bed.

Katherine staggered towards the hall and climbed the stairs, gripping tightly to the banister. Lance followed and made sure she didn't fall backwards by placing his hand in the small of her back.

Katherine went into the bathroom first. She came out looking deathly white. She climbed into bed with all the grace of a bandy-legged ostrich.

Her head hit the pillow; she clung to the bedside as the room spun. Then she was out like a light.

The only thing Lance did in the bathroom was to empty his bladder. He dropped his clothes in exactly the same place as Katherine's—the floor. Then he climbed into bed as he always did, naked.

Katherine's arm lay outside of the bed. Lance leaned over and pulling it in, slid it under the covers. Her body was warm and inviting. He tenderly kissed the nape of her neck and curled up behind her. His eyes closed and his mind wandered to visions of sex with young pretty things, all of them looking exactly like his secretary.

CHAPTER FOURTEEN

A stone chamber, of ample proportions, hid between two solid oak doors. It was a crypt in the bowels of the earth that displayed all the magnificence of the macabre. The walls were adorned with human skulls—they were the audience of the dead, in waiting. An iron wheel on a wall looked like it was going to be turned.

Beauty knelt at the feet of the Beast. A naked, horned-man stood in the richness of his conviction. In one hand he held something that shone like a dagger; in the other was a breast of Beauty. Hooded figures came from the darkness, each one fluent in his recitation of the rite.

The horned-man now also knelt. He kissed with a penetrating tongue. The dagger flashed across Beauty's neck. It slashed—blood spurted.

Lance suddenly sat upright; a horned-man's splattered bloodied face lit his vision with searing power.

Lance's nightmare-eyes burned. He began pushing his fists into their sockets, twisting them in fear, until the bloodied face scorched away amongst a wash of red. His heart was a double kick-drum playing glam-rock. His body sweat panic.

When he dared to open his eyes, into the blackness of the room, he was challenged with another face, just inches away. This face had no eyes. And yet it stared at him with a hungering look. This face was white and it masked its own shadow.

It lingered until Lance screamed. And Lance did scream. He screamed the house down.

The face dispersed into the room's darkness, the shadow hid itself away in the corners that are the blackest.

Katherine heard nothing.

When Lance finally stopped screaming, his throat was sore. He lay back down amongst his thoughts. He understood the nightmare. But what was the white face masking its shadow? He had the strangest feeling that he'd seen this shadow once before, a very long time ago.

It was 2.00 a.m. Lance stared up at the ceiling. The room was silent in its early hour.

With a renewed strength, the shadows converged to make the shape of a human-like figure. A face of white appeared out of its desire. The figure stood in the corner amongst the darkness, its face now veiled in its own fabric.

Slowly it moved. It was a whisper in the silence. When it reached the foot of the bed it knelt upon it. Lance felt the bottom of the bed dip. It was as if a heavy-laden suitcase had been placed there. But suitcases don't move. The black figure crawled up Lance's legs. Lance tried to sit up and push whatever he was feeling off him. He couldn't move. Fear gripped him.

He called out to Katherine. He called again, and again, and again. His throat was ripping. But Katherine didn't hear.

The black figure had now reached his chest. It was covering him with its body, slowly inch by inch, until the corpus necessary to absorb, was fulfilled.

Lance, with strength of mind, looked down across his body.

The figure of dense black loomed up to stare into his face. The veil fell to show a face of white, absent of eyes, yet it stared into his own, in searching.

Lance screamed. The figure absorbed the scream. Lance's scream joined all the other screams that had been collected over time. The shouts of help invited him to attend. The more he eavesdropped, the clearer he could hear. Distant voices sobbed. Crying and shouting and screaming all intermixed, yet each could be heard in their singularity. In that sound, amongst Lance's screaming, was his own crying when he was a young child. It was being woven to his teenage screams. There were other voices too; all were lost in the darkness. The sound that was once a frightened child's single cry, had now become an ensemble of cries as fragments of living souls were being interlaced to the souls of the dead. The sound was becoming deafening.

The air in Lance's lungs was being compressed and squeezed out. Lance exhaled as the figure lowered itself. The weight was unbearable—it felt like a hundred lifeless bodies were crushing him—as the white face pressed against his own. He could see a light, deep within the eye sockets. The light was calling him. He felt that the light needed him. He thought of Katherine.

Katherine turned in her sleep and put her arm over Lance's chest.

Lance suddenly inhaled. His throat burnt as his lungs expanded. Oxygen rushed to his brain—he wasn't going to die.

The figure dispersed again into shadow.

Lance sat upright. Katherine woke as her arm fell to her side.

It was now 2.09 a.m.

"Are you O.K.?" she said sleepily, as Lance lay back down. She again put her arm across his chest.

Lance's breathing was fast and loud. His kick-drum was rocking. He was drenched.

Katherine swiftly removed her arm and turned over. She opened her eyes and quickly shut them again. The room was beginning to turn again. Feeling queasy, she hung her head over the edge of the bed.

"If you've been dreaming of her again I'll…" was as far as she got before she vomited. It wasn't pretty.

Lance helped her to the bathroom where she vomited some more, luckily this time, into the toilet. He left her with her head over the rim.

"Never again," she spluttered. "I hate vodka!"

Lance cleaned up and put his rescuer back into bed, placing a bucket by her side. He looked about the darkness. The darkness didn't scare him; it was what was in the darkness that scared him. When he climbed into bed he thought about his nightmare. If that's what it was. It felt so real. To deny it was admitting to being dead, which he wasn't.

A shadow from behind the bed stretched up a hand that rested upon a shoulder. Lance felt nothing except that it would be better to think about more pleasant things. He switched his thoughts towards work. Imogen was all he saw.

The hand vanished from his shoulder.

No. 111 Padstow Avenue still had its hall lights on. Mr. Green was in his living-room. The only light he could see by was that which entered from the door left purposely ajar.

Mr. Green paced as a bear does when confined. He was waiting.

The front door opened and closed again. Mr. Green walked towards a small side-table and looked into the mirror placed above. He stared at himself and thought about what he'd said to Katherine. Soulless eyes, hollow of any emotion, stared back.

Behind him a shadow moved. It rose to a human's height and walked through him, into the mirror. Now he stared at the face of his soul captor. A white face stared back from sockets of black. It was one of The Sleeping. They were many, so which of them this was made no difference. They all looked the same to him. They all had the same purpose. How many were there? He had no idea. If he had to guess—he would say thousands.

Mr. Green explained his meeting with the Lewisham's and especially his talk with Lance. The Sleeping writhed in its mass as Mr. Green bent a little further.

He managed the pain in his spine with his own personal belief. It wasn't his fault that Lance was good at resisting. How could he be blamed for a soul that wouldn't surrender? He must try harder to break into that psyche. He would do that today, as soon as Lance paid him a visit.

CHAPTER FIFTEEN

Lance woke, climbed out of bed and threw open the curtains. For a moment he didn't know where he was. If there was anybody at the window of the house opposite they would be greeted by a naked man standing proud. There wasn't. And if there were, the exhibitionist didn't care. Not this morning.

Lance made himself presentable and went downstairs to make coffee. His stomach felt as if someone had taken it out, wrung it and turned it inside out before ham-fistedly putting it back. He also had a headache that craved painkillers.

Tablets and coffee were making their presence welcome as he recounted the previous evening. He went for the controversial file. On reading his notes of how James described his encounters, he felt a connection. He needed to see Mr. Green, urgently.

Katherine was awake and standing at the bathroom mirror. Her reflection looked ghastly. A shower was needed to wash away the decay that layered itself over every part of her. Soon water was falling through her hair, over absorbing flesh, down legs that trembled, and away. Handfuls of shower gel did nothing to remove that unfavourable feeling she had about the soulless man she'd met yesterday evening. Even though he never touched her sexually, he'd left what felt like a strange discoloration to her skin. It was something suggestive of mild sunburn—no amount of washing was going to make it go away. It remained an invisible taint.

It was 9.00 a.m. Lance knocked on the front door of No. 111 Padstow Avenue. He waited with all the nervousness of a condemned man at the gallows. *Where the hell is the executioner?*

Mr. Green opened the door.

"Please come in," he said, and stood aside.

Lance walked past Mr. Green, down the hall, into the living-room, and sat in one of the two armchairs that were beside the fireplace.

Mr. Green followed, with a lower stoop, and sat in the remaining armchair. Both looked at each other, both wanting to speak.

"I presume, from your manner, that you've had a visit from The Sleeping?" said Mr. Green. This made a perfect, poignant starting place.

Lance's reaction to Mr. Green's deduction was balanced somewhere between anxiety and professional calm. It wasn't easy.

"I feel as if I have to bow to your assumption," he said.

"Then I will continue from where we left off."

"Not more history, Mr. Green."

Mr. Green laughed. "Lance," he said, "history is part of this. Yesterday is history and so is every day before that. But I understand. Let's start with The Sleeping, shall we?"

Lance merely nodded.

"The Sleeping, as far as I've fathomed, go back to when human life began. Let's not get into anything biblical."

Lance nodded to this.

"Do you agree that bodies have souls?"

Lance again nodded.

"Well then, The Sleeping are wardens for those souls that are in the underworld."

"You mean Hell?"

"We said not to get biblical," Mr. Green said. "Each soul starts as pure light. It then, like a sponge, absorbs what the body feeds it. The soul is our very being. It is the best of us and the worst. The Sleeping suckle from those that enter into their realm. Evil is their existence. The Sleeping can enter into your world only when they come for the souls of the unwanted and only when they have a key. I am The Messenger—I am The Key.

"I told you that I have lived and died and lived again. I lived my first life as many men do; I wanted money and lots of it. I was doing well, hundreds of thousands of doing well. Then it happened, the economy collapsed. It was the blackest day in financial history, it became known as Black Tuesday. October 29th 1929 was the day I first died. I took my Pocket Hammerless—the same model that Bonnie Parker had taped to her thigh to help Clyde Barrow break out of jail—from the right-hand drawer of my beautiful burr walnut desk and shot myself. It was suicide, and my soul was instantly grasped and taken to the underworld."

Lance listened. He needed to listen, to understand. He could have simply stood up and walked out. He thought it was the description of the semi-automatic pistol that rooted him to the chair. But it was simpler than that. It was the need to know more about James Walker. He craved that knowledge.

"I was offered, in exchange for another soul, my soul," Mr. Green said. "If I helped them collect a soul from the Unwanted, then my soul would be released from their grip and allowed to enter the light—I was assigned to James Walker. I have never been far away from him. But every time he resists their calling, I am tortured by the bending of my spine. They cannot hurt my soul, for in this existence I am soulless."

"You said yesterday that your job was to tell me the truth and help me back to where I belong."

"I did."

"Then where is it that I belong?"

"Lance, my dear friend, and for all the time that I've known you, that's what you are, there is more you need to know before I can answer that directly."

"Answer me this then—what do The Sleeping look like?"

"Is this a test?"

"Yes," Lance said.

"But you know what they look like. You saw one of them last night."

"Then describe them to me, if you can."

"Very well," Mr. Green conceded. "They are like shadows…"

Lance spluttered through his laughter, "Whoa! Ghostly shadows—that's original! You've got to do better than that."

"May I continue?"

"Please do."

Mr. Green thought it funny that he wasn't being believed. But then again, Lance was a rather strange character, much like himself.

"Last night you were visited by a human-like figure that presented itself to you. It appeared as it did when James was five, when it walked out of the wardrobe, white-faced and eyeless, and yet it sees from sockets of the darkest black. When The Sleeping come in bodily form, it is because they are in great need of that soul that was created for the Unwanted. To show itself showed its need. It will continue to come, no matter how long it takes or by what measures, to take it."

Lance was no longer laughing. "Do The Sleeping want me to give them, in some way, James Walker?"

"Yes. Are you now in acceptance of me?" Mr. Green asked.

"Almost," Lance said.

Katherine was dressed and downstairs, in a hangover state. She held her head and, in the hope that it wouldn't topple from her slumped shoulders, sipped at strong coffee—the aroma made her feel sick. Coffee was meant to help, just like the painkillers that were trying to quieten the thumping inside her head. But there was no escaping, not just yet, that feeling that over-drinking brings or the furry sensation that her tongue had—she was inside an imaginary fur-lined boot that was stomping down a cobbled street.

Mr. Green looked at Lance sitting opposite. His blue-grey eyes smiled at someone he called a friend, in his own gratification that one day this friend would set his soul free from those known to both as The Sleeping.

Lance didn't smile. He didn't do anything except stare into those blue-grey eyes.

"The truth now, Lance, has to be accepted," Mr. Green said with indulgence to what he'd previously said. He was, to be truthful, unsure as to how Lance would receive this truth, but, as painful as it might be, it had to be told. "You must listen and not interrupt. Interruptions delay and neither of us want that, do we?"

Lance didn't answer—he heeded the advice.

"I will say it as plainly as possible—you are James Walker. There, I couldn't have said it any plainer."

Lance didn't respond in any other way than contemptuous silence. He digested the words and waited for more.

Mr. Green took the silence as non-committal. He continued: "James Walker was born on the 12th July 1969, his birth certificate shows the date as 2nd September 1969 and that his name is now registered as Lance—if you are in any doubt over this, you should ask Sister Miriam."

"I intend to," Lance said. He didn't say anymore, but his brain was on fire. *Why didn't my mother tell me this?*

Mr. Green read the question and answered. "You were told of your adoption when you were five—you responded badly. You said words that were meant to hurt. But they didn't. Your mother understood your anger; she loved you like you were of her flesh—she felt that she had actually given birth to you.

"And remember this, when you were given to her, she had only just given birth and lost her baby. Once you were handed to her, she instantly felt that you were hers—nothing could break that bond."

Lance sat in a chilling silence. Even Mr. Green felt the coldness, as nothing came from a mind that was thinking.

"Lance," Mr. Green said, "Your mother couldn't tell you anything about your blood-parents, because she honestly didn't know. The subject of adoption was always there for you, should you have needed to talk. You chose not to talk about it—you shut it away inside of you. You wanted to be the same as everyone else. You wanted to fit in.

"The Sleeping came for you when you were five. You saw one of them come out of the wardrobe. It conjured your name—the name your blood-mother gave you—and spat it at you. You screamed in blissful ignorance to its calling.

"To The Sleeping you are The Unwanted. And they just made a claim on your soul. It is a claim they've made many times over.

"Your childhood was a happy one—your teenage years fraught. The Sleeping's visits became irregular nightmares. Sometimes they appeared, sometimes you became as them—to be able to walk amongst the shadows and wander at will—and each time you let them closer with your curiousness. Firstly, shadows crawled over you. Then the shadows got darker and heavier, until they are as you see them today.

"The visits only occur when you are deep in thought about who you really are. All the unanswerable questions are slowly eating away at you, in a way, similar to how The Sleeping feed. There is no escaping their feeding.

"Once you were so angry about who you were, that you punched a window. The Sleeping sensed your energy, and as your fist broke the glass—which was reflecting your image as a mirror—The Sleeping appeared opposite you. You were feeding it. It wanted more. It needed more. It grabbed your wrist and pulled you in. Again you resisted, you pulled away with such force that it lost its grip. You pulled your hand back through the hole, from their world. Your reflection disappeared and your wrist was slashed by the broken glass. Your loss of blood sent you unconscious to the floor. You were lucky not to die. You still bear the scar across your right wrist, like a suicide that failed."

Lance turned his hand, palm up. Sad eyes followed his fate line down from his fingers—it touched his life line, giving the meaning that he would have to surrender his own interests to those of others. And where his fate line separated again, meant he was back in control of his life. Those same sorrowful eyes now moved over his wrist bracelets—here was the jagged white line that was his reminder of how close he came to death, and Them.

"When you met Katherine, your nightmares slid into oblivion. But it was only for a while—your happiness couldn't stall them forever. The loss of your baby daughter—heart-breaking as it was—pushed you into gloomy thoughts. You blamed yourself, and you blamed Katherine, which is a natural thing to do; only it wasn't either of your faults. You wrapped your grieving into the web of time, hoping to lose the memory. But memories, Lance, return.

"Even what your mother told you when you were five, never went away. Your dreams surfaced the memory, so much so, that you slipped between the doors of two existences. As strange as this may sound—you have a split personality. Here—today—you are as Lance. Other days—as

in weekends away—you become James. It's strange how you become…
you. I suppose it's a bit like Dr Jekyll and Mr. Hyde, don't you think?

"Are you now in acceptance of me?" he asked again.

Lance stood up. "I'm going home," he said. "I need to think."

"You'll be back with questions."

"Will I?"

"Yes."

"See you later then."

Mr. Green smiled. "By the way, Lance," he said with a teasing spar-
kle to his eyes, "Margaret Walker had two more children after she gave
you away, and kept them. Do you now feel more unwanted?"

Lance left Mr. Green sitting in his own misery—for that's what Lance
thought he must surely be in, because every time he was around this bent-
double, grey-haired old man, he felt pretty much the same.

Lance entered his own home as a living ghost. He felt everything a
hanged man felt when being taken down from the gallows—nothing. He
sat next to Katherine.

"You look as bad as I feel," Katherine said, noticing his ashen face.

"You don't know the half of it," Lance said.

"I don't want to know just yet—I don't feel very well."

Lance laid back and closed his eyes. He thought about his parents,
and the sorrow they must have endured in losing five children. He knew
their feelings, even if it was only a fifth in magnitude. Katherine thought
he hadn't feelings—but he had—he just didn't talk about them.

He found it difficult to understand, without having children of his
own, the happiness he'd brought his parents. Also, why was life so
unfair? Understanding the intricacies of life and death was beyond him.
He thought of why those that didn't want children bore them, and those
that truly did want children, couldn't bare them. It tore him apart. He

knew that if his soul ever got to its architect, then there was going to be one hell of an argument.

CHAPTER SIXTEEN

Stephanie lay face down upon the mattress—the bedding was down, below her buttocks. Imogen was beside her with wandering fingers. Those fingers curled the short hair at the nape of a dainty neck. Then they slowly, and extremely provocatively, stroked a delicate backbone before slipping down between the cheeks of a boyish backside.

Stephanie moaned, pleasurably, "Oh…" and parted her legs slightly.

"Time to wake up," Imogen whispered. "It's nearly midday."

She climbed out of bed leaving Stephanie to play with herself—which she did.

Katherine was starting to feel more human. She turned to Lance, and quite out of the blue, said;

"Do you think I'm still attractive?" She was remembering Lance's feverish state during his dream. "Am I?" she pressed.

Lance opened his eyes and was greeted by a face that appeared to look twenty years older by its blotchiness and dark-bagged eyes. It was haloed by hair that looked like it had been tossed by salad-tongs, to give it that ventilated, dragged-through-a-hedge backwards look.

"To whom?" he said.

"Thank you—that's just what I needed to hear!" She stood up and ran up the stairs in a flood of tears.

The bedroom door slammed—the noise stoked his headache.

Lance was not in the mood for a marital argument. He grabbed his jacket and car keys and left the house. He went only as far as next door. Determination hung on his brow as he knocked on Mr. Green's door.

The old man opened the door and said: "I told you you'd be back with questions."

"I don't want you to answer any questions, not just yet—What I need is a passenger who knows where to find Sister Miriam."

Mr. Green smiled.

"Get your coat—I'll be waiting for you in the car—you've got five minutes."

"Or you'll do what?" Mr. Green retaliated.

Threats—Mr. Green liked. He wanted to wait past the five minutes, just to see what would happen. But his need for his soul's release was greater than the fun of Lance's fight for his own.

Lance walked to his car. He got in and gripped the steering wheel—both hands shook with either rage or nerves. He couldn't tell which.

Four and a half minutes later and Mr. Green was sat in the passenger seat.

"Are you going to grip that wheel all day or are you going to start the car? I'm not sitting here for the fun of it." But he was—*Even the soulless can have fun once in a while*, he thought.

Lance looked at his passenger with disdain. "The only words I want to hear from you are 'left' or 'right'—anymore, and it won't only be The Sleeping that bends your spine." The words spilled so effortlessly from his mouth, that the thought of doing it gave him pleasure.

Mr. Green said nothing until the car reached the end of Padstow Avenue. "Left," he said with a smile. His thoughts directed to the car: *Nice car—I was wrong about him. I imagined him having a BMW and being the typical twat that drives it up everybody's arse. It seems I can't be right about him all the time. What's the betting he has this car for a reason?*

After one and a half hours and a multiple of verbal 'lefts' and 'rights' later, they were parked in a car park that was as close as you could possibly get to St. Thomas'. Lance got out of the car and wandered off. Minutes later, he was back with a ticket from the pay and display machine that he promptly stuck to the inside of his windscreen.

"O.K., Dead Man, walk," he said dryly.

Mr. Green got out of the car and walked in the direction of the church. Lance locked the car doors and followed.

By the time Lance caught up, Mr. Green was at the church gate. The bent-double old man craned his neck upwards to a square tower where a clock marked holy time. The steeple constructed above pierced a sky of grey and blue. His eyes lowered to the ground. Headstones leant with age—just like him.

"Praying?" Lance said, towering over the sinner at his side.

"It's you that should be praying, don't you think?" Mr. Green said, walking away. "Arrangements for my soul have already been made."

Lance walked beside Mr. Green as he walked alongside wrought-iron railings on the perimeter of the church grounds. The land inside those wrought-iron railings occupied far less than a supermarket. It said something about the way we live today—more people go to a supermarket than they do to church.

Mr. Green strode off down a narrow street that descended away from the church. Lance was as obedient as any servant, and followed behind in silence—his thoughts racing ahead on what he would say to Sister Miriam.

In file, Mr. Green showed the way with the confident manner in which he now walked.

"Try to keep up," he joked.

Lance didn't laugh; he just closed the gap between them.

"Not far now," Mr. Green said. "We're practically there."

That wasn't exactly true. Thirty minutes of walking wasn't practically there. Lance was of a different opinion. *Maybe the old man just wants to see the church first or maybe there's another reason.*

They both turned a corner and saw a length of building, built from red bricks, which seemed to stretch forever. They walked on, until they reached a large sandstone arch. Written in a block of the same stone, above the arch, were the words: The Sisters of Hope Convent.

Through the arch was spied a courtyard with neat box hedging, that was surrounded by a canopied outer walkway.

Mr. Green looked away towards a park area that was opposite—St. Thomas' Church bell struck twice. He crossed the road and wandered off into the park, through iron gates, along a tarmac path that was neatly edged by grass—where small stones and leaves had blown—and to a wooden bench that would soon be visited. It was in clear view of the sandstone arch. The surrounding rose-beds were still blooming in pinks and reds and were a playground for the squirrels, until they disappeared up the trees that were starting to lose their leaves.

Lance soon followed. He found the bent-double old man sitting on a long green bench—that easily sat six—with a handful of small stones, which he was throwing at the pigeons.

"I hate the verminous things," he said with every throw—the birds scattered and re-grouped further away.

"Why are we in a park and not at the convent?" Lance said, sitting down next to the pigeon tyrant.

"Because, Lance, Sister Miriam is a woman of habit—excuse the pun, she comes here every day at 3 o'clock and feeds the bloody pigeons."

"Including today?"

"I did say 'every day'."

Lance folded his arms and waited.

It wasn't long before Mr. Green had scooped up another handful of small stones and was in the process of scattering the birds all over again.

"Can't you stop doing that?" Lance said, indignantly.

"Why?"

"Because that's what a child would do."

"Fine," Mr. Green said, throwing what was left in his hand at one very large pigeon that was refusing to move. "Stubborn little shit, isn't it?"

Lance refused to answer; instead he looked across the road and waited for a nun to wander out with a bag of birdseed in her hand.

For the next hour, neither spoke—Lance watched the squirrels.

St. Thomas' Church bell sounded thrice. Five minutes passed and again, without word. Then, as predicted by Mr. Green, a woman in her sixties emerged clutching a clear plastic bag readily showing several handfuls of bird seed. Lance straightened his posture and waited for her arrival. He was expecting to see a woman wearing the insignia of her order; instead she was dressed in normal street clothes of a checked skirt and warm cardigan. It was only when she walked through the gates of the park, that he noticed the large wooden crucifix around her neck.

She walked with a sprightly step. Her short, grey hair was combed with a side parting—almost manly-looking—and lacquered so it didn't move. Some would say, owing to her vocation, that she had the face of an angel. It seemed to radiate warmth and love. She was in her sixties, but looked a good ten years younger.

Imogen was breathing fast and her lungs felt tight, as she walked hand-in-hand down the street with Stephanie. The squeeze to her hand showed that Stephanie was in support and pleased that her own feelings could be shown in public. Imogen didn't feel quite so thrilled.

"Relax!" Stephanie said, as she smiled at passers-by. "Neither of us looks like dykes."

Not one person gave a blind bit of notice at two women holding hands. Lots of women held hands, even straight women. Stephanie was moving like a Hollywood movie star—in her 1940s self-designed tea dress—on a Sunday afternoon walk. Imogen was also wearing one from the same collection but was feeling less confident. It was possibly the stockings and suspenders that did it. The breeze was refreshing in a naughty way. Stephanie's choices of dresses were deliberate. The accessories that brought them both into the present—apart from their hair styles—were their bags and jackets. Stephanie liked to mix and match decades. The torn-frayed Levi was genuine '70s, whilst the shoulder-bag was swinging-hippy '60s. Imogen had on a cropped, brown tweed equestrian riding jacket with a brown, leather shoulder bag—so small it held only make-up and a purse—loosely over her shoulder.

Stephanie had decided that Sunday dinner was called for; the place mustn't be too close—or far away for that matter—to make Imogen feel uncomfortable in anyway. In such an early stage in their new relationship, meeting anyone that Imogen knew, would most definitely push her back into the bisexual closet.

Imogen wasn't like Stephanie when discussing sexuality—Stephanie was a tell-the-world person, whereas Imogen was more reserved and thought it nobody's business but her own.

Stephanie recalled a conversation she'd had with her photographer, telling her about the canal area she'd moved into, and not that far away was a public-house that was apparently haunted.

Stephanie loved anything to do with ghosts—she was a firm believer in the supernatural.

This apparently haunted establishment was called 'The Rifleman' and was reputed to do a great steak and ale pie, in a very period setting. It was a place where families could go to eat, so there wouldn't be any ogling beer-bellied men eyeing up two attractive-looking women.

Imogen agreed about Sunday dinner. The steak and ale pie wasn't for her. And ghosts definitely hadn't any appeal. But if it was off their beaten track—where they wouldn't be seen—then the place sounded perfect.

Sister Miriam didn't look surprised to see Mr. Green sitting there. She'd been seeing him on and off since 1974 and at first, didn't think him real. At that time, she had no belief in ghosts—the dead were dead—or so she thought. Mr. Green was real, and was very much amongst the living. She approached in her usual way, with no fear of him and with smiley blue-grey eyes.

"Hello, Lance," she said with a heavenly smile, "I knew you'd come and see me one day."

Lance was surprised by her knowing him. Far too many questions ran in his head to speak.

Sister Miriam now turned to Mr. Green and said quite pleasantly: "Hello, Great-grandfather, are you still teasing the birds?"

"Hello, Miriam," Mr. Green said, with a broad smile—he found the experience of being with his Great-granddaughter rather amusing.

Sister Miriam sat down next to her Great-grandfather and began feeding the pigeons.

Lance didn't speak—he was feeling stunned by the whole situation.

"I see by your stoop that The Sleeping are still inflicting their fun on you," Sister Miriam said, almost laughing.

"It's not fun, Miriam, it hurts like hell."

"And so it should. But on the whole—you look well for a one-hundred and fifty-four year old."

Lance almost choked laughing.

Mr. Green cocked his thumb upwards, pointed his index finger to his mouth, and cleverly flicked his digitus medius, triggering his finger-gun. "Bang!" he said.

"That's so funny," Sister Miriam said, throwing more seed to the flocking pigeons. Mr. Green's sudden outburst did nothing to scare them. "How many times have you died now? Oh, yes. Once by your own hand and two by Their calling—can't you stay dead? It would be so much less irritating, for the both of us."

"You're so heartless, Miriam," Mr. Green said.

"I'm not heartless, Great-grandfather."

"Why are you still in disbelief of me?"

"I'm not in disbelief of you, Great-grandfather, I'd just rather you stay dead."

Lance nodded his agreement.

Sister Miriam stood up and threw the last of the bird seed into a swarm of pecking, strutting pigeons.

"Lance, dear," she said warmly, "come and see me next Sunday, at the convent—come at three, and don't bring him." Her eyes darted and flashed at her Great-grandfather, who was picking up small stones from around his feet. "I'll tell you what you want to know and I'll explain about him."

"Tell him about 'The Room of Truth', Miriam. Tell him what it is that you do in there," Mr. Green said, giving a schoolboy smirk as if he was letting out a secret.

"Shut up, Great-grandfather."

Sister Miriam walked away hastily, scattering the pigeons into a mass of grey and white. When they re-settled—Sister Miriam was gone.

"She's a flighty little thing, isn't she?" Mr. Green said.

"Just like all women," Lance said. His thoughts were on Katherine.

Mr. Green nodded and slowly raised himself from the bench. "I'll take you for something to eat. A brave lad I knew told me there's a really good pub that does Sunday lunch near here."

Lance stood up and started walking back to the car. He strode off, to distance himself. But Mr. Green was like a dog—he just wouldn't lie down and play dead.

"Corporal William Hopkins—what a grand fellow, at only nineteen—was just talking about where to eat the best steak and ale pie," Mr. Green said, walking some eight-feet behind, and quickly closing the gap, "when a bullet struck him in the head—poor boy just keeled over—he didn't know what hit him.

"Well he wouldn't, would he?" Lance joked, walking with greater speed. He suddenly came to an abrupt halt, turned and waited for the hurrying, bent-double old man to catch up. "Hang on a minute—when exactly was this?"

"December, 1916," Mr. Green said, without being the slightest bit out of breath.

Lance remembered the photographs in the boxes. Horrific images flooded his mind.

Imogen was feeling a slight disappointment. She thought being daring outside was going to be exciting. Holding hands was as daring as it was going to get—she wasn't a flaunter.

Stephanie was still giving everyone she saw a wide lipstick smile.

Ten minutes walk—without a single word—took them from their canal-renovated warehouse home to a more residential area, where rows of Victorian yellow brick houses lined the streets. They turned a corner and less than two-hundred yards away, stood The Rifleman public house.

Imogen's heart began to race again. It felt as if Stephanie—knowingly—was opening her closet-door wider, to a waiting audience. Stage fright stopped her going through the door.

Stephanie gripped a trembling hand tighter. "Trust me," she said. "No-one will blink an eye."

Stephanie pushed at the door. It opened. She stepped into a warm and welcoming atmosphere. Imogen was frozen in the doorway. Stephanie's hand pulled her into the warmth, and led the way to the bar.

Two beautiful, young women—hand in hand—approached the bar. The only eyes to look at them were the barman's from behind the counter. He was ten years past their age, heavily built; shaven headed, and fancied himself as a bit of a lady-killer. He liked what he saw, especially the one looking right at him.

Stephanie's eye contact did nothing apart from make her walk to the first available barmaid. Five minutes later and they were sat at a table by themselves. Their only accompaniment was two halves of lager.

Couples, families with children and the odd loner sat drinking and eating. The old Victorian pub had none of its separating lounge, bar, and snug walls. The large open area—it had created—gave a pleasing sweep around a long curving bar. The décor was also pleasing in a tasteful quirky-nostalgic way, where WW1 and WW2 regalia adorned every available wall space. The piece that drew everyone's attention was the photographs of a soldier in two wooden frames. One had been enlarged to A4 size, the other—the original—stood proudly by its side on the wall behind the bar, just like the very soldier in the photo. Written across the bottom right were the words: Happy 18th Birthday to my young, smiley pal Willie. Best wishes, Ambrose.

CHAPTER SEVENTEEN

The tyres of the Moggy 1000 hugged the road as Lance drove aggressively throughout Mr. Green's directions. It wasn't that the little car sped along with a heavy foot on its accelerator that made Mr. Green grip his seat—it hardly ever went over the speed limit—it was the fact that it weaved along the road overtaking, and undertaking, everything in its path. He didn't mind so much if Lance crashed and smashed up his own back, he just wished the idiot wouldn't do it when he was in the car.

"I'll get you some number 53 stickers for the doors and bonnet!" Mr. Green quipped.

"Herbie is a Volkswagen Beetle—you idiot!"

Mr. Green smiled. "Fine," he said, "I'll just get you some go-faster stripes then."

"Is that supposed to be funny?"

"Or maybe a sticker for the back windscreen that says, 'I've just been up your arse'," Mr. Green added with a snigger.

Lance seethed.

"Have you had this thing souped up?"

"Of course I have."

"I wasn't far from my original thought about you."

"And, what was that?"

"That you're a twat," Mr. Green said with immense pleasure. "By the way, what is your reason behind owning a 1969 Morris Minor?"

"She's small and beautiful, and is the same colour as Katherine's eyes."

"That's reason enough," Mr. Green approved.

The car was driven with less aggression and more restraint. The Rifleman came into clear view as Lance turned the next corner. He drove into its car park and parked next to the rubbish bins—the only available space. He wasn't the least bit happy about it.

"Say one word about the parking position and you're dead," Lance said. "If it gets scratched, I'll use your head to buff it out." He got out the car and restrained himself from slamming the door.

Mr. Green did the same and quipped: "Your temper was always—what word would you use? Oh, yes, useable. I like that. Is it nice having a useable temper? I myself don't have one."

"It's a pity you haven't. Smashing things might have resulted in us all being better off, instead of giving up and blowing your brains out."

"Touché," Mr. Green said. *It would only have altered for me, not you.*

Lance smiled and locked the car doors. He then, very hungrily and without being told, made towards the car park doors of The Rifleman.

Obediently in his trail was Mr. Green.

Lance went straight to the bar. Mr. Green followed and was soon at his side. They had entered a war museum presenting itself as a public house that had been done so tastefully, that it didn't scare or offend anyone. If anything—it was very cleverly done.

"Yes, gentlemen," the barman said.

"A pint of bitter shandy… and whatever he wants," he made a quick glance to his sidekick.

"I'll have a bottle of red wine," Mr. Green said to the barman, bending his arm backwards and reaching into his jacket pocket, from which came a hefty roll of money. He slid a twenty pound note from beneath a blue elastic band and put it on the bar, before tumbling the roll back into his pocket.

Lance said nothing. He couldn't—his mouth was open.

Mr. Green paid for the drinks and told the barman to put the change into the collection jar that he'd seen on the bar. Lance was impressed with his generosity, but wasn't surprised when he realised it was for the A.B.F. Soldiers' charity.

Lance picked up his pint and looked around for a seat. Mr. Green was busy looking at the memorabilia on the walls. His eye took him further along the bar to the picture proudly displayed. He wandered over to it and stood silent.

"Lance," he called. "Come here and look at this."

Lance stopped looking for a seat and self-consciously shuffled to Mr. Green's side.

"Can you shout just a little bit louder next time? I don't think the people in the next street quite heard you."

Mr. Green paid no attention to his sarcasm. "Look at the photos," he said. "It's Willie Hopkins."

"Who?" Lance said.

Mr. Green was too busy looking at the photos to start picking a fight. He poked Lance in the arm with his bony finger. "Read what I wrote," he said.

Lance steadied his drink and leaned over the bar to see. He read the dedication with every bit of scepticism he had.

Mr. Green sadly reflected back over ninety years, before he solemnly said, "I took that in December, 1916—it was the week before his eighteenth birthday. I presented it to him, with best wishes, on his birthday.

And he was dead the week after. He never saw Christmas or 1917 or any year after that."

"Why is it here?" Lance said, with great misgivings for asking such a question, when he knew the answer would always be undoubtedly believable.

"I would have thought that obvious," Mr. Green said with pride. "He lived here with his parents—they were the pub landlords. I told you he knew where the best steak and ale pies came from."

"You've set this up."

"Me! Why?"

"O.K., let's prove it," Lance said.

He waved to the barman to come over.

"Be with you in a second," the barman said, as he finished serving the spiky, blonde-haired woman who'd avoided him earlier. He didn't push himself upon her. His thinking was that his masculinity would work its charm. The idiot hadn't the slightest hope in hell. But he didn't know that. He was the typical male-thinking gorilla, who assumed he was God's gift to every woman.

Stephanie put her change in her bag, and raised her dress hem slightly—knowing the gorilla was watching—and adjusted her stocking top. After smoothing her dress down she picked up her drinks, shook her head at him—telling him he had no chance—and turned. Out of the corner of her eye she saw the very someone that was going to spoil everything. "Shit," she said, and flounced briskly to her seat.

The barman with a perspiring forehead—who only seconds ago, was ogling a top few inches of slender thigh flesh—made his way to the photo-debating pair.

"Yes, gentlemen," he said.

Mr. Green's eyes were following the runaway tease.

Lance was too busy scrutinising the picture of Willie to notice any such thing as a flirt.

"What can you tell me about the photograph?" he said.

"Well," began the barman, leaning on the bar, "this here is Corporal William Hopkins. He volunteered to serve King and country in 1914 and joined the regiment of…"

"The poor bloody infantry," Mr. Green interjected; with his eyes flitting to poor Willie's smiling face.

"I suppose you could say that," the barman said, studying the bent-double old man.

"There's no other way of saying it, is there? Nearly all of them died bloodily," Mr. Green said. And pointing out their inexperience of war added, "Camaraderie made us smile, and the belief that it would soon be all over."

"Zip it," Lance said, directing a finger right across Mr. Green's face. "Do you have to make a point about every damn thing?"

Mr. Green fell silent. His eyes wandered around the room, looking for the spikey-haired young woman. When Lance turned back to the bar, the barman was busy serving.

"Find a seat," Lance instructed.

Mr. Green headed off looking for an empty table. He couldn't find one, but he did see the spikey-haired young woman. He waved his hand at Lance to follow, which he did.

Imogen was studying the menu—she was not going to have steak and ale pie, no matter how many other people around her were enjoyably consuming theirs—so didn't see the bent-double old man approach.

Mr. Green stood by Stephanie, and with a big smile asked: "Would you mind if I were to sit here?"

Imogen lowered her menu and lifted her gaze upwards. Her eyes met a kind-looking, bent-double old man, and weaving his way between the tables towards them, was someone that made her heart flutter. She turned to look at Stephanie.

Stephanie was trying hard not to make her face cloud with thunder. *Go away, turn around—leave now before he gets here...* her thoughts were broken when Imogen's male desire stood just inches away. *What the hell Imogen sees in you, wife-cheater, I don't know.* She gave a false smile that was so obvious.

"Miss Swan!" Lance said.

"Mr. Lewisham!" Imogen said.

"You two know each other?" Mr. Green said.

"Please, join us," Stephanie hissed.

Lance sat opposite Imogen, before Mr. Green did. It wasn't Mr. Green's intention to sit there at all.

"I liked the playful way you handled the barman," Mr. Green said to Stephanie, as he creaked himself lower to his seat, in a winding-down clockwork fashion.

"I don't like men undressing me with their eyes."

"I don't either," Mr. Green joked.

Stephanie smiled.

Imogen clearly looked apprehensive about this unpredicted meeting.

Lance was hesitant to say anything unfavourable about the odd companion at his side. He simply introduced Mr. Green as his next door neighbour—which in truth, he was—and nothing more.

Stephanie couldn't believe that going for a meal with anyone so noticeable could be anything as mundane as neighbourly.

Mr. Green would talk for eternity, if asked something. So he just waited patiently for someone to do just that. He knew it would take some time, so to start things rolling he withdrew from his pocket the hefty roll of money and tore from it several notes before returning it to his pocket.

"Steak and ale pie—anyone?" he said.

Lance being famished said yes, as did Stephanie. Imogen said she would have a Quiche with spinach and a salad.

Mr. Green went to the bar, ordered, and returned with a bottle of bubbly and four glasses.

"It was clear to me, by the way you handled the barman, that you don't like men—sexually," he whispered to Stephanie, pouring her a drink. "And just for the record, my relationship with him is purely soul rewarding."

Stephanie whispered back, "Was I that obvious?"

"Only to me, my dear—if I can get Lance back to where he belongs, she'll be all yours," Mr. Green whispered back.

"Are you flirting, Ambrose?" Lance said shocked.

"If I had lead in my pencil, I would be trying ever so hard," Mr. Green said unashamedly.

Stephanie smiled and took a sip from her glass. The bubbles made her nose wrinkle delightfully.

Lance inhaled deeply and exhaled loudly as he scowled at Mr. Green. The extra air inflated his lungs, allowing a greater amount of oxygen to rush to his brain before he said anything stupid.

A young waitress, all in black, manoeuvred her way between tables— reminiscent of a melancholic fruit bat that was trapped in its cave—and placed four rolled up napkins, containing the utensils, on the table, along with an assortment of condiments. Her smile was plastic and words rehearsed. She would much rather be a sparrow, soaring free.

Imogen laughed aloud, out of nervousness.

Lance also laughed at his own ridiculousness in thinking that he ought to be responsible for a bent-double old man that had had more lives than he should have had. He knew that being seen anywhere with Mr. Green would inescapably lead to embarrassment, so he may as well endure it. *Let the fun begin.*

Stephanie started it.

"Do you think this place is haunted, Mr. Green?" she said.

"I don't think it, pretty lady, I know it," Mr. Green answered. This was what he'd been waiting for—the opportunity to talk about things he knew well.

"You don't believe in the supernatural do you, Stephanie?" Lance said, cutting in.

"Yes I do."

"That's a pity."

Mr. Green smiled broadly and said: "What would you say, Stephanie, if I told you that the soldier in the picture—the one hanging on the wall, behind the bar—was a friend of mine."

Stephanie looked towards the bar and narrowed her eyes.

"His name is William Hopkins and he died in 1916 from a bullet in the head."

Stephanie grimaced. "How old was he?"

"He was just eighteen, and I was with him when he died."

"That's shocking—how old were you?" Stephanie asked.

"Would you believe me if I told you I was fifty-seven?"

"No," Stephanie said flatly. "That would make you one-hundred and fifty-four."

"Correct," Mr. Green said.

Imogen was still working the maths. Lance was pleased that Mr. Green was digging his own grave. And the waitress—as if using echo location—arrived with their meals.

"After we've eaten," Mr. Green said, "Lance will show you something that will make you believe. But until then, I wish you bon appetite."

He took up his napkin and withdrew from it his knife and fork. "This better be good, Willie. It's only taken me ninety-seven years to get here." He raised his glass to the photo of Corporal William Hopkins and bowed his head in remembrance to the young man that died—needlessly, but bravely—for his country.

What have I got, thought Lance, pouring everyone some more bubbly, *that will give any weight to his story?*

The meal was eaten in almost silence. The quiet was only broken when someone commented on how good the meal was or in the ordering of more drinks, which Mr. Green insisted on going for and paying for.

It was only after a few seconds of Mr. Green's return, with more bubbly, that Lance couldn't contain himself any longer.

"Come on then, Ambrose, out with it—what have I got that'll give you credence?"

Mr. Green didn't rush his answer. He took another drink, smiled at Willie, and finally after seeing Stephanie and Imogen with jaw-dropping suspense looks, resembling two mouth-open goldfish, said: "In the boot of your car is your leather jacket. And in the inside pocket of that leather jacket is a photograph. Go and get it."

Lance stood up in an instance and left two wider-mouthed goldfish.

"I've never seen him take an order from anyone," Imogen said.

"If you told him to do it to you, he'd do it," Stephanie stated quite openly.

Imogen thought about it and smiled.

Lance returned with a postcard photograph. He placed it on the table—picture facing up—so that everyone could see.

The photo was of Mr. Green in army uniform, and more precisely, it was the typical 1916 service-dress with steel Shrapnel Helmet, S.M.L.E. rifle and 1908 pattern webbing equipment.

"Wouldn't you say I looked dashing, for someone in their fifties?" Mr. Green said.

No-one answered.

"Turn it over," Mr. Green said.

Lance turned the photograph over.

There on the back of the postcard, written in blue ink, was a short message:

Dear Martha,

I am well. Here is a portrait of myself. Have a good Christmas and New Year—sorry I can't be with you. Don't worry about me. Best wishes, Ambrose.

And in the top right-hand corner was a postal stamp.

"Now go to the bar and politely ask if you can look at the back of the small photo of Willie."

Lance got up and went.

When he returned he was pale and shaking.

"And what did you find?" Mr. Green said.

"The postmarks are the same."

"Was there anything else?"

"Yes. There was some writing."

"What did it say?"

"You tell me—it appears that you wrote it," Lance snapped. His colour was back and the shaking was now possibly due to rage.

"Well…" Mr. Green said. "I thought his parents would want to see how happy and proud he looked…"

Imogen leaned closer. "What did you write?"

"Only that I was his friend—I wasn't a young soldier like Willie… I was a middle-aged photographer. They made me wear the uniform. I had to or I couldn't do my job. Not once did I fire my rifle at a living soul. I shot people with my camera… that was my weapon."

"He can't really be one-hundred and fifty-four, can he?" Imogen said, first looking at Lance, then at Stephanie.

Lance didn't answer. He was swimming somewhere in his mind's own disbelief. He needed to hear what Sister Miriam believed. She was as close to God as he could get. Surely she wouldn't lie to him?

"Maybe he's a ghost," Stephanie said with a shiver.

"Maybe I am," Mr. Green said.

Stephanie reached under the table and pinched Mr. Green, playfully, just above his knee.

"No, you're not a ghost," she said.

"Can I do that to you?" Mr. Green asked.

"No."

"I thought not."

"Will you explain how you did the photo trick?"

"Let's just say it was done supernaturally, shall we?"

Stephanie couldn't help but like Mr. Green. Maybe it was his charm. She played along with his game. "Willie helped, didn't he?" she said with a giggle.

"Willie can be fun, when he wants to be," Mr. Green said.

Imogen's thoughts made her blush.

Stephanie shook her head, knowing that Mr. Green understood her. She didn't mind the old man trying it on. She didn't think him dirty at all, more funny if anything.

Lance's thoughts were somewhere between his own and James Walker's. It seemed there was nothing more Mr. Green could say or do to shock anymore.

Mr. Green poured the last of the bubbly; thinking now was as good a time as any to break up the party. He picked up his photo and slipped it carefully into his inside jacket pocket.

"I'm sorry, my dears, but I think it's time we left," he said, raising his glass. And with toasting words that were sincere said, "To new friends."

Stephanie and Imogen raised their glasses—Lance didn't.

Mr. Greened skimmed his view around the large room and into every corner he could see. He knew why people thought the place haunted, and it had nothing to do with Corporal William Hopkins.

A young girl—about the age of nine—was sat with crossed arms, in a small chair, just next to the fireplace. She waited in silence with a smile that was the sweetest any angel could make. She had on a navy-blue coat that was too small for her, and brown woollen-stockings. On her head—pushed well back—was a navy-blue beret, covering flaming red-hair. She looked around the room, oblivious as to anyone there.

"Don't be alarmed," Mr. Green said only to Stephanie. "Look towards the fireplace."

Stephanie looked.

"Do you see the girl wearing the beret?"

"Yes."

"Poor thing," Mr. Green said. "She shouldn't be here. She died in 1945 during an air raid—my feeling tells me she waits there for her father—I can't say anymore on that. She does have, however, an impish manner of moving things around."

Lance and Imogen looked. To them, there was no girl wearing a beret.

"Can't we help her?" Stephanie said.

"I'm not here for that," Mr. Green said.

"Please try."

Stephanie's plea would have melted any man's heart. It didn't do any such thing to Mr. Green. No soul equates to being without heart. But there was something about Stephanie which he liked. It wasn't her femininity—he had never been attracted to women.

"Go to her, take her hand and smile—don't say anything."

Stephanie stood up and slowly crossed the room to the fireplace. Her uncertainty of what might happen made her legs tremble. But when her thoughts weighed out the presence of a little girl against some horrific black apparition, her doubts floated away with the warmth her heart gave out. She knelt in front of the girl—the girl appeared to look straight through her—and took her hand with a smile. For a few short-lived seconds, the small hand felt warm with existence. The girl returned the smile. And then into a blaze of light, the girl was gone—Stephanie felt like she'd touched the girl's soul.

The people in the room were unmindful of what had just happened. Stephanie stood up and was greeted by Mr. Green.

"You're very special," he said, "I'm sure we will see each other again. One day, my soul will be happy." He then turned and made his way towards the car park doors.

Lance smiled his goodbyes and trailed after Mr. Green like a puppy.

Stephanie radiated. She had never been called special before. She took hold of Imogen's hand and left The Rifleman. Her thoughts were of where the little girl had gone. Strangely, and in her head, she could hear Mr. Green say: I know all about the dead.

Imogen's thoughts were on Lance and tomorrow.

CHAPTER EIGHTEEN

Sister Miriam felt full of love as she knelt in prayer to the Holy Trinity. An hour of prayer in her light-giving chapel gave nourishment to her faith. She asked for divine guidance in all that she did.

After prayer she began her ten-minute lonesome walk to 'The Room of Truth'. Its descending floor presented a feeling of the underworld giving invite to the person—or persons—that dared tread upon it. It was only a feeling, but you felt it nonetheless. She was advised, on her first visit, that she must—with prayer—decline the invitation, and in doing so, the feeling would go. She never heeded the advice, and besides, nothing had ever happened to her in all the years she'd made this walk down, or on her walk back.

There were two keys that Sister Miriam kept about her, at all times. The first key that unlocked and locked again the door to the hidden passage was back upon her person. The second key was in a sheath, ready in her hand. The only light inside the tunnel came from a PIR motion-sensor, and LED night-lights, placed at some ten feet apart. It gave an eerie sensation walking under light that lasted only the amount of time it took to reach the next sensor. It looked as if she was in a pool of her own spirit's light being pulled towards the dark. And in a way, that's exactly what was happening. Her spirit would stay with her for as long as she kept her faith.

Sister Miriam neared the end of her lonesome walk. The key she now withdrew resembled a four inch long, round iron bar, with a pointed end. It had several cut lines around its circumference, and a flat hitting head. The door that she had first seen—when she was only twenty-four—came into LED light. It was of solid oak, faced with shiny black iron, and encrusted with hundreds of large iron studs that jewelled in the white light. Quickly, the key was pushed upon an iron stud that it was intended for. The key slid into place easily like erotic unification—the knowing of the keyhole lay in the keeping of two minds, hers being one of them—and then with palm force, pushed on the flat head. The key released its power. A click was first heard, followed by the tumbling of locks, then a final loud clunk. The light went out. Sister Miriam, in her darkness, removed the key. The second key, like the first, was again back upon her person.

She pushed the door open, and in the few seconds it allowed her to step inside. She took another seven steps. The door did as it always did. It automatically closed behind her. The lock gave a clunk, and reversed its procedure with a tumble and a click. Lights came on. She had twenty seconds to activate her presence before the lights went out.

A surge of adrenaline—the same she got every time she entered the room—kicked in immediately, giving her an almighty burst of energy. It was a powerful preparation for her solo flight to enter the six digit code, to keep the lights on and to tell just one other person that she was down there—underground—in 'The Room of Truth'. Twenty seconds never seemed enough.

Fifteen seconds later and a pushing of six buttons, the electronic safety panel beeped its acceptance. Sister Miriam's breathing always raced as she lay under her desk—the lying down and looking up at the safety panel, always gave a second rush of energy, albeit a dizzy one. It was strange how the panic button's yellow light made the lines on her face appear eerily lizard-like. The bright colour made her eyes slit. The button was for emergency use only, and once pressed it would flash red to show that a call had been made and assistance was on its way. She prayed—as she always did—that nothing would happen to her while in this underground chamber. Panic buttons are all well and good; if you can get to them and if the other person actually receives the call and comes. She presumed it would be the other key holder, but had no knowledge of who possessed it—if indeed, anybody.

There were several reasons why Sister Miriam loved this room. Her foremost being that, for some strange reason, she felt closer to her God. Other reasons were in the literature it held and its sheer macabre beauty. There was a draft—that aired the room—which entered from a small vent above one door and left by another small vent above the only other door. The room had a life that seemed to breathe.

Sister Miriam sat at her desk and was watched by the skulls of the beautiful that died there. She looked to the iron wheel on the wall and longed to know what it did. She'd often tried to turn it—it never moved an inch.

"You're not a long time dead, Great-grandfather, are you?" she said, as she turned page after page—with white-cotton-gloved hands—of the only book she thought would hold the answer regarding her Great-grandfather.

The book had dated signatures, the earliest being from 870A.D. Its pages were beautiful in their transparency. They had been made from the skin of those servants who'd willingly given their souls to Him that was wrongly cast out of heaven, in the hope that one day Satan would again be Lucifer—the shining one—the morning star—and that they, the true worshippers, would resume their rightful place in heaven.

It had been a compulsive thirty-nine year read, the more she read, the more she understood. But there was a lot more to her work in 'The Room of Truth' than reading this one book. But since her Great-grandfather's visit in '74, her need to understand his being here burdened her.

She would stay in 'The Room of Truth' for only a few hours—longer than that, made her feel claustrophobic. Leaving was the reverse of arriving.

Lance drove with careful regard to everything that was on the road. He was in no hurry to get home.

Mr. Green watched the world go by, and thought about how he was seen then, vis-à-vis how he would be seen today.

"The young are so lucky nowadays," he said aloud.

"You think?" Lance said.

Mr. Green didn't answer, and Lance didn't chase an answer. But Mr. Green wished he was young and really alive today.

Lance was stone-faced as he parked the car on his drive. He waited a moment before switching off the engine.

"What's the matter?" Mr. Green asked.

Lance switched of the engine. "You are," he said.

"C'est la vie," Mr. Green said, opening the car door. As he eased himself out of the car he struggled with his tortured stance. The pain was bearable. He slowly walked away. "Such is life," he translated.

Lance didn't respond and sat for a few moments longer before he ventured inside. He knew the frosty atmosphere that awaited him. Katherine would avoid him for several days, and then look hurt all over again.

Mr. Green vomited steak and ale pie into his toilet. It wasn't that he didn't like the pie. The fact that he was technically a dead person, brought alive by the making of his creators, meant he couldn't physically eat anything. Wine, he found, had no ill effects upon him. He wondered if blood would be more substantial, but he wasn't created a vampire, so wouldn't try it. He hated the term 'living dead', but that's what he was. He was alive and he was dead. He was alive as long as They wanted him to be, and as dead as long as They wanted him to be. Suicide was no longer a way out.

Stephanie had led Imogen home like she was on a tender leash—her hand never once dared to release. In their living room they faced each other as lovers do. Rainbow eyes were changing colours and size.

Stephanie knelt and lifted Imogen's dress up. She kissed the soft flesh on the inside of Imogen's thighs. She kissed higher.

Imogen turned around and lifted her dress, higher. She did her famous bend over to show what she wanted kissing.

Stephanie slipped Imogen's panties down to stocking tops and did what either gender could do.

Katherine lay on her bed listening to Lance downstairs. She'd slept on and off and was now feeling a lot better. There was no way she was going to forgive Lance for his wrong answer.

She lay looking at the ceiling, wondering where he had been and whether he did love her. She would only know that if she allowed him to tell her. And she was not going to allow that until she was ready. She was her own punishment for nothing she had done wrong.

CHAPTER NINETEEN

Lance lay back in the armchair that he associated as his. His eyes looked up at the ceiling; he wondered what Katherine was thinking. His thoughts moved toward Sister Miriam and how she called his living-ghost, Great-grandfather. In a worryingly strange way, he was looking forward to seeing her again. She obviously had some answers—if not all—to his questions. Mr. Green was conspicuously a part of Sister Miriam's life.

It had just become apparent to him of how ignorant he was. He had never once asked the man about his life. Averse to his seeing of neighbours, he would go next door and be friendly to the old man. Trickery wasn't intent on his mind, but it was there nevertheless.

The knock on the door was a gentle two rap. Lance's knuckles had only just left the paintwork when the door opened.

"Mr. Green!" Lance said with surprise.

"And who were you expecting?" Mr. Green barked.

The pugnaciousness of the question took Lance off guard. He dilly-dallied in his retort. But it eventually came—sharp and to the point. "The living dead," he seriously joked.

"Then you've come to the right house—come in."

Lance stepped over the threshold. Mr. Green was quick to close the door.

His walk seemed a little straighter as he led the way to the living room. There was no warmth to the house—coldness climbed in from the foundations, then bled through the walls.

Lance shivered as he stood in the starkness of the room.

Mr. Green sat in one of the armchairs and gestured that his guest do the same. Lance took the only other available armchair.

Mr. Green spoke first.

"I take it you're here to know more about me?"

"Am I that transparent, Mr. Green?"

"What happened to calling me Ambrose?"

Lance didn't answer.

"You want to be ahead of the game before you next see Miriam," Mr. Green said with a knowing smile. "I understand that. I'll do the talking if you promise not to interrupt or ask questions."

Lance nodded his acceptance to the terms, and settled back into his chair to become as comfortable as he dared possible. His host's presence gave him the strangest feeling of being no older than five—he didn't feel cold anymore. His curiosity towards Mr. Green became ablaze, as he listened intently to Mr. Green telling a fragmentary story of his life up to his death in 1929.

It was late when Lance eventually sat in his own chair, in his own living-room. He'd left Mr. Green in the haze of his own past. It had been a one-way conversation to which Lance felt somewhat moved and illuminated. There were questions he wanted to ask—of course there were—but he was true to word of being just the listener.

The picture that was developing exposed a child that had wanted a better life and unfortunately didn't get one.

Ambrose Green's father had been sacrificial in his plight to get to England, to the point that he'd lost his entire heritage. In 1830 a twelve-year-old German Jew by the name of Maik Rosen had attached himself to a family named Grün, leaving Hamburg via steamer. He entered into the port of Hull, under the name of Michael Green.

It was only after he'd married—at the age of twenty-two—that anything more could be said about Michael. There was simply no knowledge within the files of Mr. Green's mind to explain what his father did in those ten missing years or, in fact, for any years prior to him coming to England. And so it was in 1840 that Michael Green married the sixteen-year-old Sarah Jones.

Ambrose Green's memory recalled his mother telling it as a marriage made from love. It was more likely a marriage made from necessity—for six months after the marriage, followed their first child. Over the next nineteen years there followed more and more children—nine in total—with Ambrose being the youngest. The eight between 1840 - 1858 all died in infancy. Two died from the 'Blue death'—named due to the patient's skin turning a bluish-grey hue from extreme loss of fluids—known as Cholera, three from Tuberculosis, and the other three were not known or, more likely, not remembered.

Lance had been moved by these deaths, whereas Mr. Green showed no emotion whatsoever. His reason was a simple one—it all happened before he was born.

Mr. Green had recounted his childhood as difficult. His recollection of his father was next to nothing. He recalled the strap—a wide leather belt—and how much it had hurt him, and his mother for seeing his father use it. The sting of that leather never got easier. It ended when he reached ten.

Michael Green died in 1869—at the age of fifty-one—when his fall down the house stairs snapped his neck. He was in a drunken state when it happened and his death was recorded as accidental. It was possibly due to his feet catching in his trouser hem, due to him not wearing his belt. Mr. Green had smiled approvingly when he told Lance this.

It was with repentance what Ambrose recounted further. He and his mother lived a poor life—if not happier—for the next five years. It was when Ambrose was fifteen and working in a popular music hall—his duties were varied from cleaning to operating props—that his mother, who was now fifty, fell in love with a man of similar age, with a plan to live in New Zealand. She told Ambrose of her love for this man and that he'd asked her to travel with him to New Zealand. Her plan was to send for Ambrose soon after they had settled. Ambrose wholeheartedly gave his blessing.

The Cospatrick—a wooden, three-masted, full-rigged sailing ship—voyaged from Gravesend, England to Auckland, New Zealand on 11th September 1874 with four-hundred and thirty-three passengers and forty-four crew members—Sarah Green and her gentleman friend were among the passengers. The ship caught fire south of the Cape of Good Hope, on the 17th November.

Sarah Green and her gentleman friend didn't survive what was of one of the worst shipping tragedies to a merchant vessel during the 19th century. Of the four-hundred and seventy-two persons on board, only three ultimately survived.

Ambrose was devastated at the loss of his mother. He now told Lance that he turned to God for answers. His answer came after five years of him going to church, in the form of love. He lived with his love for the next seven years—nothing more was said on that matter.

Lance wondered what life the twelve-year-old Maik Rosen would have had, if he had not set foot out of Germany. Thought makes irrepressible conclusions.

Lance had learnt nothing more of Mr. Green's life, until he got married in 1897 to a Martha Brent, and that he'd become a father at forty.

Mr. Green simply ended their one-way conversation with the simple fact that he'd gone to America in 1920 and shot himself in 1929, aged seventy.

Lance closed his eyes to the dark behind his lids. There immediately followed a sound like feet stepping onto an iced-over pond. His eyes sprang open into blackness. He was now in a standing position and couldn't see anything—there was no differentiation between his eyes being open or closed. And it was at that precise moment that he knew he was not in his own living room. Whatever lay beneath his feet produced a cracking sound that pricked his ears. Not daring to do anything other than to understand what he was standing on, he crouched down. It was with unease that he touched the area around his feet. There was nothing whatsoever to touch—fear struck.

Lance cried out a question: "Where am I?"

The darkness engulfed the question, and gave nothing in reply.

Lance's head spun. He swayed left, right and forwards—there was nothing to give him balance, so he tumbled—and landed on all fours, just like a cat.

Several minutes passed—in catlike position—to fear. His hands remained flat on the ground that he couldn't feel earlier. Slowly, he began to inch forward into the darkness. It was with the first placement of his right hand that, again, he felt there was nothing to touch. He withdrew it quickly back.

It was over the next half hour that he tried that same manoeuvre—only to get the exact same result—to every degree of the circle he travelled. His registered data meant that there was nowhere he could go—it was utterly ridiculous.

Lance had to do something—his kneeling there served no purpose whatever. He began to think he was dead. And if that was the case, then nothing worse could happen to him.

Fear can only last so long until it turns in on itself. Anger takes its place, and with anger he stood up.

"Fuck you," he yelled at the top of his voice.

Nothing came back—not even an echo.

There was nothing logical in what Lance did next.

He jumped up and down, portraying a three-year-old succumbing to a tantrum. Cracking again pricked his ears. He immediately stopped jumping, and clapped his hands together in wild applause until they stung. His next action was bold—he blindly held out his hands and took a giant step forward.

He didn't fall. He took an extra step—again he didn't fall. He again crouched down and touched the area around his feet. There was nothing whatsoever to touch.

He started to run into the blackness—it went on forever. His direction never changed from steaming straight on ahead. It was only after one hour of pushing himself to exhaustion that he stopped. He once again crouched down and touched the area around his feet.

"Fuck you!" he shouted, as his fingers touched nothing. "Am I dead? And if I am dead, then who am I in the presence of?"

Time passed. How much time passed? Lance hadn't a clue. All he knew was that he could go in any direction and not get anywhere, or so it seemed. He didn't feel thirsty or hungry.

Suddenly something changed. In the far distance a spark of light hovered. Lance took to his heels and ran towards it. *That must be the beginning of the tunnel you see when you pass over*, he thought. *Shit! I must be dead.*

The spark of light grew. But it wasn't a tunnel; it was a small glass box no bigger than your hand, which floated and turned about on its own axis. It was emitting light. Whatever was inside the box was also a prisoner to the dark, but unlike Lance, it couldn't go anywhere.

Lance tried to stop the box from turning. It took all his strength—eventually he managed it. He couldn't take it from its fixed position but he could examine it. Etched into all of its sides was the name Ambrose Green. Lance's head exploded into a world of light. He saw himself alongside himself. Both incarnations were alike and yet different. The light closed in and swallowed them whole. Darkness returned. Lance let go of the box and stepped backwards—the glass object rotated again.

Lance again took to his heels. When he looked over his shoulder there was only darkness. He stopped running and sat. He shouted loudly in a continuous chain of obscenity.

Water hit him hard in the face. "What the fuck!" he spluttered.

Katherine was standing angrily with her sick bucket—which seconds ago, she'd filled with cold water, and seconds ago emptied into her husband's blaspheming mouth.

"Fuck you, too," she said, and left without saying another word.

Lance sat in his own chair, in his own living-room and had never been so glad to be there. He might be soaking wet, but he wasn't dead. He could have been, had Katherine done what was really in her mind. The only thing that had stopped her was the mess she'd have made.

CHAPTER TWENTY

Lance hadn't the slightest experience of evaluating dreams about death. But he figured that Mr. Green had, and that he would be delighted to explain this one. If he had to be truly honest, he would have to be on the side of Mr. Green. Seeing the man's soul imprisoned in a glass box, and imprisoned in a world of just black, gave him sympathy for the old man.

He gave extensive thought towards his sudden kindness. But when the sympathetic is in danger of one's soul being in the same environment as the soul he'd just seen, then just how sympathetic should one be? It was all becoming too difficult to translate, and yet here he was trying to do just that. The more he troubled himself with this quantum problem, the more he lost elucidation of all events. He couldn't kill Mr. Green because Mr. Green was already dead, and if he killed this incarnation, then The Sleeping would just simply materialise Mr. Green again. There really was no answer other than to stop being sympathetic at the cost of one's own life. Sister Miriam would help, he was sure of it.

After getting showered, Lance climbed under the duvet in the spare bedroom. His mind—as it often did—floated towards Imogen.

It had been the first time he'd seen her out of work hours, and to be honest, he wished he'd been alone with her. He couldn't help feel that her friend Stephanie was cold towards him. There was only one reason for her unfriendliness towards him, and that was she knew about the filing routine and didn't approve. And that meant she had feelings for Imogen and wanted her to herself. He'd been blind. When he'd seen them holding hands, it had never occurred to him that Imogen might be bisexual. Stephanie—he guessed—was at the end of her sexual line and furthest away from the island, and possibly always had been.

Lance had full understanding of the sexual line. At one end you had the homosexual and at the other the heterosexual—the heterosexuals were on an island, only joined to the line by a bridge. To travel was to cross the bridge by accepting your homosexual feelings—no matter how small. Leaving the island was termed 'to travel', in his university under-standing. That's accurate in its accepting. But the difficulty is in the understanding of every other point on the line. And the line was a long one with many, many variations of sexuality, all leading to the individual you. He always tried to pin-point where on the line he would be, if he had to evaluate his own sexuality. He was biased; of course he was, given the fact that he had always portrayed himself as straight. He preferred to stay on the island where all hot-blooded men are. Basically because his love—foremost—was for women. He'd heard professors at university say that to see the world you had to travel—those professors were obviously travellers.

Stephanie's looks for example, could be tricky. She was very pretty and was as feminine as you would expect any good-looking woman to be. But even though her body parts were one-hundred per cent her own, her physique was boyish. So why did he find her attractive, as so many other men did? Where on the sexual line did that actually put him? Again he stood on the heterosexual island. His eyelids shuttered to see his office filing cabinet, and to that wonderful filing display Miss Swan put on for him. Self sexual gratification was needed.

It was 6.30 a.m. and Katherine woke—as usual—to the sound of her alarm clock. She trudged to the bathroom and slammed the door hard behind her. The toilet was repeatedly flushed—with the banging of the lid—for a full five faffing-around minutes, before she eventually climbed into the shower and sang at the top of her voice with accompanied claps, all made by flipper-stamping feet. After her shower she brushed her teeth and gave a wonderful version of 'The lord is my shepherd', whilst gargling with mouthwash. The toilet flushed one more time, and in a flourish of toilet-seat-splendour, banged her goodbyes to the tune of a very familiar Sinatra song—this was most definitely 'her way', not his. The bathroom door slammed again—Katherine was still in a mood.

If Lance wanted to confront Katherine's temper, now was the time. He listened to her crashing about downstairs and decided against such a fight. *Let the storm blow over,* he thought, as he rolled out of bed. He knew when she'd left the house, because the slamming of the front door shook the walls.

Lance sleepily left the spare room, took a shower, got dressed, had breakfast, and then vacated the house. He'd just got into his car when Mr. Green appeared.

"Don't go to that place again," he said.

Lance smiled. "Thank you, Ambrose. It's been a long time since anybody gave me such considerate advice."

Mr. Green turned and walked away.

Lance reversed the car off the drive, almost running Mr. Green over.

"Idiot," Mr. Green scolded, hitting the bonnet of the car with his fist.

"Damage her and you're dead," Lance shouted through the back windscreen. "Oops! Sorry. You're already dead." He drove off feeling somewhat different.

It was Lance that set off to his office, but it was James who arrived there—personalities were piecing themselves together.

It was Lance that said to Miss Swan: 'Good morning... coffee would be nice,' and it was Lance that entered his office. But it was James—for no other reason than to seduce Imogen—that took the position behind the desk.

Miss Swan arrived with fresh coffee and pulse-racing scent. She handed over the coffee and took Friday's files off the desk. She walked that short distance to the filing-cabinet and did her bend-over. She performed it magnificently.

She smiled before saying: "Is there anything else I can do for you?"

"Yes, there is, Imogen," James said, "please come here." He gestured, with a wagging finger, that she came and stood before him.

Imogen did as she was asked. She would do anything James asked.

James put his hands on her waist and brought her closer still. He rested his head against her breasts. He could hear her heart beat. He then slipped his hand up her skirt. He heard her heart beat faster.

Just then the door to reception opened and closed.

"We have a patient," Imogen said.

"And I have a hard-on."

Imogen chuckled.

"O.K., Miss Swan, go and see to our patient."

Imogen reluctantly removed James' hand from beneath her skirt. She sighed and turned.

"Miss Swan," Lance said.

"Yes."

"Would you tell Imogen that James would like to see her during Lance's lunch break?"

"Very good, Mr. Lewisham, please tell James that Imogen will see him then. And tell James... to be naughty."

Lance smiled as Miss Swan left the office. He hadn't been this excited about lunch since his first day at school.

The lunch break manifested into James going off like a rocket and Imogen exploding into stars.

James' sex life hadn't been this good for... he couldn't remember.

Lance told Imogen not to tell Stephanie, and that he understood there was a relationship between them both. Imogen tried to give her explanation, but whatever she said only confirmed that she was having difficulty about her sexuality. He jokingly said that he'd love to watch. Imogen blushed like a schoolgirl. But Lance wasn't joking... it was a fantasy of his. The only thing now was he had two real women to fantasise about.

After work, Lance drove his beloved Moggy 1000 to Flat 2 of No. 17 St Patrick Crescent—it was in an area he didn't know well. How to get to and from there was all he knew. And even after intense thinking, he still had no other knowledge of the area. Maybe that's why he chose it all those years ago—to fall into anonymity.

He parked his car, and like so many times before, took his leather jacket from the boot. He extracted keys that hung on a Watneys red barrel keyring, from the jacket's deep inside pocket—the one that once kept Mr. Green's photograph—and put the largest key in the lock that led to a stark white vestibule. Inside, he looked at the picture on the wall. He was thankful it was only water that Katherine poured over him.

The door to Flat 1 seemed to stare at him. He used the smaller key to open Flat 2, and found it funny how the number 1207 turned off the alarm. He climbed the stairs.

Lance was standing in James' flat. Lance's understanding—as Mr. Green had tried to tell him—was that he had been hiding under another name. Mr. Green was right again in that he was being himself, and using his birth name—that he'd shut away, but not forgotten—James Walker, and that when under that transformation, he had no knowledge of himself as Lance. It sounded confusing, but at least he hadn't been Napoleon Bonaparte. Now that would have been a split personality!

It soon became more apparent when this first happened. It was when his daughter Claire was delivered stillborn, and he deliberately made the decision not to see her. His only sympathetic thought as to why he persuaded Katherine into doing the same was—in his rash-thinking mind—for her protection. He now also understood what a self-centred idiot he'd been. It was now that he emphatically understood Katherine's pain. He could fight his own demons—for his reasons into not looking—but not hers.

He sent Katherine a text.

Lance went to the bedroom and sat down upon the bed. It was now, for the first time in fifteen years, that he cried for his daughter. Unprecedented tears fell into his hands.

Katherine received a text:

I won't be home tonight—don't feel like arguing. Don't worry.

She wasn't worried in the least. And as far as the argument was concerned… she wasn't going to start one. Nothing was sent back. The message was deleted.

Lance pulled himself together. Sore-eyed, he looked around the bedroom. Polished wooden floorboards lay in beautiful splendour, beneath his feet.

White walls and a black leather double bed gave a monochrome touch, while an interesting industrial steel wardrobe and a tea-chest bedside table gave eclectic comfort. The only other two items in the room were a lamp and clock—with red LED displays of hours, minutes and seconds—that stood atop the tea-chest.

Lance walked out of the room and closed the door. It squeaked. The living room was just as eclectic. The walls again were white. The floor was as beautiful as the bedrooms, if not more so, by its centre-piece of a coffee table made from six red 1960s Dansette record players—each one in fully operational order. Around the Dansettes, sat four red leather Cadillac rear car seats, crafted upon chrome tubular frames. The bottom length of one wall was lined in LP records, another in 45s. The best sound quality to these vinyl discs came from a '70s Marantz separate system with Celestion speakers, which could take the windows out if they had a mind to. The pièce de résistance was standing in the corner—it was a '58 Fender Precision Bass. She had a two-tone sunburst finish, soft V-shaped one-piece maple neck with skunk stripe, and gold anodized pickguard. The split coil pickup—with raised A string poles—still had its chrome cover. The bridge also sported its chrome ashtray. The thumb-rest was missing—but who cared. This beauty was in museum condition and weighed 8.2 lbs.—her bed partner was a Vox AC30/6.

Lance wondered if his other love would be jealous, and why wasn't the amp in his office? Wondering apart, he left the room and went into the kitchen. The kitchen walls were again white—he obviously liked white. The units were typical rental accommodation DIY type—cheap and nasty—but at least the appliances were built in and functionally set out. A genuine Victorian farmhouse table and four chairs—scrubbed, not painted—graced itself along the window wall. He opened the fridge. It was empty. Late-night shopping was needed.

CHAPTER TWENTY-ONE

Katherine sat in Lance's chair—his dreaming chair. It was dark outside and the inside imitated it. She thought that the dark could hide her feelings.

The doorbell rang. Katherine ignored it. It rang again. She ignored it again. It rang again. This time she wouldn't ignore it. She rushed to the door and with a mouth full of obscenities, snatched it open.

"Fuck! Not you?" she said.

"I'm afraid so," laughed Mr. Green. He held up two bottles of Pinot Noir.

Katherine saw the bottles. Red wine never made her sick.

"Is it French?" she asked.

"Yes."

"Then you better come in."

Mr. Green made his way to the kitchen and sat at the table. Katherine followed, and got the corkscrew and glasses.

"Light would be nice," Mr. Green said. "I'm not a lover of the dark."

Light was asked for, so light was given. It was the decent thing to do as a host, especially as the guest had brought refreshment.

Katherine poured the wine and took a hearty swig.

"Don't say a word about letting it breathe," she said.

"I wouldn't dare."

Katherine hooted with laughter. "You're not scared of me, are you?"

"No. The only ones to scare me are those that control me."

Katherine thought about that, and may have misunderstood Mr. Green's meaning.

"Yeah… bosses can be bastards at times. We don't need them," she said in a doleful tone. She took another mouthful of wine and said: "You frighten me."

"Me! Why?"

"Because…"

"Yes."

"…How old did you say you were when you wrote that?" Katherine pointed to the art print on the wall.

"I didn't."

Katherine didn't say anything. She drank. She would wait for the answer.

Mr. Green finally gave the answer: "I was seventy, it was the 29th October 1929, and it was the day I shot myself."

"See… that's why I'm scared."

"Because I killed myself or because I'm now one-hundred and fifty-four?"

"Both."

"Please understand that I'm not here to hurt you," Mr. Green said reassuringly.

Katherine emptied her glass and filled it again. "No?"

"No," Mr. Green said with a smile.

Mr. Green and Katherine talked. They didn't argue—there was no point.

The same story that Mr. Green told Lance about James Walker had now been told to Katherine.

Katherine was now up to speed with Mr. Green's plight, as well as her husband's.

"I don't know whether to believe you," Katherine said.

"What have I to lie for?" Mr. Green asked.

Both drank some more wine.

Mr. Green had spent a whole two hours talking with Katherine. It had been a deliberate visit that would leave Katherine swimming in her own thoughts.

She'd said 'O.K., dead man, will I see you again?' when Mr. Green had given his excuses to leave.

Mr. Green's honest reply to that was 'Of course, my job isn't finished yet'—he was starting to like Katherine's attitude.

At home he stood in front of the mirror. His recounted actions were listened to. There was no twisting of the spine.

Katherine opened her lap-top and sent an e-mail to someone she knew could help:

Pee-Pee, I need to see you in my office at 10.00 tomorrow morning— it's urgent!

Perry Parkinson—affectionately known as Pee-Pee because of his initials and the fact that he always rushed to the toilet after half a pint of lager, suggesting he had a weak bladder—was a master at finding people. If anybody could find any truth in Mr. Green's story, then he could. Some of Pee-Pee's methods were illegal. But illegality in the legal system was sometimes needed, in Katherine's view. She'd see him at work tomorrow and give him verbal details of his assignment.

She shut her lap-top, turned off the lights, and went upstairs. She stood at the window and looked out into the darkness. She knew—

according to Mr. Green's story telling—where her husband was. She closed the curtains, undressed, and climbed into bed. The wine made her glow—she felt pleasantly drunk as she fell into peaceful sleep.

In an incandescent, white-burning flame Lance's eyes were washed with pain. He rubbed them with ferocity until they bled. Bloodied tears trickled down his cheeks—falling, falling...

Lance stood—where? He didn't know. Nothing was everywhere in its whiteness. If he had to choose between the light and the dark, then he would choose the light—if only to not feel alone. This time he didn't touch the ground—he knew it wasn't there—and he didn't run. Where was there to run? Instead he waited... and waited... and waited—fear was not with him, and in a strange way he felt at peace.

In the distance, a small flesh-coloured circle came. Its centre glistened. This sparkling nucleus grew as it got closer. Lance watched it with the deepest affection. Soon he stood before a small circle of life. The life exhibited itself. A new-born baby—not yet breathing, not moving—hovered in white nothingness.

Lance's eyes bled.

Suddenly, both gasped—Lance in his understanding and the child in taking its first breath. The baby vanished, in its place stood a girl of fifteen. She was beautiful. She smiled. She was gone.

The light below Lance's feet diminished. Blackness pulled him down.

A burning cross appeared—it became a crucified man, he was travelling and pointing into the light. Lance reached and grabbed. He held the legs of the man tight and watched his finger glow until they became molten—where was his faith? He left the traveller and the light.

This time, Lance knew where he was standing. He stood upon the dead. Bodies moved like sand beneath his feet, decaying into liquid tissue that washed upon more bodies, like waves upon the shoreline. This island of death—in its putrid stench of evil—was heaven compared to the darkness. Fear returned to him as he looked up to a burning sky that was sparked with his own anxiety.

Lance buckled to his knees and prayed. He was now in a stone room. Skulls watched over him, as he knelt without strength in either his pride or his hope. From a stone table walked one of The Sleeping. And yet it wasn't—it was human, dressed like a spectre.

Lance looked into eyes that reflected nothing—soulless eyes stared back and only saw a man whose dreams were about to be broken. A dagger flashed across his neck. It sliced—blood sprayed.

Lance suddenly sat upright; a monstrous man's splattered blood face lit his vision with searing power.

Lance's lungs shallowly, yet rapidly in their intake of air, inhaled in successive gasps. He rubbed his fists into his eyes until he burnt away his vision. Had he been asleep and dreaming? He assumed he had, because he wasn't dead. He didn't want to look at the time, but he did. A red LED display showed him it was seven minutes after midnight. There was no need to put the light on—The Sleeping weren't there.

He tried to piece together images from his dream. The art print hanging in the kitchen at No. 113 Padstow Avenue scorched in his mind.

Sister Miriam had spent quite a lot of time researching Mr. Green. And not because she didn't believe in him or the fact that he was a real-life ghost—he simply interested her. She kept that to herself—she didn't want her Great-grandfather feeling immensely proud that his Great-granddaughter had some fascination toward him.

L. Sydney Abel

She'd put her findings into a documented order:

Maik Rosen/Michael Green (1818-1886) = 1840 Sarah Jones (1824-1874)

Ambrose Green (1859-1929) = 1897 Martha Rose Brent (1866-1941)

Frederick Green (1899-1956) = 1932 Ethel May Robinson (1897-1933)

Vivien Green (1933-2010) = 1949 Samuel Drake (1920-1952)

Miriam Drake (1950-

Michael Green married age 22—died age 51 / age when 9th child born—41

Sarah Jones married age 16—died age 50 / age when 9th child born—35

Ambrose Green married age 38—died age 70 / age when son born—40

Martha Rose Brent married age 31—died age 75 / age when son born—33

Frederick Green married age 33—died age 57 / age when daughter born—34

Ethel May Robinson married age 35—died age 36 /age when daughter born—36

Vivien Green married age 16—died age 77 / age when daughter born—17

Samuel Drake married age 29—died age 32 / age when daughter born—30

The other Sunday was the first time she'd seen Lance in forty-four years. She would have known him anywhere. She always knew that one day he'd find her and want to ask questions. The days were counting until they met again.

CHAPTER TWENTY-TWO

For Lance to obey his own rules of office protocol was hard. And Lance tended to be hard, firstly, when Miss Swan did her bend-over, and at lunch. Relief from rules was given by both participants during lunch. Food wasn't the only thing on the menu. Relief wasn't every lunch-time—Lance didn't want to appear greedy.

Imogen was keeping her promise—Stephanie hadn't a clue what her lover was up to behind office closed doors.

It was now six days and nights that Lance hadn't seen Katherine. He felt like he needed space, and besides, he knew she wasn't missing him—she'd made it clear, many times, that she wasn't demonstrative.

The precision bass was getting a lot of attention. Slight nerviness about holding her pristine body made the hairs on the back of his neck stand on end. It was funny how things of beauty made things stand on end. If he had to choose between Jazz and precision, then the lovely that wasn't there with him won hands down. Her finish may have been a little rough, but she had all the handling that made her feel—well, almost alive.

Seven days was ample time for Perry Parkinson to be successful. He sent Katherine an e-mail:

Can I see you tomorrow?

Katherine consulted her work diary. She sent an e-mail back:

11.00 a.m.—My office :-)

It was a sunny Sunday afternoon, with a chill. The blue sky that summer gave now waned cold in its clarity.

Lance had parked his car in the same pay-and-display car park as last Sunday, and sat—one hour early—on the exact same park bench. He even started to throw small stones at the gathering pigeons. The roses in their beds were losing depth of hue. The trees looked even more leafless as their skeletal form now stretched for warmth towards the sun, rather than hiding from its summertime heat.

A shiver gave Lance the feeling of Mr. Green's presence. He looked around for the decrepit old man. Mr. Green wasn't physically anywhere to be seen.

Lance's skin crawled with unease. The air hung in silence as he waited.

St. Thomas' Church bell sounded thrice. It was time, he got up and walked.

Sister Miriam left her prayers and walked towards the courtyard. When she got there, Lance was just walking beneath the large sandstone arch. She waved to him. He waved back.

Time seemed to flutter in dreams—for the next moment Lance was seated and Sister Miriam was holding his hand.

A look passed into Lance's eyes that said one minute drifts into forty-four years without a word.

He felt as guilty as hell.

Lance's explanation surrounding his expulsion about his adoption sounded feeble. His wanting to fit in and not to be judged differently made perfect sense—to him anyway.

Sister Miriam told him everything about his arrival and departure from her life—it was something she'd never forgotten. She never explained her reason for what she did. It was obvious—she did what she thought was best.

Sister Miriam still had hold of Lance's hand as she smiled and said: "But you knew all that, didn't you?"

"Yes. Mr. Green told me."

"The old goat didn't get his knowledge from me."

"I know. It's where and who he got it from that scares me."

"And me," Sister Miriam said with a look that told more than she was, at this moment, letting on.

For a moment neither spoke. But the subject of Mr. Green was inevitable.

"Has my Great-grandfather told you about his life?"

"He skated over it."

"How his parents died?"

"Yes."

"Did you believe him when he said his father fell down the stairs?"

"Yes."

"You did?"

"Yes." Lance said adamantly. "Are you're implying he was pushed?"

"Yes I am," Sister Miriam said.

"I'm positive Mr. Green would have taken immense pleasure in telling me if he'd pushed his father down the stairs."

"I never said that he pushed him."

Lance thought and pictured the scene. He was visualising a frightened child and a mother fighting back against their aggressor. *Accidents do happen, and if it wasn't an accident—well, at least the beatings stopped.*

"Does it really matter after all this time?" he said, trying to understand what relevance this had on a man that was supposedly dead.

Sister Miriam just shrugged her shoulders. "Who am I to judge?"

Lance changed the subject.

"After his mother died he said he turned to the church, and after five years he found love. I take it that his faith must have finally spoken to him, and that he lived with that love for the next seven years. What happened to stop his newly-found faith?" Lance said, looking deep into Sister Miriam's eyes for the answer.

Sister Miriam cried with laughter.

Lance couldn't understand what was amusing.

Sister Miriam controlled herself—it wasn't easy. She giggled like a little girl that saw something rude in what was supposed to be totally innocent.

"Would you care to explain?" Lance said.

"With pleasure," Sister Miriam sniggered. "Please excuse me… it's not my Great-grandfather I'm laughing at—it's you."

"Enlighten me," Lance said with a look that said let's be serious.

Sister Miriam gave a small cough to put stop to her girlish behaviour.

"He did indeed turn to the church. But not for spiritual gratification," she said. "It was for fulfilment of a different worship he sought. He'd seen someone whose vocation was to the church—a man aged forty who fought his condition through God—that made his heart flutter."

"I'm sorry! Are you saying Mr. Green is gay?"

"Yes I am. He was fifteen when he started relations with this man. After five years their love for each other was so strong that they'd made the decision to live together as a couple. Seven years after that, it ended." She said it so matter-of-factly, that it sounded like a soap opera.

"Why did their relationship end?"

"Ambrose's lover died."

Lance assumed that Sister Miriam's use of her Great-grandfather's first name was to imply removal of her family tie to a part of his life that she didn't approve of. *Understandably she has every right to her point of view.*

"What was his name and how did he die?" he asked.

"Does it matter?"

"No, not really."

Sister Miriam let go of Lance's hand. She took from her skirt pocket a piece of paper, and with both hands unfolded it to its A4 size. She laid it flat on her knee. Lance looked at it. It was a family tree running down from her Great-great-grandfather to herself, and was in printed form for ease of reading.

"Impressive," said Lance with a twang that cried his pain that he couldn't do the same for his blood line.

"If you look here," Sister Miriam said, pointing. "He married at age thirty-eight, and my Grandfather was born when he was forty."

"Yes, I know that," Lance said. "And he left for America after twenty-three years of marriage when his son was twenty-one—why?"

"His marriage was a sham, he's gay remember. His son loathed him."

"I see," Lance said, feeling pity.

"Mr. Green is my Great-grandfather, Lance. I've researched him." She then unfolded another piece of A4 paper. This one was handwritten. It read:

Mr. Green's resurrections:

139

He died in 1929 age 70.

He was raised in 1974 after 45 years in the darkness. Technically he looks 70.

He died again in 1979. He was here for five years. Technically he is now 75.

He was raised again in 1998. Technically he is still 75.

He died again in 2013. He was here for fifteen years. Technically he is now 90.

He was raised again, almost straight away.

He says he is The Messenger for The Sleeping.

Lance studied the dates.

'74 was when he first met the old man and '79 sounded about right for him dying. Lance recollected he was about ten at the time. 1998 stood out bolder than anything else. He thought about Claire. He knew why Mr. Green was here. But did Mr. Green's Great-granddaughter know? He believed she did.

"What has he told you, Lance?" Sister Miriam said wryly.

"Why do you ask what you already know?"

Sister Miriam smiled.

"Can you stop him?" Lance asked.

"Are you suggesting exorcism?"

"I don't know what I'm suggesting," Lance said truthfully. "Have you ever seen The Sleeping?"

"No."

"Do you believe in them?"

"I've read about them."

"Yes, of course… and was that in 'The Room of Truth'?" Lance dared to mention.

Sister Miriam dropped her smile. Her lips thinned and her eyes blackened. She took hold of his hand again, squeezed it gently, and then let go.

She stood up letting the two A4's fall to the ground. "Goodbye, Lance. I know we will see each other again," she said.

Time fluttered again—in the next moment, Lance sat alone and Sister Miriam was walking away. He picked up the two pieces of paper, folded them, and put them in his pocket.

Sister Miriam's sudden change towards him told him that the hidden room existed. And why shouldn't it? As far as Mr. Green was concerned, he hadn't lied about anything—in fact, he was candid about everything.

Lance struggled with the truth of that. *A secret is a secret. But if she had verbally admitted about the room, then what could she have told me about The Sleeping?*

Thirty minutes later and he was in his car. He started to drive to Flat 2 of No. 17 St Patrick Crescent, but he changed his mind and headed for No. 113 Padstow Avenue instead.

Katherine heard the car come onto the drive. Lance's arrival in the living room was greeted with a slap to his face. It stung. He bit his lip to offset the pain, and to stop himself doing anything foolish—like hitting back. Katherine slapped him again.

"Is that your new way of greeting?" Lance said, rubbing away the sting. "I'd much prefer a kiss."

"You're not getting one."

"I thought not. Still cross?"

"Damn right I am."

Lance turned and left the room. Katherine was fuming at this. She sat and tried to calm down. *He walks in after a week away and expects... what does he expect?*

There was a lot of noise coming from above Katherine's head. It was as if an elephant was in the loft. When it stopped, Lance came back into the living room. He was carrying something small.

Katherine looked at him with tears in her eyes.

"I think we have a problem," Lance said.

"I know. He lives next door."

There was a long silence.

"I think you should take this—it used to reside in the right-hand drawer of my office desk," Lance said, and handed over a shoebox.

Katherine took it and lifted its lid. What she saw frightened her—for there was something that took life, and she knew whose life it had taken. It was a Colt M1903 Pocket Hammerless.

"Promise me that you will keep it with you at all times. Be careful—it's loaded," Lance said.

"I promise, but haven't we another problem?"

"Yes. But I don't know how to deal with that one just yet. If I don't do something about the first problem then there will be no second problem to sort out." It sounded confusing but it was correct. Fix one, then fix another or let the first eradicate the second. He knew what he had to do—what he'd always done—to keep on fighting.

Katherine put down the shoebox.

There was another long silence.

"I saw Sister Miriam today," Lance said. "She confirmed things—she couldn't tell me anything I didn't already know." He sighed, and for a moment said nothing. Then he remembered. He took from his pocket the pieces of paper Sister Miriam had dropped. "She'd made a family tree and made dates regarding his deaths and resurrections. I can't imagine her lying, can you?" He handed over the pieces of paper. "There's something else…"

Katherine looked up at him with frightened eyes.

"Mr. Green's gay." He said it as if it mattered, which in all honesty, it didn't.

Katherine gave a sigh that said she couldn't care less about the old goat. She put the papers next to the shoebox. "Am I losing you?" she said as her anxiety began to climb again.

Lance took Katherine's hand. He gently led her up the stairs and into their bedroom. There he kissed her. She didn't resist. He caressed her breasts. She didn't resist. Passion took Katherine over. Love-making lasted three hours.

It was late when Lance left. Katherine hadn't wanted him to go, but as he'd explained: 'The further he was away from The Messenger next-door, the safer they both were'. She hadn't agreed—he was pig-headed in his decision.

It was even later when Lance climbed into bed. He was tired to the point where as soon as his head hit the pillow, he was out like a light. He slept like a baby.

CHAPTER TWENTY-THREE

Perry Parkinson died at 4.00 in the morning. Death can be as abrupt as that. The car he was driving had overturned when taking a bend in the road. Perry was barely conscious when the police arrived. He mumbled that he felt no pain and fretted about his passenger.

Perry described his passenger as being over six-foot, very pale-faced and wearing something black with a hood. He recollected, with some difficulty, that his passenger had suddenly grabbed the wheel. When the paramedics arrived, Perry was dead. His spine had been crushed. No passenger was found in the car or anywhere in the vicinity of the car.

Perry's wife was taking the news in a shocked state. It was 6.30 in the morning. She had absolutely no knowledge of her husband leaving during the night and couldn't understand where he was going and with whom. The only absolute fact she did know, was that he wouldn't be doing it again.

The phone rang as Katherine was just about to lock the door and make for work. She hated Monday mornings. She took the call and responded in apologetic shock. She put the phone down and thought about what she'd asked Pee-Pee to do. She questioned her reasons for getting him in-volved—she had no doubt he was dead because of that. She wondered what he'd found out.

She sat on a kitchen chair for an hour, with the Colt M1903 Pocket Hammerless held tightly in her hand. The hour passed like a minute. During that fleeting time, she read the two A4's that Lance had left, and understood that Pee-Pee had been on a fool's errand. And it was she who had been the fool. She decided it was time to eradicate the problem herself. Consulting Lance would be futile—he would talk her out of it, for sure.

At 9.30 a.m. Katherine marched next door and knocked on Mr. Green's front door. Her face was ashen, yet determined.

Mr. Green answered the door with a smile.

"Good morning, Katherine," he said.

He didn't say another word. Katherine pointed the gun at the mouth of a bent-double old man.

"Perform oral sex on this, you sick bastard," she spat.

Mr. Green twisted his smile, nodded and opened his mouth. His face suddenly contorted. He wrapped his arms about his body and fell into a heap.

Katherine just stood and watched Mr. Green's life disappear. She sighed in relief as the old man exhaled. She kicked him hard—he was dead.

"Let's go into your living room shall we?" Katherine mocked, as she dragged Mr. Green's body. She left him in the middle of the floor and returned to the front door. She stood there for a few seconds and listened—nothing. She closed the door and returned to her corpse. Sitting in a chair, she looked at the pitiful sight lying sideways, in its foetal position. She imagined that's how he must have slept. It would have been impossible for him to sleep in any other way, other than sitting up—*the poor bastard.*

Sitting there with a dead man at your feet and with nothing but your thoughts to keep you company is not the best situation to be in, especially when a gun is still in your hand. Realisation of the situation, sooner or later, will kick in.

Katherine's mind was of the assumption that Mr. Green had died of a heart attack. And indeed, that's what it had looked like. But if she had thought seriously about what she had just witnessed, she would have realised that a man that is already dead cannot die from such things as heart failure—it's simply impossible. It was like someone had just switched him off, and for reasons only they knew.

If she left now he would probably be a rotting cadaver before anyone found him. *Who was there to find him?*

"Bye, Ambrose," she said, as she started walking away.

She got no further than the door when she heard his voice.

"I hate the darkness."

Katherine turned back into the room. Mr. Green had manoeuvred himself into a seated position. He was cradling his side from where Katherine had kicked him.

"Help me to a chair," he said coldly.

Mr. Green had been dead for only twenty minutes. Katherine didn't know why she hadn't run. She did as he bade. Soon they were facing each other.

And so it was that a woman with a gun and a living-dead talked.

"You just died."

"That's right—first time in 1929..."

"And then again in 1979..."

"Yes, and twice this year."

"Can't you stay dead?"

"It doesn't seem so."

Katherine didn't think when she asked the next question—she hadn't been thinking all morning.

"Did you kill Perry?"

"I didn't. But The Sleeping did."

"Why?"

"I don't answer for them, I just answer to them. And if you saw where they keep me when I'm with them, then you would be just like me."

"I wouldn't."

"You really have no idea, do you?"

His explanation of the darkness made not one iota of sense to Katherine. Trying to get her to imagine nothing wasn't easy. Saying that all her soulless body would have, would be the thoughts in her head, also didn't register.

"Try this," he said. "Again, you are in a universe of absolute nothing. Time doesn't exist. All you have is thought. Imagine now after an insane amount of time searching—time is only relevant in your head—that you find your soul. Then the keepers of your soul say to you 'Would you like it back, so you can be with the one you love for all eternity'. You would do anything they asked, wouldn't you?"

Katherine sat in silence and closed her eyes. She imagined—she thought of Claire.

"I would do anything," she said.

Mr. Green nodded. There was nothing more at that moment to be said.

Katherine returned home and sat in a disorientated state. The Colt M1903 Pocket Hammerless was still held tightly in her hand. It took her a good few seconds to prize it away—a finger at a time—and put it in her bag that was hung casually over her neck and shoulder.

Everything she had been told struggled to make sense. In her head there was no such thing as an unwanted child—her Lance was wanted. Ghosts didn't exist. The Sleeping didn't exist. Heaven was somewhere and Hell was on Earth. Only one person had risen from the dead, and that took some believing. And yet, if she was to believe in Mr. Green—which was becoming more likely—then she really would do anything to be with Claire. Her childhood attendance at Sunday school never gave a guarantee that she was even going to go to Heaven. She understood that her job bordered on the ethical. In her early days, she found it difficult to represent someone she believed to be guilty. Then it became easier to become impartial and let the judge or jury decide. Personal thought was a lawyer's noose. She would, one day, be judged on all that she'd done.

I'm as guilty as Hell, she thought.

Katherine finally left for work. The bag containing the gun went with her. She made a decision about her living dead neighbour; it was to avoid him at all costs.

Weeks passed without incident of Mr. Green or The Sleeping. December started cold and wet. The wind blew like God was angry. Sister Miriam still fed the pigeons.

Katherine had taken things into her own hands and e-mailed the Sisters of Hope Convent, in the hope that Sister Miriam could help. Sister Miriam answered the e-mail and there began a series of correspondences.

In Katherine's e-mails she told everything regarding Mr. Green's introduction, and of the recent incident when darkness took him and returned him. In return, she had learnt why Mr. Green had finally made such a close and revealing contact—it wasn't that he was running out of time. Lance's barrier was down. James had at last come home. Lance's hardened shell was now as weak as when he was born. He was alone and exposed. The predators had finally convinced their prey of its calling. Sister Miriam's closing e-mail was one of hope. She asked for belief in the positivity of what she was about to do, and not to breathe a word of anything that had recently happened to Lance. She would be in touch, shortly.

Lance was still staying at Flat 2 of No. 17 St Patrick Crescent. Not once had he asked Imogen to stay over. He kept in touch with Katherine by e-mails.

Imogen understood that her relationship with Lance probably wouldn't last. She knew her lover still loved his wife. But while the offer of sex was on the table—or so to speak—she wasn't going to refuse it. She was being a bad girl and liked it. Sometimes she only wanted to please Lance. She loved to see him in only his silk boxer shorts, working his hands as Rocky did. Seeing him sweat as his muscles stiffened, turned her on. It was with a fervent hand that she would pleasure him, while he was in a state of high adrenaline.

She broke off her relationship with Stephanie. The excuse was that she wasn't 100 per cent ready to pledge her love. That was all true enough. Imogen was clever, but when it came to percentages, she hadn't a clue on proportions—only that Lance was winning, because he had a bigger proportion. Stephanie didn't argue. Instead she quickly found a new lover who modelled for her. She was tall—her legs went on forever—and went by her modelling name of Sylvie Verlaine. Sylvie looked as a Snow Queen from Narnia should look—strangely beautiful with deep-green eyes and long silvery-blonde hair. She was androgynous in her appearance. Unfortunately she had all the personality of a backward donkey—which made her appealingly child-like—but she was ravenous when it came to being in the bedroom with another woman, which was all Stephanie wanted. Her intention was to make Imogen just as green-eyed.

If Stephanie had wanted a stimulating conversation, she'd have chatted up a very pretty lady librarian.

CHAPTER TWENTY-FOUR

Mr. Green sat on a bench and threw stones at the pigeons. His spine creaked as he picked up more stones. The trees stood bare; their branches stretching up for sunlight, slumbering in their effort of doing so.

It was when St. Thomas' Church bell sounded thrice that Sister Miriam appeared. She crossed the road and was greeted by a mass of swarming pigeons. Winter always brought more birds. She approached her Great-grandfather garbed in a long coat of black—it billowed like a raven spreading its wings.

"Hello, Great-grandfather," she said.

"Hello, Miriam, it's nice to see you again."

Sister Miriam roosted next to him and fed the birds.

"I'm trying to understand why you feed the birds," Mr. Green said. "Do you think you do it because it gives you the emotion of satisfaction in doing something good?"

"Yes." It was a plain and honest answer.

"Wouldn't stopping my suffering be the greatest emotion you could receive? Think how your Lord would reward you. You could see him in all his glory. Won't you help me?"

"It could be done," Sister Miriam said, looking with pity towards her Great-grandfather. "But someone will get hurt."

"Someone has to get hurt."

"What's written requires sacrifice."

"If that what's written, then so be it. Will you help me?"

Sister Miriam continued to feed the pigeons, until all the seed was gone. The pigeons, knowing there was no more seed, flew away.

"I'll send you a letter explaining," She said smiling.

"The last letter I received from you was disappointing."

"Sorry. I've now learnt a lot more."

"So you'll help?"

"Maybe, so long as you don't talk to anyone living. You talk to the dead because I know you do. But to be honest, Great-grandfather, I'd rather you didn't talk to them at any time."

Sister Miriam seemed to fly as a shadow, as she left her Great-grandfather. Mr. Green stood creaking to his ridiculous bent height, in a state of optimism. He raised his face towards the heavens and smiled. His back twisted some more—he bore the pain.

In 'The Room of Truth,' Sister Miriam studied. The winter solstice was forthcoming. The 21st-22nd of December was its beginning, as the Sun entered the sign of the goat that symbolized Satan. The hours of daylight got longer—it was a time for celebration. If she had to do anything in her call of help, then it must be on the night of December 21st. That night was the uppermost Satanic Holy Night of the year. She knew there had to be a ceremony. She had to be ready on the night when devotion was to the Lord Satan. It was a night to make personal resolutions. She must write her resolutions on a piece of paper and present them on the night's ritual. At the high point of the ritual the paper must be burnt—Satan would pact his help for an offering of a sacrifice.

The more she understood about what she must do, the more challenging it looked to undertake. Her sacrament was to include six:

One must be The Custodian.
One must be The Key.
Another had to be The Reason.
Another must be The Protector.
Two more must be Pretty Things.

Sister Miriam knew four of the above—herself being the first. Two others eluded her.

The first week of December was when Stephanie liked to put up the Christmas decorations. She had bought a new tree deliberately—it was white and tall. It was only going to be covered in blue and pink and silver glass baubles, with lots and lots of twinkling clear lights. She hated coloured lights—they reminded her of a fun-fair, and she hated fun-fairs. Earlier on, when she and Imogen had confided secrets, she had sobbed when explaining her first penetrating interaction with the male species. It was rough and painful and felt like she was being raped—she was only thirteen. No boy had ever put his finger—or his apparatus—in her since. She found the idea disgusting.

Stephanie was extremely happy being attracted to other women, as long as they looked like women. She loved the softness of their curves, the smell of their perfume, their femininity. Butch did absolutely nothing. If she hadn't been attracted to the female form, then what happened to her as a teenager would have no doubt made her a frigid bitch. Instead, she was promiscuously content being a lesbian. She could still be a bitch, when she wanted. When she was asked—at school and by bitchy teenage girls—how many times had she done it, she would answer, truthfully, 'just once'—making her a really good girl. Never was she asked about female fingers or tongues.

Imogen's response to a white and tall tree didn't make her green-eyed. The significance of hair colour and height seemed to wash over her head. Instead she liked the idea.

Fuck, thought Stephanie. *Maybe she's becoming a donkey.*

Shopping every night for a week had resulted in Stephanie amassing a wide variety of tree decorations. It was Friday evening and all the decorations lay in the middle of the floor, as did Stephanie.

She had her panties down around her ankles. Sylvie's head was up between Stephanie's thighs. The hi-fi was kicking out the line 'Rudolph with your nose so bright, won't you guide my sleigh tonight', when Imogen walked in amongst the frolicking.

"I see you're feeding the reindeer?" Imogen quipped, as she stood there, shocked by the sheer ignominy of what she was seeing—the look of pleasure on her past lover's face was like she'd just got the best Christmas present ever. Hazel-brown eyes were starting to change colour.

Stephanie glanced up as Imogen left the room in awkwardness. She smiled and pulled herself away from Sylvie. She stood up, kicked her panties off, and climbed onto Sylvie's back, kicking her heels against soft thighs. "To the bedroom, vixen," she called, gripping tightly to a mane of silvery-blonde. Vixen stood to her full height and obeyed.

From the kitchen came a clattering. Imogen was making coffee, very loudly. From the bedroom came noises that, thankfully, Imogen couldn't hear. The kitchen was being utilised as a sound barrier. In this room Imogen made herself an omelette. You would think the eggs she used were the heads of the cavorting couple in the room next door, by the way she cracked them and beat them. The omelette tasted good with all the unspoken words added to it. Calm prevailed.

By the time the bedroom door opened and a red-cheeked spikey-haired pretty thing emerged, the Christmas tree was decorated. Imogen had excelled herself. It had been the first time she had decorated a tree alone. The hi-fi was playing a cd of Christmas songs, by legendary crooners.

"Hi," Stephanie said. "That looks lovely."

Imogen didn't answer straightaway; she was busy tidying the ornament boxes away. "Would you like to turn the lights on?" she said with a smile. She could easily forgive.

"Please," Stephanie said, walking over. She bent down to the plug socket and clicked the switch. The tree burst into an illumination of twinkling stars that reflected million-fold into blue and pink and silver. "You even put the silver baubles on."

"I know—they're only baubles," Imogen smiled.

"It was a game."

"I know. I also play games."

"I know."

They both stood in silence looking at the tree. Memories were recalled.

A loud crack shot into the air—it sent two reminiscing young women into each other's arms as the cd skipped every track and stopped. Sylvie screamed and burst from the bedroom. A naked Snow Queen dropped to the floor in a flood of tears, in front of Stephanie, Imogen and a sparkling Christmas tree—she looked like she was melting.

No other noise came. For a few minutes the only sound was Sylvie's crying. Imogen took a shawl from off the couch and wrapped it around Sylvie's nakedness, and held her close to give comfort. Stephanie gave an objectionable glare.

Imogen took Sylvie to the couch; they both sat and listened—silence. Both looked at Stephanie to do something.

"Fine," she whispered. "You're both cowards."

Imogen and Sylvie nodded.

It took some guts, but in the end Stephanie—armed with only a kitchen knife—stormed the bedroom in a shouting assault. Her bed was a mess—obviously. But no-one was there. It was then she noticed the sliding wardrobe mirrored door. It had a massive crack in it. *What the fuck?*

"I've got a gun," she said, quickly sliding the door and stepping back while projecting a flashing blade. The only things in the wardrobe were clothes. She returned to the twinkling living room, shaking.

She dropped herself onto the couch next to two vulnerable, pretty women—if she hadn't been so scared she might have initiated a three-some. Imogen removed the knife from a quivering hand and put it on the floor.

Sylvie began to mumble something about being watched. It took a while to get anything coherent from her. They got her to start, slowly, from the beginning, which she did through a great deal of sobbing.

Stephanie coaxed her to tell past the sex, to when she must have, and obviously did, fall asleep. But Sylvie stuck to her guns. She was determined that she was being watched from the wardrobe before she fell asleep, and thought it was a kinky game.

Stephanie shook her head, to display her disgust. But really she liked the idea. Why hadn't she thought of it?

Imogen could see a faint, twisted smile on Stephanie's face. She gave her a dig in the ribs.

"Never ever," she said.

Stephanie held her side. *What if Lance were to watch?*

Girl telepathy struck.

No, Imogen glared.

It was just a thought.

Sylvie described a vault-like room. She was in the room and yet wasn't—she was floating like a tendril of white smoke that seemed to be able to leave the room and return whenever it pleased. In one door she freely went and out the other she freely went. But she kept returning to the room like a ghost. Six people were in the room and none of them saw her.

Sylvie covered her tear-lined face and shivered. She continued by recalling the room itself:

"The room wasn't as cold as I thought a room of stone would be. All the faces on the wall were smiling warmth at me." She then burst out in a hysterical cry, "They can see me!"

Stephanie's eyes widened. She suddenly thought of Mr. Green and shivered, knowing that he knew about the faces.

"They're only in your dream," Imogen told her.

"But there were hundreds, and they were all wearing skull masks," Sylvie recalled. "The six had on gowns, bar one. That one wore only his skin and had horns coming from his head…" she paused as if something terrible was about to happen. But there was nothing more about the dream that she could remember.

Stephanie prodded her to go on. "And then what?"

"Then there was a loud crack..." Sylvie said. "Someone came out of the wardrobe. He was tall and draped all in black… he hadn't a face… he hadn't any eyes… but he was staring right at me."

"It's O.K., it was just part of the same dream," Imogen said, pulling Sylvie into a warm embrace.

Sylvie's body crumpled into Imogen's hug.

The mirror cracking wasn't a dream. They all agreed on that. But not one of them could come up with why it cracked. Sylvie was in no state to go home. Two out of three decided it was best they all slept in one bed that night. The two agreed it had to be Imogen's bed.

In bed, Imogen cuddled Sylvie like a teddy-bear in her struggle to go to sleep. The bedside light remained on.

Stephanie's eyes where turning green, and most possibly by the reflection of the clock's digital display by her side. She looked at the time—it read: 11:34. Her imagination turned it upside down, to read the word: hell.

Out of the corner of her eye, she saw the same little girl she had seen in 'The Riflemen' weeks earlier. The girl smiled sweetly and then faded away. Stephanie didn't feel afraid. She closed her eyes and slipped into sleep.

It was 3.00 in the morning when a letter was dropped through the letterbox of No. 111 Padstow Avenue. Mr. Green was not asleep. He was standing in front of the mirror. A white face in his reflection communicated.

It was at 4.30 in the morning that his eyes looked over the letter. It read:

Black Mass at the Winter Solstice
Below are listed who should attend:

Miriam Drake..........The Custodian
Ambrose Green..........The Key / The Messenger
Lance Lewisham..........The Reason (James Walker... The Unwanted)
Katherine Lewisham..........The Protector
? .... A Pretty Thing
? .... A Pretty Thing

"Thank you, Great-granddaughter. I know of two Pretty Things," Mr. Green said, as he straightened up a bit. "That's clever… A sentence of six words, followed by another of six, and followed by the attending six."

He burned the letter.

CHAPTER TWENTY-FIVE

Fingers skated across the keyboard. Sister Miriam was half awake as she sent an e-mail to Katherine. She inwardly laughed as she turned off her PC. She knelt and prayed—as she always did—before going to breakfast. It was 7.00 in the morning. It was raining.

Katherine received an e-mail that simply said:

I will come to your house. I will be there at 11 a.m. The result is in us both.

At 11.00 a.m. Katherine was waiting by the door. She peered through the side window and saw a large black umbrella; under it sheltered a sprightly woman walking. She had short grey hair that didn't move an inch. She smiled like an angel at Katherine's peering face.

Katherine opened the door.

"Hello, Katherine," Sister Miriam said warmly. She looked at the bag casually hung across Katherine and smiled.

Katherine smiled back and said: "Welcome," as she stepped aside, gesturing her guest in.

Sister Miriam closed her umbrella and shook it before entering. It flapped like a gigantic black bat, dispelling water from its wings. When she stepped over the threshold of No. 113 Padstow Avenue, it was as if she was Katherine's mother, paying a visit. The love she brought was hopefully going to be welcomed.

Sister Miriam stood her umbrella next to the front door.

Time seemed to flutter in dreams because before Katherine knew it, Sister Miriam's coat was upon a hook in the hallway—keeping the umbrella company—and she was sat at the kitchen table with her visitor and two cups of coffee. She could hear a warm voice saying how delighted she was to meet her. She extended her delight back.

Sister Miriam read—silently—the words of yellow upon a brown earth background that stared at her from the printed art work upon the kitchen wall.

Niceties over—seriousness began.

Each looked at each other in an examining way. Coffee was finished before another word was spoken.

Katherine looked at the cross around Sister Miriam's neck and wondered about what it was like giving yourself to God. *Did God really want that?*

Finally Sister Miriam spoke: "Do you trust me, Katherine?"

"I think so," Katherine deliberated.

Sister Miriam spoke again: "Will you trust me, Katherine?"

"Yes."

"Good," Sister Miriam said. "Isn't it strange, don't you think, that the words God and good share the same letters?"

Katherine thought about it. *Do people really think things like that?*

"Trust starts from now," Sister Miriam said. "We need to go next door."

Katherine thought about trust. "O.K.," she said, "when?"

"Now would be as good a time as any. I ask you to listen and not speak. We will talk when we return here."

There was a knock on the door of No. 111 Padstow Avenue. Mr. Green answered it.

Katherine gazed unsympathetically at a bent-double old man, from under a large black umbrella. Sister Miriam simply smiled.

"I offer welcome to The Custodian and The Protector," Mr. Green said. "Please come in."

"Thank you, Great-grandfather," Sister Miriam said.

Katherine looked puzzled. She did as she was bid and didn't say a word. *Hello, Soulless Fucker,* she said callously in her head.

Into the living room went The Custodian and The Protector, followed by The Messenger.

Sister Miriam saw the mirror in its sparse surroundings. She turned her eyes away and said without emotion: "We are here to offer The Unwanted in altercation for The Messenger—peace will hopefully come to both."

Mr. Green then sat in one chair as his Great-granddaughter sat in the other. Katherine was a noticeable fly on the wall.

The conversation between the two seated began:

"I know of the two we need," Mr. Green said.

"Good. Who are they?"

"The Pretty Things are Imogen Swan and her ex-lover Stephanie Duke."

Katherine recognised the name of her jealousy. *She's had a woman lover?* Imogen's nakedness filled her mind.

Sister Miriam put her hand to her chin in thought.

"Who is Miss Duke's lover now?" she asked.

161

"I'm of the understanding it's a model named Sylvie Verlaine… and yes, she's pretty. Fashion designer Stephanie Duke wouldn't be interested otherwise."

Sister Miriam still had her hand to her chin in thought.

"We'll replace Miss Swan with Miss Verlaine," she said without any emotion.

Katherine was now thinking about her husband's secretary. *Who's her lover now?*

"Which one will sacrifice her life?" Mr. Green asked.

Katherine gasped in horror. *Oh my God!* She clutched at her bag.

Sister Miriam shot a sideways look. "I haven't decided yet."

Katherine covered her mouth.

Sister Miriam stood up and walked over to Katherine. For a moment, Katherine was scared… A calm and gentle hand rested upon a trembling hand that was reaching into a shoulder bag. A soft voice said: "Trust."

Mr. Green turned his head. It was only a brief glance. He returned his stare back towards the empty chair.

Sister Miriam, again, sat opposite her Great-grandfather. She said very sweetly: "The Protector will bring The Pretty Things."

"Of course," Mr. Green said. "It's your call."

"I'll see you at 10.00 on the evening of the 21st." Sister Miriam stood up. "Hopefully, that will be the last time we see each other." She gestured Katherine to leave.

Katherine turned and caught herself in the mirror. Her reflection looked soullessly back. She quickly looked elsewhere and made her way to where the black bat umbrella rested against the front door.

Sister Miriam, very vigilantly, whispered into her Great-grandfather's ear: "If you fail to obey my every command, then you will stay in the darkness for all eternity." Her Great-grandfather nodded. She looked into the mirror only to see herself. She cocked her head and winked.

Time fluttered as a dream. Katherine was making fresh coffee. Sister Miriam was sitting patiently at the table.

When Katherine sat, Sister Miriam was looking pleased as she viewed a dark, clouded sky out of the kitchen window. The rain was relentless.

"Katherine," she said warmly, "let me tell you what has to happen…"

"No," Katherine said with such strength, that Sister Miriam's eyes darkened as they narrowed to form a frown. "I'm not going to be part of a murder."

The sky thundered and rain lashed hard against the windows. The room became dark to the point where it mimicked night. Sister Miriam's eyes widened at the sky's response.

"No-one will be murdered… trust me," she said.

Deep down, Katherine knew that something had to be done about Mr. Green. In her mind Pee-Pee was dead because of that Soulless Fucker. She needed to listen. She looked across the table into an angelic face. *I need to trust her.*

She began to describe her understanding of things: "I know that Lance was adopted, and that—according to that sicko next-door—The Sleeping want to claim his soul because he was not created out of want."

"Correct."

"And that Mr. Green committed suicide in 1929, and therefore went straight to Hell…" She paused briefly to think. "My husband's first encounter with The Sleeping was when he was five—that was also when he met Mr. Green, who after forty-five years in the darkness had made a pact with The Sleeping."

"Again, correct."

"So, to put it in a nutshell, so to speak, The Sleeping will reunite Mr. Green with his soul, once he gives them my husband's soul?"

"Spot on."

Katherine glowered. *And you think I'll allow that?*

Sister Miriam had listened. Now it was her time to speak: "You can't kill my Great-grandfather...," she gave Katherine a see-into-the-mind look, "but you already know that. We agree he is The Messenger for The Sleeping—The Messenger is also The Key that opens the door between worlds.

"What I am proposing is that by trusting in me, all will be sorted. I can't tell you anything about the night of the 21st other than that you are your husband's protector, and that you will protect him.

"As The Custodian, I will hold a black mass." Katherine's eyes enlarged. "The Messenger will be the object of debate. The Unwanted is The Reason; he is the whole reason why. And you, as The Protector, must attend with a forceful act. And lastly, we draw our attention to The Pretty Things—unfortunately one must be the sacrifice."

Katherine heard the word once before and said nothing. This second time she wasn't going to remain silent. She said in a voice that was full of fear and confusion: "You said no-one would be murdered."

"Yes, I did, and no-one will be. But there must be a sacrifice."

"If you're going to sacrifice a life—I'd call that murder."

"Katherine, I told you no-one will die." Sister Miriam didn't say anymore.

Believe, Katherine told herself. *For Christ's sake, this is a woman of God—if she said no-one will die, then no-one will die.*

Silence took hold.

Katherine had never had any interest in witchcraft, tarot cards or any of that malarkey. She hadn't the faintest idea of what a black mass really was. But she was beginning to understand that if a nun and a living-dead, and hellish-things—such as The Sleeping—were involved, then it was most definitely something very, very dark that she was going to witness.

A wood, a clearing, and a moon at midnight—where men and women dressed in long robes watched others performing sexual acts with more than one other—sprung to mind. *I'm going to be involved in Devil worship... will I be part of the orgy?*

Sister Miriam looked deep into Katherine's eyes and repeated: "Do you trust me, Katherine?"

"Yes," Katherine said. And she meant it.

"Good," Sister Miriam said. "If you fail to obey my every command, then you will never be free of my Great-grandfather. Bring the Pocket Hammerless that you carry with you on the night."

Katherine nodded. She had no intention of going anywhere without it. She was keeping Lance's promise of not letting it out of her sight.

Sister Miriam again observed the art print that hung on the kitchen wall. Softly she said: "When there are no eyes watching over you, and the air is sparked with fear. No strength of pride and hope. One man and his dreams are broken."

"You also know it," Katherine said.

"Yes. It was written by a man that lost love and faith—do you think my Great-grandfather deserves them back?"

Katherine didn't say anything. She had no pity as she thought about the man next door: *I personally wouldn't give that Soulless Fucker anything more than he deserves.* She wondered how this was all going to end.

Time fluttered as a dream again. Sister Miriam was at the door with her coat on. As she stepped outside, she put up her umbrella and said: "Let me know when you have convinced The Pretty Things to attend. Do it quickly—we don't have much time. I hope to see you again at 10.00 on the evening of the 21st. You know the place—you heard The Messenger talk about it to The Reason. Don't dress up—appropriate dress will be provided."

With that, she turned and went. The rain showed signs of relenting, as a gap, oval in shape within the black clouds, revealed the sun. The clouds drifted, making the sun resemble a golden pupil moving from one side of a Godly eye to the other, in watchfulness.

CHAPTER TWENTY-SIX

The working week's start was cold. The forecast said snow was on the way. Lance sat at his desk watching the lovely Miss Swan do her perfected bend-over—his pulse still raced. His mobile burst into song. His heart missed a beat.

It was Katherine calling.

Miss Swan eloquently left the room—she knew it must be some sort of an emergency because the last time she heard Lance's phone play his wife's favourite '70s song, was when Katherine's mother had died. She remembered Lance's singing 'Hip! Hip! Hooray! The mother-in-law died today!' after the call ended.

"Katherine, what's wrong?" Lance said panicky. All he could hear was road noise and hard breathing.

A bus that was late, carrying commuters it had made late, rumbled by. Beeping taxis only added to the chaos. Walkers noisily jostled for space like drunks.

Katherine talked loudly above the sound as she walked: "Don't worry—everything's O.K., it's just that I spoke to Sister Miriam and she's come up with a solution to our problem."

"What have you been doing?" Lance snapped.

"I need to see you so I can explain what's going to happen."

"Why, what's going to happen?"

"It's to do with The Sleeping and that Soulless Fucker we have living next door."

Lance didn't say anything straight away. He listened to the traffic blast his eardrum as he tried to think. Finally he said: "I'll come and see you tonight—are you keeping to your promise?"

"Yes. It's with me always," Katherine shouted. "What are you do-ing… hitting the leather… twanging that old piece of wood… or eyeing up your Imogen?" Her voice sounded more aggressive the further down the list she went.

"Neither. I'm talking to you," Lance said dryly.

Men… they can never multi-task. "I'll see you tonight. By the way, talking of your beloved secretary… did you know about her and her female flatmate being lovers? I bet that's turning you on…"

It was either no signal that broke communication or she had hung up.

The conversation left Lance's head spinning.

After work, Lance drove to see Katherine. He parked on his drive, turned off the engine, and sat for a moment. The warm car soon began to get cold—the temperature was dropping like a stone down a well. Through the windscreen the sky was void of moon and stars. Snow was imminent.

When he walked into the kitchen, the air wasn't as bitter as it was outside. Katherine looked pleased to see him.

"So, what is going to happen?" he said.

"Hello, darling, it's nice to see you too."

Lance gave a broad smile—the one Katherine found charming. It was possibly the first thing she'd liked about him when they'd met.

"Is this going to be a friendly evening?" Katherine said, uncorking a bottle of red.

"Do you want it to be?"

"Yes." She poured two large glasses and handed one to Lance.

"I take it I'm staying the night?"

"This is your house as much as mine. We are married, aren't we? We are in love, aren't we?"

One minute passed in uncomfortable silence as Lance sipped his wine. He quite openly said: "Of course we are… but we are having some troubles."

Katherine was looking at him with big eyes.

"We are. And we will get through them." She drank her wine like water. "Do you want to screw me?" Lance's mouth fell open. She took him by the hand and led him into the living room. She undid his belt and pulled his trousers and boxers down, below his knees. There wasn't a time—that she could remember—when her husband wasn't ready. She pushed him into a seated position on the couch.

Katherine undressed, straddled and lowered herself. She moaned pleasurably. Lance looked shocked and pleased at the same time.

"Are you screwing your secretary?" she asked.

Lance hated the word screw or fuck when used sexually. He preferred the term 'making love', so he answered: "No."

"Are you screwing me?" Katherine asked.

"No," Lance said.

"That answers a lot," Katherine said. She didn't stop what she was doing.

After they had taken a shower together and were tucking into a Chinese take-away—F4 special for 2 persons, that consisted of: House Hors D'oeuvres, Crispy Duck, Chicken with Cashew Nuts, Crispy Chili Beef, Sweet & Sour Prawns, Mixed Vegetables, and Special Fried Rice—it was Katherine that talked and Lance who listened. After all, that was why he was there. Sex was secondary.

When he heard about her going next door, he was so mad that he shook with anger. Katherine made light of it, but there was no disguising the fear that was in her eyes. He held her hand comfortingly. He could be sensitive when he wanted.

The more Katherine told, the less he shook. His anger was being substituted by shock. When he'd heard everything, his first words were: "Can we trust her?"

"Do we have a choice?" Katherine said.

"No… I don't suppose we have." He stood up and wandered to the window. Looking at next door, he saw only one window with a light on. *The Messenger is home*—his thoughts became furious in questioning—*Are Great-grandfather and Great-granddaughter working together? Is all this part of their plan to give The Sleeping my soul? If so, what's going to happen to me? Why the hell was I unwanted? What happens to others like me? Are we surrounded by Soulless Fuckers like Mr. Green and colluding bitches like Sister Miriam… Why, God, why? Why did you take Claire?*

Snow started to fall.

"I'm putting the car away," he said. He went outside to feel the snow on his face. Tiny flakes landed upon him as he stared intently up towards heaven. He couldn't feel tranquillity—as some claim—when he thought about God. His only comfort was in what he'd recently dreamt and that his dear daughter was somewhere in the great creation of things.

When the car was safe in the garage, he again stood looking up. The snow floated down—it looked like it might settle. He didn't feel at all cold. When at last he came back indoors, Katherine had changed for bed. She shook her head and crooked a smile that said it all: I don't know why things happen—but someone does.

"Let's go to bed," she said. "You'll never be unwanted to me."

Lance smiled sadly. No matter what his wife said, or how much love he'd received from his parents, he would always feel unwanted. The truth never hides.

Katherine was asleep as soon as her head hit the pillow. She breathed softly into the room. Lance listened absorbedly. Nothing else could he hear. The gentle falling snow had a strange way of making noise redundant.

He pondered over what he had heard tonight, and thought even more deeply about such things as: Is it a coincidence that The Messenger is an ancestor of The Custodian? What are the chances that The Custodian of 'The Room of Truth' would ever have known The Unwanted? Is it all for a reason? As he fell asleep he thought he knew the answers.

Lance was standing barefoot in an empty room. He felt a connection to the room, he was certain he had been there before. There were footprints in the dust upon the bare wooden boards. He suddenly realised that it wasn't himself that had been before, but James. He felt strangely disconnected. It was as if he was a stranger in his own body.

Light from the street lamps poured into the room the last time he visited. Moonlight and streetlight had now become its cover. It was a depressing nightfall that stifled his breathing—time was leisurely decaying him, and yet he didn't feel afraid or alone in its doing. He wandered over to the window and stood in the pale blue light of the moon. The moon was blue in reflection of his heart's sorrow.

When he looked out into the night, he only saw himself. The glass had become a mirror in its similarity by reflection. He stared past himself—there he could make out shapes. He knew what they were; he had seen them enough times to recognise who they were.

Faces of white came closer. Lance didn't step away as tens of faces now looked at him from unforgettable black hollows. He stared back with all the emotion they showed. The faces blurred and shimmered like heat on a hot road. He had made them angry.

"Welcome to my world," he said mordantly, as he tried to fix his gaze onto their bleached faces.

There followed a venomous hissing.

Lance grinned. He was antagonising them—he liked it.

And then they were gone. He saw only his reflection.

It came to him in an instant. His mind spoke to his soulless self behind the glass: *Sister Miriam was my first Protector. I was adopted by the two most wonderful people in the world. Their love was so natural, that in their eyes, I was made for them. Their love made a shield around me. My love for them was its strength. My mother was now my Protector.*

When I first saw The Sleeping, I was unwell and sleeping between my parents in their bed. My shield was secure because they were near. When The Sleeping came again, I fought and screamed because I recognised their presence. I had become a good fighter.

Katherine came into my life. The love she pledged strengthened my shield to the point that when my parents died, the shield was as strong as ever. She was now The Protector...

Understanding lost when he questioned why he became James. His only assumption was that to protect himself from a weakening shield—due to their loss of Claire—he let The Sleeping come for James. As long as he shut his mind to James, The Sleeping couldn't touch Lance. That made as much sense as why falling cats land on their feet. It was as simple as 'because they could'—it was for their protection. Why he hadn't fully understood all this before was beyond him. His shield was now weakening, and it was his own fault.

The light from the window became bluer. He felt faint and leant against the wall. The disturbed dust upon the bare wooden boards glittered like stars in an unknown universe. Without warning, his nose bled backwards into his mouth. He started spitting and swallowing his own blood. His put his index finger into his inkwell mouth and inscribed across the wallpaper...

Katherine woke to the sound of her name. It was faint in the darkness. She switched on the bedside light to find that Lance was not beside her— he was standing facing the bedroom wall, dipping his finger into his mouth and scratching across the wall's surface with his nail, like a quill. He was quietly calling her name, over and over again.

Katherine rushed to his side. Her touch instantly woke him.

Lance had no idea what he'd done or why. All he knew was it had something to do with Katherine. He had defaced their bedroom wall in his sleep. The words he wrote were dark red. His mouth dripped the very ink in which they were written:

The blue moon's gonna shine away—the blue moon's gonna shine...
Don't call on the broken-hearted
Don't tell me that to comfort me
The words won't touch in the right places
Run among a million flowers...
Falling—forever touching wishes
Falling—while we sleep
Falling—shower me with kisses
Falling—love is deep...
Now your smile is breaking through
Sometimes you have to hold on me
And your touch is reaching in
Pin down the clouds and cover me...
Torture the small who wonder
When the blue moon shines away

See through the words
Wait for the Beast to come out to play

Lance was led dazed and confused to the bathroom. Katherine sat him on the edge of the bath and cleaned him of his blood. Neither spoke.

Lance took control and washed his hands and rinsed his mouth. Katherine returned to the room. When she saw the words 'wait for the Beast to come out to play' she went and got a knife and scraped the wallpaper from the wall. She put the mess in a bin-bag and dropped it outside the backdoor, onto a thin layer of snow.

Katherine then got back into bed. Her husband was by her side. He looked to be asleep.

"I can't do this on my own. I don't even know this Stephanie. What on earth do I say to her?" she said so pathetically, that it didn't sound like her at all.

"Katherine, I'll worry about that tomorrow. Go to sleep."

"You want to sleep?"

"Yes."

"Aren't you frightened?"

"No."

"Well I am."

Katherine next saw her husband at the kitchen table, drinking coffee. She had been so deep in sleep that she hadn't heard him get up. She stood looking at him in panic.

Lance looked up and smiled.

"I thought they'd taken you," she said through a trembling smile.

"If that had happened, then I would be dead in bed." He said it so matter-of-factly that it hit her right between the eyes.

"Of course… it's only your soul they want." She sarcastically added, "That makes me feel a whole lot better."

Lance sipped away at his coffee. He was trying hard to figure out a way of convincing a woman who disliked him to come to a black mass and bring her new lover, so that one of them could be sacrificed in a rite that presumably involved the giving of souls. He had to tell her something plausible, but what?

By the time Katherine had showered and was applying her make-up for work, Lance had only come up with one idea. He was still sipping coffee as he contemplated his future. It was transparently apparent that Sister Miriam had his life in her hands.

Katherine walked into the kitchen looking lovely. She'd done her war-paint purposely different. Out with characterless—in with noticeable. She now looked office-stunning and her breasts looked fabulously perky in her new work clothes. She had spent the last few weeks, secretly, working on her new look. She loved it, but would everybody else? Her husband was going to be her first audience. She gave him a big smile and waited for his reaction.

Lance gaped with widened eyes that said everything. He could have said lots of things, but thought it best not to comment. Whatever words tumbled out of his mouth about her beauty, were bound to be read in a totally different way. He so wanted to fondle her breasts.

He moved his eyes away from her breasts and looked her imaginatively in the eye, saying: "What if you sent Miss Duke and her partner an invitation to a winter solstice celebration, saying that the fucker next-door will be there and he would very much like them both to be part of the event. Add that there might be some ghosts present… that will get her interest. Oh, and don't use the word 'fucker', use Ambrose."

175

Katherine had got the reaction she wanted. If her husband thought she looked anything other than wonderful, he'd have said so. There was no way he would let her out the house looking anything but respectfully beautiful. She looked and felt a good fifteen years younger.

Katherine thought about her husband's suggestion: *Good idea.* But she wasn't going to tell him that. She didn't want him going to work with a bigger head than he already had. "What's her address?"

Lance shrugged.

Katherine gave a dubious stare. "She co-habits with your secretary and you don't know where she lives?"

"No. Do you know your secretarial staff's addresses?"

"E-mail me her address when you get to work."

Lance drank the dregs of his coffee and put the cup down assertively. He stood up, walked over to Katherine, and kissed her softly on the lips. He then furtively fondled her breast. Her slightly open blouse exhibited an adorable cleavage.

"Pervert," she said with a smile.

CHAPTER TWENTY-SEVEN

The start to the working day was crisp with a light dusting of snow. It was nothing to cause disruption for the thousands of city commuters as they poured into their workplaces, wrapped up tight and warm. Nearly all were looking forward to the Christmas break. There were always the few humbug-bosses that needed a visit from three spirits to give them a good kicking up the backside; or maybe deplete that surplus population by whatever means they saw fit. Such miserable bastards should understand that the people that work for them—all year round—are the ones that toil, while they are spending two to three weeks in the Bahamas every year enjoying themselves, and spending ridiculous amounts of money on either their wife or, more likely, some dyed-blonde, fake-breasted bimbo. Oh! How the workers hated that sort of person. They are the fake with the tan.

Stephanie was wandering through her place of work. It was a lofty open-plan office apartment with enormous glass windows, which gave a fantastic view over roof-tops and looked as if it was in Andy Warhol's creative corner of his Factory. If that was only true—it was only in its appearance and not its location. She had bought the space some years back when her father died from the disease that claimed someone from everyone's family sometime or another. She'd vowed never to say the word that began with a capital C. Her father had told her: 'Live *your* dream, for there are no second chances. Be who *you* are—love who *you* want'. She'd promised she would. It was his money that made her dream—she was doing it all for him. She called her 'Factory' the provocative name 'Velvet'. If anyone was dumb enough to ask why, then they deserved not to be answered. For Christ's sake, there was enough Velvet Underground album covers on the walls to give the clue. Her father was a big Velvets fan. The music was drummed into her. She had grown to love it. As a teenager, she'd had a crush on Christa Päffgen—known mostly by her adopted modelling and singing name, Nico. She was probably the reason why Stephanie had chosen her career. A vision of Nico in shiny, shiny, shiny boots of leather always turned her on. Sometimes, a few different coloured tears fell, especially when listening to the husky-sexy singing of 'Sunday Morning'. At those times, gloomy thoughts made her feel that all the people she ever loved, were in the world behind her.

Today, Velvet was empty of models and clients. Tuesday was her alone day at work. It was when her finest ideas flowed best—solitude always gave her a unique creativity. Stephanie sat amongst her latest inspired drawings for a New York lingerie company that loved her ideas. They'd approached her—apparently falling in love with her heterogeneous style. It had always been known that big-name companies watch and observe creative talent. When, and if ever they needed them, became another matter. Stephanie felt she was in the right place at the right time. And how clichéd was that?

Lance had obtained Imogen's address from his files and forwarded it to Katherine. Today he was only window-shopping. He was being the unresponsive, desire-hiding, Mr. Lewisham.

Miss Swan had deduced that office protocol was back on the menu. She was wondering what she had done wrong.

Katherine had turned heads. She felt wonderful. Why hadn't she done it before? The female staff complimented her new makeover. The straight male staff said nothing. She could see them lower their eyes to her most noticeable, lifted bosom, when she spoke to them. She had watched the hunky ones' arses enough times, to not feel sexually harassed.

Katherine sat at her desk and ignored the e-mail from her husband—it was just a test. She searched the internet for Stephanie Duke:

Stephanie Duke
www.Dukefashion.com
Stephanie Duke—UK address and phone number—192.com
Stephanie Duke profiles | LinkedIn
Stephanie Duke—Image Results
Stephanie Duke | Facebook
Velvet—Design by Stephanie Duke
www.Dukefashion.com

Katherine clicked on the website. *Mmm, very impressive,* she thought. Her eyes were pulled towards a very pretty young woman looking very self-assured—Stephanie's blue hair seemed to be electric in the photographer's flash. Her androgynous appearance made the page-viewer search her body with curiosity.

The cursor was moved over the site's viewable pages. It passed over biography and hovered over lingerie. Click. *Mmm, those are absolutely lovely.* Eyes flitted from woman to woman, looking for the blue-haired pixie. She wasn't there. *Does she wear them?* Her eyes fell to a tall blonde. She saw Sylvie Verlaine in white silk knickers and bra. *She is beautifully ghost-like.* She moved the cursor over contact. Click. *Bingo!* There was her e-mail address.

She clicked the address.
She wrote the e-mail:

Dear Stephanie,

Please let me introduce myself. I am the next door neighbour and good friend of Mr. Green. He has told me so much about you. It is at his request that I invite you to a small gathering this coming winter solstice. The invitation is for yourself and Sylvie Verlaine—your partner—to attend what will be a rather special evening. If you are both otherwise engaged on the evening 21st December, Ambrose and myself will of course understand. I, personally, would love you to join us on what promises to be a very supernatural night. Please forward your address for invitation :-)

Regards,
Katherine Lewisham.

Sent was clicked.

Stephanie wondered how Katherine knew about Sylvie. A smile came, knowing that Imogen must be truly jealous. *Mr. Green hadn't met Sylvie, so it must have been Lance that told her. Lance must have heard about the reindeer from Imogen—I'm already embarrassed about meeting her. Why am I? I'm me!*

An hour later, a response came. It was short and sweet—saying: Yes, we would love to come and thank you. It was warmly smiled upon. The address was copied down. All that was needed now was an invitation card. The invite would in no way lie. It just wouldn't say the whole truth. An e-mail was sent back, saying an invite would be put through her letterbox the following day.

Katherine had always felt that a point in her life would come when she would need to put her entire trust in another human being's hands. That point in time was going to be 21st December—the Devil's night. But whose hands was she really putting her trust in? Lord only knows! She sent an e-mail to Sister Miriam saying that the Pretty Things would indeed be attending mass.

Wednesday became the eleventh day of the twelfth month of the thirteenth year of the second millennium. Sister Miriam was not her usual self—her eyes looked milky, her skin lighter. She hadn't been to chapel or communicated with anyone since she last spoke to Katherine. She had also taken to wearing a white habit and absolutely nothing else but the sandals upon her feet. She looked like a wistful bride. The large wooden crucifix from around her neck lay in the darkness of a drawer. Her time was spent either in her room or in 'The Room of Truth', reading. She needed to be ready. She had to be ready.

This woman—who had always given her love to her Lord—was in considerable pain as once again she took to prayer, kneeling in front of the wall of skulls. Her aged, slender shoulder blades felt like something was cutting its way out of her back. She breathed deeply and said aloud: "Merciful Lord, I give to you myself, as I have always done. Be pleased with me…" The rest of her supplication fell silent. The Lord hears those that speak to him.

Each skull—barring one—saw what it had seen before, all heard nothing. The silence was so crushing, that if a spider walked you would hear it.

A pain so severe pushed the prayer flat-faced to the ground and who, without perception of her actions, spread her arms out to form a crucifix. Blood soaked into the cloth between her shoulders, making two scarlet lines about six inches long. Sister Miriam didn't scream. She bore her pain. Pain was part of living. Her hands, which had spreading clawing fingers, burnt upon the floor as she continued to pray in silence.

After hours of painful praying, Sister Miriam left 'The Room of Truth' and returned to her own room. There, she removed her habit and looked at her pitiful reflection in the only mirror she dared keep—the mirror had always been in her room and was full length. Its frame was gilded and looked out of place in such humble surroundings of white-washed walls and bare-boarded floor. She had once removed it from the wall, but when she'd seen the Lord's Prayer written upon the back, she wisely put it back. It had obviously been put there for a good reason, which—as time went by—she fully understood.

"Are you watching?" she said. Her reflection showed her naked truth. She looked washed-out, like she was nearing death's door. Twenty years had somehow been added over the past few days. Her flesh was wafer thin. It hung onto her by God's will only.

As she turned, the mirror rippled to give the impression that she was swimming amongst others. Hundreds of wrinkly, old hags squirmed together in a boiling pot of loathing, hissing at what could be seen.

Her reproduced image showed there was nothing on her back to give any indication of where the blood came from. Nonetheless, it was her blood that was on her habit, which had spread out to form—in appearance—a pair of glossy reddish-brown wings.

When at last she washed in her simple stone bowl of crystal-clear cold water, she felt a much needed revitalisation. A clean body was adorned by a fresh white habit; it covered a multitude of sins and two keys that never left her. She stood in front of the mirror with renewed vigour. Her eyes stared deeply through herself. She couldn't see anyone but herself, yet she knew she was being watched. She casually winked and turned and lay upon her metal framed bed.

There, staring at the ceiling, she gave thoughtful acumen into the date on which this had just happened. It was with mathematics that she pondered over its significance. She subtracted the satanic numbers associated with the Beast from the day, month and year. She was left with five, six and seven floating in her mind's eye. She added them to make eighteen. The Beast's numbers added together also made eighteen.

She frantically sat up. Two shaky legs felt like they couldn't support her weight as she tried to stand. She sat down hard, almost knocking the wind out of her frail body. As she looked at the floor it became a whirl-pool—she felt sick. She focused on the wall; it remained a wall and not a swirling sea. Her continuous study and refusal to eat was making her ill. She needed more than mental sustenance—it was food that fed the body, not learning. How stupid had she been?

If the number eighteen was to have any relevance, she had yet to find out. But one thing about her stupid arrangement of putting knowledge before food, made her realise that she needed to be ready and clear in her mind of what needed to be done, by one week today. She knew she needed to study more. She also knew she needed to eat.

CHAPTER TWENTY-EIGHT

Stephanie showed a smile of expectance as she arrived home from a day full of modelling try-outs, and slid her keycard into the mechanical lock. Its click allowed her into the entrance hall of its warehouse complex of eight flats, where she speedily opened letterbox 6 in the wall. A broader smile beamed at a small, white envelope that had no stamp. Her name, written in a flamboyant, flowing line, begged her to take it.

It was no sooner in her hand, than she was running up the stairs, two at a time, mouthing excitedly in a whisper, so no-one else could hear: "I'm going to a party." When she got through her front door, she frenziedly ripped open the envelope. Her eyes flashed wide at what was written:

Guests: Stephanie Duke & Sylvie Verlaine
Occasion: Black Mass
Venue: The Room of Truth
Date: 21st December 2013
Time: 10.00 p.m.
Theme: Appropriate dress will be provided on the night
Arrangements: A car will pick you up at 9.30 p.m.—be there or be square.

Looking forward to meeting you,
Katherine Lewisham x

"How cool is that?" she said aloud. "'Dress will be provided'… what in God's name will we be wearing?"

The invite was left propped up on the mantelpiece, as Stephanie switched on the tree lights and went into the kitchen. A fluttering was in her stomach. A drink was needed when anxiety reared its head. *Aren't orgies practised at a black mass? Don't they wear gowns? I hope mine isn't black. I don't look good in black—it makes me look even thinner.* Ice was dropped into a tumbler of vodka and coke, as she had second thoughts about attending. A minute later and she was up for it again. *I'm definitely going!*

Imogen felt very much on a downer. Work was extremely busy—being the last two weeks before the holidays—and was giving her no time to talk to Lance. Why it was that every legal representative who dealt with them had to have a professional evaluation of their client in their possession before the end of the year was beyond her—lawyers never rushed at any other time of the year. The idea that it was to get some poor innocent sod out on bail, so that he could have a supposedly joyful Christmas, quickly vaporised from her mind. It wasn't even the thought of the large Christmas bonuses those money-grabbing leeches got, which was depressing her. The truth was, that she was feeling neglected and unloved. The world was full of taking and not giving.

Her eyes welled as she entered her flat. She knew she was a taker of sorts, but she knew she was also a giver. Her mind flooded with the image of the man she loved. As a tear trickled down her cheek, she felt shame for her womanly desire. She wiped away the tear and told herself, in a positive way, that love was worth fighting for. That was all the justification she needed. The New Year would rightly be a time for resolutions.

She removed her coat, kicked off her shoes, and walked into the living room. Her eyes roamed for a friendly face—the tree lights flashed their welcome. A propped up envelope on the mantelpiece drew her attention. She reached for it, and wrongly opened it, and nosily read it. She felt sick with jealousy. She threw the invite and envelope in rage, and went storming into the kitchen.

Stephanie's sweeping smile was swiped from her face. Imogen's hand stung as she ran crying to her room.

Stephanie was numb. She poured another drink. She debated taking it to the green-eyed bitch that had just struck her, but thought against it. The side of her face was smarting, and besides, she wasn't in the mood for any sort of fighting. She couldn't care less that Imogen had talked about her lover to Lance, and that Lance repeated it all to his wife. What did it matter? She wasn't afraid of being who she was.

Mr. Green sat alone with his thoughts. His skin was bluer than ever, his back more bent. He arrogantly bore his pain with the knowledge that it wouldn't be for much longer. Visualising 'The Room of Truth' and his soul's future gave him his strength.

He thought about his life as if it were a book. It didn't start promisingly. The middle failed to grab. And as for the end—it was obvious and boring. If he'd read it as somebody else's life, he would have had tears flowing down his face—the drama of a child struggling to survive, the loss of a hated father, the tragic loss of a dear mother, the love for an older man, the marriage that should never have been, the horror of war, the greed for wealth, the loss of a fortune, and to top it all, a suicide. And yet here he was, tearless. He couldn't cry, not for his life. He knew he hadn't understood what he'd had until he threw it away. His thoughts became lost in the harrowing images his camera-eye had caught. It was those poor souls that deserved his tears. It was life that had shown him death, and it was death that had shown him life. Understanding was all too late.

Beneath the brightness of his lone ceiling light, the mirror beckoned. His refusal to look in its direction was not accepted. His eyes pained within their sockets for his obstinacy. His eyes shot to the reflecting surface that rippled as if it were a still pool into which a pebble had just been tossed. Mr. Green tried hard to avert his gaze. The reflecting surface became a volcanic mass that spat.

Shards of silver knifed into already hurting eyes. The pain doubled. His summoned frame tiredly raised itself from the chair, and in agony made its way towards the mirror. It stood there—this feeble and distorted structure of a man—and stared at itself. It saw all the immorality that was in him. Slowly, eyes closed in shame.

Mr. Green wished for release. He wanted his soul to be free. Out of the mirror stretched centuries-dead leather grey hands that pulled his head back and ripped open his eyes. Through his pain, he heard hundreds of high-pitched voices screaming in unison: "This is your last chance".

Then silence slashed and a helpless fool fell crippled to the floor. The mirror now reflected only the sparse room as it returned to its still self— eyes would remain forever watching.

In a crumpled heap, blood trickled from Mr. Green's ears and nose. He lay there thinking his Great-granddaughter was his savour—she was the light and the light would not turn away from those held in the dark, seeking salvation. Her light gave what all living souls felt, and that's the tranquillity of hope. She was a sedative to his pain.

It was Friday the 13th and Lance stood looking out of his office window at the sky, lost in thought. He was in no way gullible as to think that bad things happened on this day. The clouds were a substance that wiped away blue, to make white. Snow was still predicted, but it was a guessing game as to when below would be as white as above. The season was calling for a white one.

Lance's working day usually started with Miss Swan doing her damn hardest to entice. This morning, she walked into the office, picked up yesterday's files and crouched in front of the filing cabinet as ordinarily as she possible could. The files went directly to their correct allocation. "Good morning, Mr. Lewisham," she said, upon standing up.

Lance guessed why the bend-over's had stopped. "Good morning, Miss Swan," he said. "James will miss the routine."

Miss Swan smiled. She wanted to grip Lance in her hand and excite him. She wanted Lance to take her panties down and pleasure her.

Lance walked over to her and took her hand. She didn't object. He pulled her close. She let him. He kissed her softly upon the lips. She was melting. She wanted to make love, there and then, on the office floor. If she had looked deeper into his eyes, she would have seen that he was stressed and not himself. He was drowning in his thoughts. He had fallen out of his small boat at sea, in a terrible storm, and was in no way capable of swimming to save his life. He was sinking between the waves of nightmares.

"Imogen..." he said, letting go of her hand and stepping back. "I wanted to wish you a Merry Christmas."

Imogen stepped forward, took his hand and pulled him back towards her. She kissed him tenderly. "Merry Christmas, James," she whispered magically into his ear. "Won't you come out to play?"

Lance looked like a lost puppy.

"Tell me, is it Lance or James that will miss my bending?" she whispered.

"Lance will miss it."

"After Christmas, would Lance like me to file in my usual way?"

"He would."

"Good… be sure to let me know when Lance wants to play," Imogen said, placing her hand upon his manhood.

"I will."

"Merry Christmas, Lance," Imogen said. She smiled, turned and left the office, leaving Lance with a swelling that was going to ache all morning.

The cold of the linoleum floor numbed Mr. Green to the bone. The floor had been his sanctuary for all the night and half the morning, but it was now more a tomb than a refuge. He had to think hard on why he was laying there. Looking up and seeing the mirror, was as if someone had stabbed Atropine into his heart. He sat up with a jolt, crawled to his chair and somehow managed to sit in it.

It was there that he thought only about his Great-granddaughter. It was there that he would stay until 10.00 p.m. on the night of the 21st. There was nothing more he could do.

Every day, in 'The Room of Truth', Sister Miriam went through agonising pain as she memorised the ritual for the mass of the dead. As her dark spirit strengthened, her body showed a woman in her thirties—beautiful, with flowing dark hair. It was only as she returned to her room, that her body withered again. Washing herself with blessed water filled her lined skin with the Holy Spirit's love; it was with that love that she prayed again. The dark pair of glossy reddish-brown wings her habit bore, had grown increasingly larger. She now displayed two parallel slits that ran vertically between her shoulder blades, each of which were 18 inches long.

Those behind the mirror watched Sister Miriam's transformation. They knew she didn't fear them, whatever form she was in. This made them spit and scowl at her. It was as she stood in front of the mirror that she taunted them, by slipping on a clean, white habit. The mirror rippled its disgust. Her devotion to her faith was her asylum. She was an inmate of Faith's calling. Her faith was her life, as it would be her death. It was her choosing.

CHAPTER TWENTY-NINE

Saturday 21st December was a cold, frost-biting day. The sky grew whiter as the hours of the day passed. It was 9 a.m. when Katherine graced her presence upon the day. She got up with feverish vigour, took to the shower with a delight that only someone expecting something good from the day would feel, and then flounced into the kitchen with nothing on but a dressing-gown and a smile. Her consciousness was aflame—all she could think about was what magic the night would bring. She knew that three others had differing feelings. One had selfish feelings, one had god-knows-what feelings and the one which mattered most to her, had hesitant feelings, or maybe, he had none at all. She hadn't seen him for over a week, so had really no idea of his thinking or his doing. But today wasn't a day to wonder about her husband's state of mind—today was a focusing day. She continued to focus on Sister Miriam's positivity. All she knew was that tonight, in some way, would remove Mr. Green from her husband's life. And if that meant giving all her trust to that Soulless Fucker's Great-granddaughter, then so be it.

Lance had no doubt believing The Sleeping existed. He had grown up knowing this since he was five. He also had Mr. Green telling him the same thing. That was all well and good in his head. The fact that Mr. Green died in 1929 aged 70, was firmly understood. But the hard fact that his childhood next door neighbour was the same Mr. Green, and aged

115, was difficult to believe. Plus the fact that Mr. Green had recently lived in the flat below him, and was, at this moment, residing in the house next to his wife, was a far cry from tooting-dandy. To say Mr. Green was now a living-dead 154-year old was beyond anyone's belief.

Lance had visions of men in white coats for those facts. If they had to give an analysis as to him being James, based on his sleep paralysis astral travels, then the van with the square wheels would surely be transporting him to pill-sedation heaven.

He had a condescending thought: *Aren't we all, sometimes, a little mad?*

His drooping eye-lids made his jaw slightly drop. His mask looked like he was indeed on medication. Sleep deprivation can only last so long—he hadn't slept for 72 hours.

A scream punctured emptiness. Lance was standing in the dark. He immediately thought he was back in the darkness that had nothing but Mr. Green's soul. He sat and refused to play The Sleeping's games.

Other screams came. His refusal was the same. Crying filled the space around him. His face felt wet with tears. They weren't his own.

A pinprick of glittering light appeared in the far distance. Lance immediately stood up, and without any conscious decision, started running towards it. Running wasn't as easy as his last visit here. It was as if a bungee cord was attached to him, and somebody was pulling it to prevent him from getting anywhere near the growing light.

The distant light called out the word: "Daddy."

Lance's heart tightened. He fell to the floor clutching his chest. Something snapped and he was liberated from his body. He stepped out of himself and walked freely towards the light.

A shape formed, giving a cloudy brightness to all around. Lance had seen this shape before. It was the burning cross of a man. One hand was showing him the way to the glittering light, the other, back the way he came.

From way back in the dark, starting as a faint whisper, he heard his name float up to him.

From the distant light, he again heard: "Daddy."

"Carry me with you…" the burning cross said, "for I am the light that will guide you."

Lance's mask now looked tortured. His eyes were wide and afire, as struggling to move was ripping him apart. He twisted his mouth to shout, but no words came. His body was as the burning cross. He twisted his mouth again and felt his face split open. Light shone from his body's abyss. He managed a weak cry to the woman he loved—his protector, Katherine.

From the dark corner of his room, a shadowy figure emerged and glared at him from eyeless sockets. It crossed the room, took hold of him, and pulled him upright. Lance looked deep into the face that was whiter than the place he had just been in. He stared down the black holes of sight. Far inside was a burning cross of a man.

Again he heard someone calling his name and believing it to be Katherine, he called to her.

The shadowy figure slipped back into its dark corner.

Lance stood in his bedroom, wearing only what he was born in. He slipped to the floor as if he had just been delivered into this world, warm and wet. The light of day would soon be advancing towards the darkest of nights.

He sat huddled in his own arms, feeling—as he often did—alone. The dark thoughts of rejection numbed the goodness that surrounded him. It had been hundreds of times that he had wished for his birth mother to seek him. It had been hundreds of times that he had cursed her for what she had done. It had been hundreds of times that he had forgiven her. And it was now, in his darkness, that he knew she would never come. He was suffering all her guilt for being born. He was a pawn in his life's shitty chess-game. Pawn takes pawn. Knight tries to take pawn—The Sleeping, wielding swords on horseback, charge towards him.

Standing up, Lance yelled: "Come and get me, you bastards," and raising his fist in anger spat, "come on—bastard takes bastard." Sometimes the darkness slept across him like an anaesthetist's mask, feeding him thoughts of self-loathing.

Light flooded his dark eyes. Hooves were heard galloping away. It wouldn't be light for long—today was the day with the shortest amount of daylight. Lance glanced at the clock; it was flashing 12:07:00. He immediately unplugged it and hurled it across the room. The clock hit the wall with a crack, sending plastic pieces in all directions. The red LED display, on the printed circuit board, still flashed with a life of its own. Lance picked it up and snapped it in half. The display fizzled as it died. Lance had a twisted smile on his face like he was The Sleeping, snapping Mr. Green's back.

The coffee cups rattled as Stephanie began making her first drink of the day. She had been up only fifteen minutes. It was now midday.

Imogen trudged into the kitchen, looking like a park-bench sleeper. Her bleary eyes smiled as she yawned.

"Make me one," she said.

"Morning," Stephanie said.

Imogen smiled. "Where's the White Witch?"

"Do you have to call her that?"

"Would you prefer I called her Rudolf?"

Stephanie's face colour matched the famous nose.

Sylvie walked into the kitchen, looking every bit a Snow Queen. She hadn't a silver hair out of place. Her skin was as white as her silk dressing-gown, which flowed open, revealing everything. She kissed Stephanie good morning, and smiled at Imogen.

Imogen gave her a look that said: Bitch. *How can anybody look that good when they've just crawled out of bed?*

"Are you going to the party tonight?" Sylvie said, still smiling.

Imogen wanted to slap the smile off Sylvie's face. "NO," she said with hidden anger. It had taken days to get over her disappointment, and now she had an albino stick insect attempting to scratch her eyes out—mockingly. "Do you believe in God, Sylvie?" she asked.

Sylvie looked bemused. "Maybe I do and maybe I don't. But no God can prevent anything happening to us whilst we are on this mortal earth," she said.

"That's so profound," Imogen said.

"No, it's a Gucci," Sylvie said, running her hands over her silk dressing-gown. She took Imogen's coffee and left the kitchen like a cold breeze.

"Hee-haw, hee-haw," Stephanie said, making another cup of coffee. "She can make a good point for an argument."

"Yes, I know, and I know you're only with her for her looks," Imogen said, feeling altogether ridiculous in agreeing with the donkey and at the same time being jealous of her.

"No," Stephanie said. "I'm with her because I'm not with you."

Imogen took her coffee in pensive thought. She actually wished she was incapable of love.

The hours of daylight vanquished to a thick-with-snow dark sky. Snowflakes finally fell. In a strange way, everything seemed to be lighter. The streetlights illuminated every ice crystal, giving them a divine vivacity.

Mr. Green had moved from chair to window, to view the spectacle. Katherine opened the front door and peered up into the heavens, like a child. Stephanie and Sylvie stood on the roof-garden and let the snow fall delicately onto their faces. Their eyelashes swept like car wipers. Imogen stood and watched in envy—her thoughts stormed as she imagined the night's festivity to which she wasn't invited. Lance was pensive as he sat looking at the snow falling past his window. He was thinking about the four other children born by his birth mother. He saw the snow as his childish, frozen tears falling down upon his wondering as to why they'd never sought him out or if they even knew he existed. The latter was reason enough to make him feel unwanted.

Sister Miriam was in chapel, praying. Sustenance of food had been her only reason to lapse from her beseeching for the heavenly kingdom's favour.

The snow was prettily falling, making everywhere look—for the time being—like a winter's picture postcard. Sister Miriam felt statue-cold as her giving heart pumped her blood loudly. The white habit she wore hung dishevelled and sack-like over her pained body. It gave her discomfort as she prayed, whilst giving thanks to the floor for its seeping coldness that numbed her torn flesh between her shoulder blades. *Merciful Lord...*

CHAPTER THIRTY

At 9.30 p.m. a taxi pulled up alongside a very smart red brick warehouse conversion to flats. All was quiet as the snow lay as a damper to the wheels upon the cobbled street. Katherine sat in the back of the taxi and looked out of the side window, towards the canal. Her eyes followed the straight lined blackness—that was even more of a perpetual scare in this now white covered land—until it repelled her to look anymore. She closed her eyes distastefully at the ugliness created by the Industrial Revolution in the mid-18th century, for its greedy demand on an economical and reliable way to transport goods in large quantities, and altered her view to the door from which, hopefully, two Pretty Things would excitedly emerge.

Like magic, the spikey-haired, delicately framed Stephanie opened the front door from safety, to let an androgynous beauty out into a night that was to swallow her into its darkest depths. Katherine's heart fluttered with anxieties.

The rear taxi door opened and the two scrambled in. They both wore skinny jeans—so tight, that nothing was left to the imagination—and calf-length boots. Brown fur bomber-jackets completed their identical evening look.

Stephanie's face radiated childlike warmth, whereas Sylvie's portrayed cool glamour as they both said: "Hi."

Katherine felt somewhat old in her flared jeans and jacket, as she warmheartedly smiled her welcome. "Hello," she said back.

The taxi slowly drove off. The compacting snow beneath its wheels crunched in the gentle falling snow. Stephanie looked out of the back window and waved up at Imogen leaning over the roof garden railings, blowing kisses. The furrows upon the snow-covered cobbles were already disappearing.

When Imogen faded from view, Stephanie turned and looked out through the windscreen at the falling snow glittering in the headlights of cars. She took hold of Katherine's hand as if it was the most natural thing to do. Katherine squeezed a child-like hand and prayed that her trust in Sister Miriam was defensible when it came to the protection she was going to give her husband.

It was Sylvie that spoke first: "Do we get to wear witches' robes?" she asked nonchalantly.

Stephanie grinned at Katherine.

Katherine really didn't know what they would be wearing, but assumed that the Pretty Things would be wearing some sort of sacrificial gown. Stabbing in the dark she said: "I think you will both be dressed in white."

The snow queen smiled happily. For the remaining period of the car ride, her mind was gone to the cat-walk in white-witch-robes amidst a blaze of photographic flash. Simple things pleased simple minds.

When Mr. Green stepped out of his front door, hopefully for the last time, he was exhausted and feeble. His torturous dead life's outcome would be in a few hours—his fate he had put in his Great-granddaughter's hands. He walked away from No. 111 Padstow Avenue with The Sleeping's grip tightening around his spine.

"Patience—for tonight he will be yours," he said. The words crystallised in the cold night air before vanishing into the falling snow. Rewardingly, the grip upon his spine was released.

Mr. Green craned his neck up and cast a soulless look into the night's abyss. The falling snow engulfed him as he disappeared into the dark of night.

Lance stood in the white-walled vestibule that led to flats 1 and 2 of No. 17 St Patrick Crescent, wearing—for luck—James' leather jacket. The white walls merged with the world outside in a cold, foreboding way. The thought of being with Mr. Green—in less than 30 minutes—made his skin crawl. That soulless old man, without a doubt, would call upon his haunting visions. Tonight was not a fight between The Unwanted and The Sleeping, but between The Unwanted and The Messenger. Would he spit in the face of his opponent or shake his hand and wish him luck? He would decide that later, as he closed the door to James' world—for what he hoped would be the last time—and trudged ankle-deep in snow, to his white covered Moggy 1000. His hands brushed the windows clear, and stung in doing so. A fighting life was still within him.

It was 9.55 p.m. when the taxi carrying The Protector and the Pretty Things pulled up outside the Sisters of Hope Convent. Katherine paid the driver handsomely, and wishing him a Merry Christmas, followed Stephanie and Sylvie onto the snow-deep pavement. Soon all three were huddled under the large sandstone arch, in shelter. The taxi drove away along the slushed lines made by other cars.

Lance came around the corner, just as St. Thomas' Church bell began to chime the hour. When the last ring of the bell echoed the night air, he was also under the large sandstone arch greeting his wife with a hug and kiss.

Stephanie felt oddly uncomfortable. She gave a reticent stare into Lance's face, as he looked at her with entreating eyes. The smile she gave was nonchalant—she pulled Sylvie closer to her to show she had no intention of hanging out his dirty laundry.

Lance warmly smiled back. "Hello, Stephanie," he said.

"Hi, Lance," she dryly replied.

In the park opposite, an unusual gust of wind swirled the snow into a glass-snowstorm effect. It was from the swirling that Mr. Green walked. The bent-double and grey-haired old man crossed the road with remarkable ease—he hadn't a flake of snow upon him. When he reached the others, his gaze craned upwards. It was only Stephanie who smiled a welcome.

Time fluttered—within a moment Sister Miriam was there. She opened her hands in welcome; from them glowed warmth.

"Tonight will be etched upon your eyes for all eternity—remember the Lord is always with you," she said, looking at each in turn. Her eyes stopped upon her Great-grandfather—sadness flooded from one, happiness spilled from the other—and blinked her thought: *Why me?*

A tender hand wiped the tears away as only a Great-grandfather could do. "We do what we do because it has to be done, not because it is right or wrong."

Sister Miriam turned and said: "Please, this way."

'Follow the Leader' began under the large sandstone arch and wound along an empty corridor, where it stopped briefly inside a room that used to be the infirmary—not used since the H1N1 influenza virus struck down several nuns in December 1920.

It was a cold room; the once clinical white-washed walls—that now took the colour of piss-stained mattresses—closed heavily their neglect about them. Several bare metal bedsteads flanked the walls and beside each were white dividing curtains. Even these were imitative of the piss-stained colour of decay. Upon the mesh of the beds, neatly folded, robes of linen waited—2 white, 2 green, 1 black, and 1 royal-blue.

"Miriam, this place has the stench of the dead," Mr. Green said.

"I haven't noticed, Great-grandfather, but try not to let it bother you. Now, please, everyone take the robe I hand to you, undress and slip the robe over your naked body."

The Pretty Things received white—Stephanie and Sylvie stood together and drew the dirty curtains. Giggling was heard as they undressed.

The Protector received light-green—Katherine hid behind her curtain. She undressed as quickly as she could. From her bag she took the Colt M1903 Pocket Hammerless and hung it about her flushed neck, as if it was a religious prettification.

The Unwanted received dark-green—Lance followed suit and changed.

The Messenger took his robe of ink-blue—Mr. Green, without any hesitation, did as he was bid.

The Custodian hid herself behind her curtain and stripped before her Lord. She knelt and prayed before covering herself in the colour of death's veil. The two parallel slits, which ran vertically between her shoulder blades, suddenly oozed a yellow pus in lubrication of what was to follow. She bared her hands, palms up, and said: "Merciful Lord, into your hands I place my soul." The two keys upon her person felt magnetically attached. She felt an unbelievable strength. She felt invincible.

Everyone was now standing in the middle of the room dressed in ritual accordance. The comfort of the robe felt different upon each wearer.

To The Pretty Things it was as if silk caressed their bodies.

To The Protector it was non-existent—she felt naked and free.

The Unwanted suffered coarseness, which caused him to itch.

The Messenger—who was under no illusion about fabric trickery—felt death's endearing cloak of coldness.

The Custodian felt fire upon her skin and a breeze foretelling the coming transformation.

"Why is this room so awful?" Sylvie said.

"Because the nun in the corner likes it that way," Stephanie explained.

Sylvie looked into each of the four corners with child-scared eyes and whispered: "I don't see anyone in the corner."

"I see a troubled ghost," Mr. Green said.

"Don't mess with the apparition," Sister Miriam said sharply. "It can be rather unpleasant when it chooses to—it remains here for self-punishment—and is never spoken to."

The apparition, being aware that it was seen, vomited violently on the floor. The stench of death tried to permeate into the soles of the bare feet of five.

The Pretty Things clung to each other. Lance, being a gentleman, led the scared things out through the infirmary doors into the corridor. Katherine shadowed, she didn't like what she couldn't see. Mr. Green accepted the nun's fate and also left the room.

Time fluttered as Sister Miriam stole the show again, 'Follow the Leader' continued away from the room where death lingered. Time fluttered again. The next thing, they were all standing inside a brick tunnel and Sister Miriam was locking a door behind them.

Here began the ten-minute walk.

Sister Miriam led the way along the descending floor to 'The Room of Truth'—everyone felt the underworld giving invite. The first key that unlocked and locked again the door to this hidden passage, was again about her person. The second key within its sheath was now in her hand.

The PIR motion sensor LED night-lights came into action as each person was detected, and triggered on/off unpredictably, until a uniform human chain kept all the lights on within the sensor's range. As the next light came on and the last went out, it could easily have been beheld as a mass of burning souls travelling down to hell.

The walk came to its end. A four-inch long round iron bar, with a pointed end was held before an encrusted, iron stud door that jewelled in the white light. The key was pushed into the correct iron stud and struck with the palm of the hand. Sister Miriam groaned sexual pleasure.

The key released its power, tumbling locks clicked and clunked. A final loud clunk gave authorisation for the lights going out. Three of the six screamed.

In the darkness, Sister Miriam removed the key, and like always, hid it about her person. Her gashed back seeped pus, pleasurably. A rush of energy gave her the strength to push open the door.

The door wouldn't let pass anyone into the room that was not named by The Custodian.

"I ask you humbly to allow The Unwanted, The Protector and The Pretty Things into your presence," Sister Miriam beseeched.

A breeze blew from the room, and upon it hundreds of voices could be heard talking in whispers. The door remained open. The lights remained off.

Sister Miriam commanded those she had brought.

"Come to me, Lance," she said.

Lance stepped forward to the voice.

"Take twelve steps forward," Sister Miriam instructed. "Allow entrance to Lance—The Unwanted."

Lance was positioned to walk the twelve steps. He did so and stood in anticipation.

"Come to me, Katherine," Sister Miriam said.

Katherine stepped forward to the voice.

"Take eleven steps forward," Sister Miriam instructed. "Allow entrance to Katherine—The Protector."

Katherine was positioned to walk the eleven steps. She did so and stood in anticipation.

"Come to me, Stephanie," Sister Miriam said.

Stephanie let go of Sylvie's hand and stepped forward to the voice.

"Take ten steps forward," Sister Miriam instructed. "Allow entrance to Stephanie—The Pretty Thing."

Stephanie was positioned to walk the ten steps. She did so and stopped promptly behind Katherine.

"Come to me, Sylvie," Sister Miriam said.

Sylvie, who was almost wetting herself, stepped forward to the voice.

"Take nine steps forward," Sister Miriam instructed. "Allow entrance to Sylvie—The Pretty Thing."

Sylvie was positioned to walk the nine steps. She nervously did so, while groping for Stephanie's hand. Stephanie took the hand in the dark, and held it tightly. She prayed it wasn't the ghostly nun.

"Great-grandfather, you must make your own way," Sister Miriam said. "The room will not refuse The Key."

Mr. Green walked the way without any guidance. The dark, he knew well. Whispering voices welcomed him into their world.

The Custodian finally took her seven steps. The door shut itself behind her. The lock tumbled and clicked. The lights came on. A surge of adrenaline gave Sister Miriam solo flight to enter the six digit code. Fifteen seconds later and the electronic safety panel beeped her acceptance. The panic button lit up The Custodian's face a sickly yellow. A breeze came from the only two vents in the room, giving breath of life. James had watched everything.

CHAPTER THIRTY-ONE

Mr. Green's face was full of surprise—he had expected supreme wonder. What greeted him was restrained horror. To him, the room was as evocative as a crypt—the walls were of stone, the ceiling arched as in a church. The wall of skulls was breathtakingly beautiful, in its macabre simplicity. Skull upon skull looked upon the room's guests. Each look bequeathed love of faith. The 'room' was first and simply a place for the initiated. The 'truth' was in its literature, and that combined, made its magnificence.

His Great-granddaughter's desk was a simple trestle of oak, and was bare of any goods. Standing by its side, against the wall, rested its smaller brother. As a book-shelf, it was covered several books deep, in spines of cracked leather. It was the iron wheel on the wall that drew his attention. *What did it do?*

Lance walked from oak door to oak door—both identically covered in shiny black iron and studs, both solid, both locked. He had no idea which one he had just passed through, into what he could only interpret as the inside of a tomb. It gave the same feeling as the vestibule of No. 17 St Patrick Crescent—except the painting that did nothing to cheer was now wall-size. There was no mistaking which way up this one was meant to be. To him, it was there for the sole purpose of saying: "Your head goes here after they devour you." There was no way in hell that he was going to apologise for his unimportance. The iron wheel on the wall worried him. *What the hell did it do?*

Katherine stood in respect to those that gave their life willingly. She was in no way going to give her husband's life willingly, not as long as she had something around her neck that could blow away the fucker that wanted her to. Her eyes moved to the iron wheel on the wall. *What in God's name did it do?*

Stephanie's hand slipped from Sylvie's. Both Pretty Things looked at the wall of skulls in adoration. Both heard whispering that implored union.

Sister Miriam moved around like a wasp on attack, touching the walls in ritual declaration and positioning the assembled. This was how the symbol of the 'Heavenly body' or more commonly known as the penta-gram, was made. Upon the five wounds of Jesus stood The Pretty Things, The Protector, The Messenger and The Unwanted—Stephanie and Sylvie stood at the top of the pentagram, closest to the wall of skulls. Lance was at the bottom. Katherine was on the right and Mr. Green was on the left. All stood silent under The Custodian's touch—spellbound. The Pretty Things were given a free spirit's touch.

Finally, Sister Miriam stopped central to the pentagram and bowed to the wall of skulls. She muttered words that were meant only for the dead to hear, and it was only the dead that heard. Twelve of the dead an-swered.

One skull fell from the wall. It hit the floor—shattering in conse-quence. Sister Miriam slipped off her black robe to reveal her pained and weeping wounds. Eleven more skulls fell from the wall, all shattered like the first.

Twelve broken skulls crumbled to dust and blew about the room. Sister Miriam spread her arms in crucifix fashion. The dust flew to her and veiled her aged body.

As her dark spirit strengthened, her body showed a woman in her thirties, beautiful and dark-haired. Small closed wings pushed out through the slits upon her back and rested in dark majesty. The dust now appeared as a black, backless gown that covered her lusty nakedness.

The Custodian breathed deeply and said aloud: "Merciful Lord, I give to you myself as I have always done. Be pleased with me…" The remainder of her prayer was silent. The Lord heard the believer that spoke to him. The silence crushed upon the ears of those present.

The believer lay flat-faced to the ground, and fully aware of her actions, spread out her arms again. The wings upon her back grew painfully. The distance between oozing rip and winged carpal joint reached eighteen inches.

The Custodian didn't scream—she bore her pain. Pain was part of her living. Her hands, which had spreading clawing fingers, burnt upon the floor as she continued to pray in silence. Finally the wings spread out to cover and appease the burning of her fingers. The silent prayer finished.

The Custodian slowly raised herself and stood to her full magnificent glory. Raven-black wings slowly closed. The Custodian was whole—once again.

She decreed to 'The Room of Truth': "My breath is in the wind. Upon my calling of your name, you shall come and be worshipped. You are the darkness from which there is true light. You are no longer the fallen, but the risen that will shine upon all who follow. Your light will engulf us all."

The Custodian walked around the wounds of Jesus in an anti-clockwise direction, touching and releasing only three from her spell.

Lance knew the feeling of sleep paralysis well. Like always, he was sweat-wet-through, and hard. His robe bulged embarrassingly. The angel of death before him was bewitchingly beautiful. Fantasy saw a sex-wicked Imogen, in dark-angel wings. In his head, he recited the Lord's Prayer and faltered... *Why is it I always get stuck at the point 'as we forgive those who trespass against us'?*

Katherine looked disgusted at her husband's arousal, as she struggled with wobbling like a drunk. Under these circumstances she could forgive him. She checked to see if what was about her neck was still there—a deep breath confirmed. She had no idea if what she had just witnessed was real or not. But whatever the creature was that took Sister Miriam's place, it still commanded her trust.

Sister Miriam's transformation smiled at her in a knowing way.

"Faith," The Custodian said.

Mr. Green looked no different. He had been captivated by the sheer brilliance of his Great-granddaughter and not by any hypnotic charm—he had stood and watched willingly. He would do anything asked.

The Pretty Things, in their spellbound state, were steered to stand with the others, in a line, facing the cranium sculpture.

The Custodian touched the walls, muttering prayers. She returned to the centre of the room again and said, in a calm and collected voice to the iron wheel:

"For those who ask for you... you shall come.

"For those that follow you... you shall come.

"For those that give themselves to you... you shall come.

"For those that call to you… you shall appear.

"I call to you… Lord Lucifer."

The iron wheel on the wall began to slowly turn, anti-clockwise. The room shuddered on a Richter scale of 4.0. The quaking ground produced a rectangle of dust that hissed into the air—the vacuity between the two worlds had been broken.

From the bowels of 'The Room of Truth' emerged a slab of stone, large enough for a body to lie. Its surface shimmered like a tarmac road in summer heat. Three of the assembled stood captivated. The iron wheel stopped its slow, anti-clockwise turn.

"The Key is needed," The Custodian said.

Mr. Green stepped forward.

With a jerk, The Custodian pulled from deep within her wing, a feather with no pigment.

"Raise your sleeve from your left arm," she said.

The Key did as he was bid. The shaft of the feather was driven hard into old white flesh that hung from the bone. There was a small spurt of blood, the feather absorbed until it was saturated. Mr. Green didn't flinch.

The blood-red feather was withdrawn and tossed upon the table. It landed as hard as a striker hitting its cast metal resonator. The bell sound bled into the stone of the table.

Nine times this was done. It was midnight. It was time.

Lance held Katherine close—she was shivering with fear. The Pretty Things stood as vacant puppets, held by the kind, free spirits The Custodian had called to the room. No expression revealed what they were going through behind that kept state of being.

Mr. Green, on The Custodian's command, positioned himself by the table and cradling an arm that felt lifeless, placed it upon its surface.

L. Sydney Abel

Blackness flowed from open wounds until a dark shadow lay amidst the shimmer. The Key was rejected from its lock with a force that sent Mr. Green flying backwards. The Key hit the wall, not with a clatter but with a sickening thud. A hurt Mr. Green rose to his feet and stretched his back in defiance. He spat at the table to show his rage.

Katherine was beginning to feel pity for the thing that was in cahoots with its captor. She had a feeling that she was not in 'The Room of Truth' only for her husband.

A black, shapeless form slipped from the table and like a serpent, crossed the floor. When it reached The Custodian, it stood as a man, naked and with horns—decaying black flesh filled the air with the stench of death.

"You dare to use The Key to bring me," it hissed. Its glare shot towards Lance.

"I do," The Custodian said. "In 'The Room of Truth,' The Sleeping are at my command."

The naked, horned man hissed.

Lance instinctively knew the time. He looked at the face that wasn't hidden behind a mask and felt his muscles go—he slumped to the floor like he hadn't a bone in his body.

The Custodian spread her wings in power and flapped them provocatively, cloaking The Sleeping. When she closed her mantle, she stood there as a naked man with horns. Dust formed a covering of black, to hide a thick and lengthy erection from view. Womanly power drew from this male all its potency, until the consumed was flaccid and useless.

Katherine began begging her husband to stand, but the words implored made no impact. Lance was twitching and whimpering like a dog.

Lance was shielded by a woman that loved him. Katherine's hand reached for the object that was tied around her neck. Her hand shook as she withdrew the Colt M1903 Pocket Hammerless. It steadied as soon as

210

it pointed at the face of the winged man with horns. Her finger was itching to pull the trigger.

"Who are you?" Katherine screamed.

"I am The Custodian—I am its transformation and I am The Sleeping… I stand as all of those, but inside, I remain the one in whom you placed your faith, Sister Miriam."

Katherine searched the eyes of the creature that stood before her. The eyes were Sister Miriam's soulful smiling eyes. Katherine's finger seemed glued to the trigger. It took several seconds before it relaxed and the gun lowered.

"Faith is all-powerful," The Custodian said.

CHAPTER THIRTY-TWO

The haze on the table grew tall; it moved feverishly about, secreting him from the call of a breath of wind.

A hooded figure was summoned from shadows.

"Bring forth the soul of The Messenger, Ambrose Green," commanded The Custodian.

The shadows drew back the hooded figure as Mr. Green stood a little straighter.

A spark of light appeared and grew; a small glass box, no bigger than your hand, floated and turned about on its own axis. It emitted beautiful rainbow light from all sides.

Mr. Green smiled his gratefulness towards his Great-granddaughter's manifestation. It didn't return the smile.

"I say to all The Sleeping: This soul is now in 'The Room of Truth', under the gaze of him who commands you, and is in my keeping," The Custodian said powerfully.

Hissing from the shadows disapproved of such actions.

"A body that is living and yet dead can only be destroyed by the tool that bequeathed death," The Custodian said to him that was on the table.

No response was indication enough to continue.

The Custodian caused time to flutter—Mr. Green knelt at the feet of The Protector.

Katherine now understood why she was asked to bring Mr. Green's Pocket Hammerless.

Mr. Green closed his eyes, and Katherine did what she so naively tried to do the last time she was alone with the man that was bargaining for her husband's soul—she shot him in the head. The noise and recoil it gave resulted in her dropping the gun—it hit the floor the same time as Mr. Green. It wasn't the way she'd put the cold steel on the space between his eyebrows and just above his nose, the craniometric point, which had scared her. It was the way that it had indented into his skull that had made her realise he was indeed human and might have regrets. She also hadn't asked him if he was sorry for what he had done. Being judgemental in seconds can spit doubt at you afterwards.

Katherine looked down at the corpse with the dark red growing halo, and had no misgivings. *That soulless fucker deserved it.* And yet, it was the strange smile that curled upon a peaceful face, which gave her the odd feeling that she had done the man an immense favour.

Wings flapped and the naked, horned man was released—decaying, black flesh filled the air with the stench of death again. Powerless, The Sleeping slithered away and was seized upon the table. It lay stretched out amongst the haze and cried its agony. Katherine held her hands over her ears to prevent the screams from boring into her brain. The high-pitched frequency made her stomach turn.

The nauseating cries bled into the walls and eventually stopped.

The Custodian stood in her full magnificent glory. Raven-black wings slowly closed. The Custodian was again a woman in her thirties—beautiful with dark flowing hair.

The body of Mr. Green remained lifeless upon the floor. Beautiful rainbow light covered a blood-haloed corpse, like a shroud.

Lance was running around his dark world shouting: "Take me, you horned bastard!" He was eager for the one that he could recognise to retaliate. He had visions of ripping the horns from its head and slashing them deep across black, rotting skin. He wanted this merciless attack… he wanted the fight so much.

The stench of death flooded Lance's nostrils. He lurched and vomited uncontrollably—he wasn't alone in the dark any longer. *I cannot fight something I cannot see!*

He felt cowardly and shouted from his darkness: "KATHERINE!"

Katherine shook her whimpering dog.

Lance jolted and cried: "I can't fight anymore."

"You must," Katherine begged. "You have to."

"I don't want to."

"I know, my darling."

Tears streamed down Lance's face—he was broken.

The Custodian bent down and took the hand of The Unwanted. "James, every time you break away from their world, you win—consider yourself victorious again."

Lance stood up with the feeling he had only won on a technicality. Deep inside, he knew that winning was the only thing that really mattered. How he won wasn't worth fighting himself over.

The Custodian saw The Unwanted rekindle. She embraced him with her wings. Her hands held his manhood; his pleasure became her pleasure as she drew potency from him. Seconds later, he was flaccid and useless. Wings closed. Lance had no doubt as to who'd won that fight—even though there had been no fight in him.

The look on Katherine's face was one of bewilderment. The look The Custodian gave her was again of 'TRUST'.

Lance withdrew; he again stood by his wife's side. His heart skipped a beat when he saw Mr. Green's lifeless body bathed in rainbow light. His shocked heart fell in empty pity and almost simultaneously rose to bursting serenity—his eyes smiled through watery vision at the soul that hovered there.

The Custodian had taken all but one of the powers the room had to offer. Stopping where she did was the lowly thing to do—someone supremely greater had once gone further.

It was time to make personal resolutions. She withdrew from her person, a piece of paper that had written resolves—it was time for it to be burnt. She offered it to the haze. The haze took it and burnt it in a blaze of blue. She knew what it meant—Satan would pact his help for an offering of a sacrifice.

The haze upon the table fell like a whore's knickers—quickly from payment and for the promise that more was to come.

The Custodian had demonstrated her power. Him, from whom a breath in the wind called, looked pleased. What was expected came down from the table. He was everything The Custodian had visualised. He was nothing at all like the image Lance or Katherine perceived. He was a man of flawless physical beauty—skin as dark as the place he had been sent to, radiated lightness. He was hairless and wingless—fire had devoured his outward facade. His appearance, as naked as he was, showed his immense power—it was everything you had been told it was.

"My Lord Lucifer," The Custodian said, with a courteous bow.

Satan smiled at the use of his heavenly name.

"My beautiful angel," he said. And on cupping the calling's face with his hands, whispered: "You are not what you appear."

The Custodian said nothing; she felt him enter her and caress her soul. She swooned.

215

"Has your learning, Miriam, brought you closer to me?" Satan said, walking towards the Pretty Things.

"It has, my Lord."

"Do you think that demonstrating your power shows devotion to me?"

"Yes, my Lord."

"We shall see," Satan sneered. A proud walk was made towards Katherine.

Katherine stood before her husband; she outwardly stretched her arms in defiance to display her loving shield. It was without concern for her own soul that she forcefully said the word: "No."

Satan only had to smile to make such a futile stance perish in its innocence, but with respect to The Protector, he stepped away. The Sleeping collects the souls of the unwanted; it had always been that way.

When he did smile, arms fell to their sides and obedience was evident.

"Katherine," he whispered upon the air. And with the invisible pressure of a kiss upon her lips, spoke directly into her head: *I can be your Beast if you so desire.*

Katherine looked at him with a hunger. Widening eyes moved over his body and to the area she evaded looking at before—she was not disappointed. It took the willpower given by an angel to look away.

Katherine was red-faced when she eventually shut her eyes.

Another time then, floated into her head.

The Custodian opened her eyes and withdrew from deep concentration.

Satan moved over towards Lance's side.

Lance was refusing to show fear—he was so determined, that he deliberately looked straight into eyes that burnt at his soul.

Satan spoke to the room: "I see a servant of God and the Lord Jesus Christ."

The shadows hissed loudly.

"Greetings, James," Satan said with a spitting tongue. "A double-minded man is unstable in all his ways."

The hissing turned to awkward laughter.

Satan glided like a shadow and appeared alongside his dark angel. "My presence requires more than that which is merely for The Sleeping," he said.

The Custodian brought forth a Pretty Thing—an offering for her requirement. She removed from the dispensable the white gown which covered desired flesh. Countless shadows took the form of their God— harmless mimicking apparitions chanted the rite of welcome.

The Custodian lifted her spell for the Beast to cast his own.

Beauty stood before the Beast. A naked man stood in aroused excitement. He placed one hand over Sylvie's breast, cupping it acceptably; the other hand now slid down her tummy and over her pubic bone, and under—his finger slipped gently inside her.

Minutes later he withdrew his finger and playfully sucked on it. Her taste was of mermaid that had leapt from the waves to fly upon the ocean breeze—free-spirited.

Beauty knelt at the feet of the Beast.

The Beast now also knelt. He kissed with a penetrating tongue, commanding his prey to bring him to climax.

Sylvie did as she was told; her mane of hair was held by the tamer of horses as she, in her act of oral stimulation, brought her Poseidon to foam.

Lengthening fingernails flashed at Sylvie's neck. They slashed—blood sprayed. A body fell to the floor. The shadows bathed in beauty, as her soul danced out of the waves and into the fire.

Katherine's screams ripped at her own throat. "Fuck you, whatever you are," she cried, as she dropped to the floor in a crawl for the gun. Picking it up, she pulled the trigger—the bullet penetrated Satan's blackened skin. A puff of smoke, with a spit of fire, showed the point of entry between his shoulder blades.

The Beast rose to his feet and turned. The look he gave Katherine was of pure pleasure. An orgasmic open mouth allowed the bullet to travel through all damnation and drip from its keeper's tongue.

Katherine lunged forward. *Fine! So the gun was only Mr. Green's Achilles' heel. What or who, is yours?*

Her attack was like scratching smoke in which she fell to the ground, angry and frustrated. It seemed that the Beast could imitate shadow for protection—not that he needed protection. He liked the play of this particular spirited woman—if he wanted too, he could take her. He wouldn't, not forcibly. When her fight with him was over, he would, with open arms, welcome her—that was when she would submit to any request he made, willingly.

"You fucking coward!" she screamed.

"If you plan to keep her, James, you must leash her," Satan said sarcastically.

James was trying—the kicking and biting he received was evidence of him trying to do just that—it took all Lance had to hold her down.

Sylvie lay flat upon her back. Blood was pumping from her neck.

The Custodian spread her wings and covered the bloodied body. The fever of death, under cover of black, broke. The snow queen became heavenly—the soul that danced amongst fire ceased its torment and returned to the waves—as the wings of The Custodian turned white. Blood from the lamb sent amongst wolves, soaked into snowy feather. White gorged until it could become no redder.

CHAPTER THIRTY-THREE

A new transformation flamed its power. The blood was returned from whence it came and white wings fluttered restoratively. Sylvie lay in a dream—the slash to her throat was like a flapping gill.

The transformed was standing before Satan. Spreading her wings, she sent a few feathers to fall and cover the wound made by the hand of the sinner.

The shadows screamed their condemnation as they hid amongst the skulls that saw. The dust forming The Custodian's backless gown, fled holy flesh and reformed as the watching upon the wall.

Satan screeched. The Sleeping—in their hoards—were called.

Black animations with white faces began coming through the walls. Grasping hands appeared, skeletal faces emanated.

Lance cowered in his wife's embrace; the gun in her hand was as useful as a spent oxygen tank under water—Lance was going to drown.

No complete entity managed to get through. Screams tore at the very soul of existence.

"'The Room of Truth' permits entry to those only of my calling," The Custodian said, in her glowing naked truth.

"And shadows," Satan sneered.

"Shadows are everywhere, my Lord, and we know that shadows, in whatever imitating form, cannot harm."

The wall of skulls suddenly burnt in a pure light—the souls of sinners were being pulled back from the darkness. The light the souls exuded cast The Custodian's shadow upon the Beast. The inverted cross was Satan's sign, but seen from the sender, then it was a cross that was holy.

The Custodian folded her wings and knelt before her Lord. Standing in her wake, was a man with his arms outstretched in crucifix fashion; he burnt with the fire of love—Lance had seen this vision at least twice before.

The light filled every part of the room, obliterating shadow. Lance dropped to the floor as if in prayer. Katherine stood and felt as a new-born child—pure of heart. Stephanie was oblivious to all happenings. Sylvie slept in healing dreams.

Satan grasped at the source of the rainbow light, committing the glass box to collapse into non-being. Mr. Green's body rose again, this time by the Devil's command. A crumpled, old man looked down towards Lance and heaved a heavy sigh. His eyes then moved to Katherine and his sorrow showed. When he looked at his Great-granddaughter, her eyes were full with tears. They exchanged loving smiles.

The burning cross pointed into the pure light. Mr. Green walked frailly towards it. His body was pained by years of abuse; his mind on the other hand, felt suddenly at peace. Satan squeezed at the soul within his grasp. Rainbow light splintered out from between black fingers and fragmented into incongruous angles. Mr. Green bent like a twig, his spine twisted and turned. But he kept on walking until he burnt in the light. His body's cremation was blessed by a ball of rainbow light leaving Satan's hand and appearing in the hand of the burning cross.

Satan screeched again. The Sleeping—in their hoards—screamed their withdrawal and returned to the underworld.

The burning cross burnt brighter. Satan felt his power diminish and stumbled to all fours like the Beast he was. Whimpering, he crawled to the table and leapt upon it, his eyes searched out Katherine. Beseeching-ly, he looked into her eyes and saw her pity. Then a mountainous mist appeared as a veil and surrounded the Beast. Through the mist, a hand snatched at The Custodian. A piece of her was taken before the Beast dissolved amongst the mist, dropping as rain to the place of his sending. The wheel on the wall turned clockwise, reinstating the stone table as part of the floor.

The burning cross extinguished with the light. The wall of skulls re-mained, but only as cranium bone and nothing more.

"A soul for a soul, a messenger for a messenger, a key for the sleep-ing," was heard from deep within the shadows.

The Custodian still knelt; she was also no longer a beauty of youth. She was herself and a good twenty years more—she looked weakened. Naked, she trembled. Her wings had changed yet again—there was at this moment no reason nor understanding—in appearance, they resembled the pigeons she fed every day.

Katherine rushed to cover her—the black gown was slipped over wrinkled flesh and brown speckled-wing.

Sister Miriam observed Katherine with soulless eyes.

Katherine shrank back; the fear that Sister Miriam had taken her Great-grandfather's place was too much to take.

Sister Miriam spoke kindly: "I'm not a living dead, Katherine, but heaven knows, I feel as my Great-grandfather did. A soul has to leave the dead. But a soul cannot fully leave a living body, even if given freely. Fragments linger on living tissue, like memories. I just have to build on that memory in order to survive, but it is not going to be easy. I can see into the dark world of shadow now. I hear their voices call to me. I am now The Messenger. And I will refuse The Sleeping."

The Sleeping, in their understanding of obstinacy, used command by directing pain. Sister Miriam's back began to bend. She was going to be very much like her Great-grandfather.

Lance was as far away from his old enemy's guise as he could possibly get. His back was pressed hard up against the door. He needed to get out. Katherine might have faith in this woman, but he hadn't. He could handle a bent-double and grey-haired old man—he could pummel his head with his fists, if he needed to, but he couldn't, for any reason, hit a woman.

An image of yellow light suddenly came into his mind. It was Claire who put it there; she was standing in a small room playing with a yellow orb—she kept tapping it. On first thought, he assumed it was Ambrose who was the orb and that Claire was waking him up from years of dark sleep. His second thought had a slow lucidity to it.

It seemed that Claire wanted him to act upon something—she was jabbing at the yellow orb fiercely and mouthing one word. His mind's vision popped like a balloon and the noise it made sounded like: BUTTON.

It appeared that Sister Miriam heard it too. Her soulless eyes shot at him with the same desires as The Sleeping—she was seeing as they do. Lance moved like lightning. He slid across the floor and was facing heavenly, when he came to his stop beneath the trestle desk. The panic button's yellow light lit his face—his eyes slit and tracked sideways. Sister Miriam was on her feet; she sidestepped Katherine and moved like shadow. This was her first time manipulation by The Sleeping. She slithered alongside Lance and was equally slit-eyed. Lance quickly pressed the button. Next thing, it flashed red. Lance spun from under the desk as Sister Miriam's back bent again. The agony she cried made her fall into unconsciousness. She was now in the darkness. The key was used to open the void between worlds.

The Sleeping started coming through the walls, as Katherine was frantically trying to pull the emaciated Sister Miriam out from under the desk. The flashing red light lit the hollows of the nun's cheeks like a dropped flare that hit the sides of a chasm as it fell, making her look like the phantom of hell.

The Sleeping came into the room like the Schutz-Staffel—this was no protection party. It was Nazi S.S. looking their decaying worst, whose all-black uniform was designed by Death itself. Masked white faces, carrying soulless searching eye-sockets, advanced towards The Unwanted.

If God moved in mysterious ways, then this was one of his worst performances, as the lights suddenly went out. The Sleeping were now darkness within the darkness—home from home, and groping with expertise.

It was from no intervention on God's behalf that the lights went out. It was down to human manipulation with the light's timer, or the use of the panic button. Darkness was deemed a defence, but not in this case. The blinking, red light flashed upon the floor like the reflection of an exploding bonfire night cracker, putting stars into the eyes of the living.

Some of The Sleeping took the time to explore the entranced Stephanie—she was unknowingly emitting a rainbow aura as a shield. They hissed to her in secret whispers. It was then, in their understanding vibrations of her lack of concern in such matters, that they made the slither nearer towards The Unwanted. Not once did any of them approach Sylvie—she had a more celestial protection.

The Sleeping gathered around Lance; they buried him within their own darkness. Some punctured his veins and travelled in some drug rush to his brain. Others mixed with the air he breathed and became his need to live. He was their junkie, and he was going on a bad trip. Simplicity would be if they could physically kill, but such as they were, that was impossible. Their need or trick was human terror; they would feed from the heavenly soul and eat away at its goodness until the living gave up life, freely. The wrong things done in Lance's life were traits of others that had sucked upon his soul. Wickedness moves in shadowy ways.

The panic button had been flashing once every second—now the countdown of sixty was up. The locks inside the door, on behalf of emergency calling, began to tumble—loose chains had become taut, giving movement to weights within the walls.

Feeling choked by the stench of decay, Lance coughed his lungs up. His mouth had the taste of the putrid water that lapped upon the shore of hell, where the wretched dead putrefied.

Lance frantically tore at the blackness around him. He had fragments of decayed weave fall between his fingers, only to return to whichever of The Sleeping's garb it was ripped from.

The door clunked as it unlocked and opened outward like the hand of offering. Lance, again, heard the voice of the burning cross: "Carry me with you… for I am the light that will guide you."

Lance held his breath and ripped away at the darkness. He cleared his mind and thought only of goodness. Katherine became his beacon. Then there came his light—it burnt a hole in the dark—and Lance ran towards it. The Sleeping pulled at him without avail.

The Unwanted was outside 'The Room of Truth', in a passageway that was lit by a multitude of stark, florescent strip-lights that ran above head height for over a mile. Under this bright light, the walls, which were of yellow brick, replicated the colour of blood-streaked urine, as the earth behind leaked its way through. The Sleeping knew it impossible to follow into such a place. Hissing loudly, they retreated back into the walls from which they came. This fight was far from over.

Katherine had Sister Miriam in her arms; she rocked the unconscious nun like a child.

Lance bitterly tried to get back into the room, by using physical means, towards an invisible barrier. His leaving 'The Room of Truth' was cancelation to The Custodian's request of entry. All his kicking and punching was useless. It was like trying to break through a wall made of two-inch thick Plexiglas with all the characteristics of jelly—plainly not possible. He could clearly see his wife cradling a bent-double, grey-haired old woman who was exactly the same as her Great-grandfather was—a problem.

"Katherine," Lance called into the room.

Katherine looked up with tears in her eyes.

A problem-solving thought suddenly hit Lance: *What if Katherine had shot her?*

Sister Miriam opened her eyes. "That would be murder, James, and you've seen where murderers go."

CHAPTER THIRTY-FOUR

Sister Miriam pushed herself from Katherine's arms. In pain, she crawled to the trestle desk and lying under it, pushed the button. Yellow, again, slit the eyes of The Custodian, as she blindly punched in an emission code. The lights came on. A signal was sent...

Sister Miriam's faith was starting to give her the will to fight those that had the power to manipulate her. Her back twisted—she would learn to endure her pain.

Within the walls, devices clanked—the door began to close. Lance tried holding the door open—it swung shut, almost taking his fingers.

Katherine slumped against the door. Her back had pushed against it with all the failings of pushing back the tide. Her eyes stung with tears and her throat burnt emotion.

"Lance..." Sister Miriam called, "Katherine, for the time being, will be safer with me... she played her part well... she'll see you soon... now go."

Lance thumped and kicked at the door. He shouted his wife's name, he pleaded for her, but it was all in vain, the room had silenced the outside world. Katherine heard nothing, but she did feel as if her back was pressing against a panicking heart—just as it often did when in bed and Lance was being visited by The Sleeping. She touched the door, as if she was waking her dreamer. The panic stopped.

There was no alternative for Lance but to go. Spookily, Mr. Green's account about 'The Room of Truth' being at the end of an 11th century brick tunnel, far beneath St. Thomas' Church, came suddenly to the forefront of all his thoughts. *If this is that tunnel, then all I have to do is follow it until I find myself above ground, inside a church dating back to 1571. There, I'll make my way back to the Convent, and back to Katherine.*

He set off in the direction of what he hoped would be St. Thomas' Church. *Was Mr. Green telling the truth?* He ran with urgency, for new hope was his power. He tried not to worry about Katherine—she was more than capable of looking after herself. *After all, she has the Pocket Hammerless.*

Some of the overhead lights would sometimes dim, go out, and then flicker fiercely as if they had faulty starters. He needed the light to keep the shadows at bay.

An anxious, large man wearing pink-silk pyjamas was carpet-slipper running down a tunnel. He looked quite the simpleton, but was far from it. In his hand he clutched a medical bag, which he hoped he would not have to use.

Only minutes ago, the alarm device on his person had almost frightened the life out of him. He was woken violently to find his bed clothes clinging to him as all around flashed red. His thoughts were that the sheets had manifested as dark demons and that the devil was rising from hell. And here was the scenario—he was heading to a room were shadows took to shape and a wheel on the wall led to a stone in the floor that brought the Devil himself.

As far as he could remember, his predecessor and his predecessor's predecessor had never received the secret emergency call and so, he assumed he never would. It gave him plenty of thought as to how an emergency was called and answered before electronics came into play. He had taken his offered employment in the safety of never being made redundant or homeless. The supplementary money, for the extra duty, of which only the few knew about, was an added bonus. He was to be part of a team of sextons, and to be seen as the fat one with little brain. The few saw his given disguise as perfect, as they told him his jobs' true meaning. He was a sacristan, a name derived from the Medieval Latin word sacristanus, meaning 'custodian of sacred objects'. His loyalty and faith had earned him the right to swear his oath of secrecy concerning 'The Room of Truth,' even though he had no idea what was kept beyond its door or what its purpose was today. He obeyed the ruling to never use the keys for any reason other than the room calling for emergency. His alarm device—apart from its ability to flash red and wail at 75db—also had a yellow LED that lit whenever the room was occupied. He could never see himself escorting a Pretty Thing to their Lord, as he much preferred his pretty priests-to-be to come to his rooms, and be his alone. He could play the queen and remove them from court if he so wished. He had the ability to see auras and if they looked anything like his then, after becoming conversant, bedroom calls were talked about for his assurance to keep their fleshly urgings a secret and for him to say good things—on the topic of their devoutness—to the right people. Scratch my back and I'll scratch yours. Blackmail is ugly, sin is expected, but the results of accepting—as in these cases—were on most occasions enjoyed by those partaking. Ask and your sins will be forgiven.

Several things weighed on this individual's mind, two being foremost at this time:

1 – The weight of the tons of earth above his head.

2 – Would he lose his position if he couldn't help the person he was being called to?

He ran with his hand to his chest and over the device. He was ready to silence it again if it suddenly repeated its wail. The red light lit his pyjamas like a flashing neon sign at a brothel.

Sister Miriam released Stephanie—the free spirits had been glad to help someone who they were evident to. Their protection was to blind and deafen, to talk of faith and for remembrance to only the good. Their explanation about Mr. Green's absence from the room was told with the approbation the man deserved. Stephanie would, in time, understand.

Stephanie looked happily spaced-out. She could recall everything leading up to the positioning before the wall of skulls and nothing of the horrors afterwards. It was that memory of Mr. Green's prediction of his soul's happiness that gave her the soppy smile, which shone unashamedly into a room that until recently, had seen the worship of the sinful to the sinner.

The wondrous power of heavenly-angel feathers had finished washing the Beast's touch from Sylvie's flesh. An irremovable scar across her pretty white neck would one day become as white—rendering it almost invisible. God's reminder is God's goodness.

Sylvie sat up as a mere mortal, somewhat slightly dazed and as naked as the day she was born. She remained like most individuals, not able to understand what had been seen or felt. It had all been horribly nightmar-ish—its truth was in the visible reminder it left, to show how frightening-ly real it had all been.

A free spirit's kiss upon the white neck sent the scarf of feathers to fall softly over breasts and gather between legs. It was then that Sylvie felt the goodness of heaven enter her and warm her soul. The nightmare was forgotten—it simply dissolved from all thought.

It was Sister Miriam who covered Sylvie's body—firstly with her arms and then with the white robe—before leading her, by the hand, to the door from which they'd entered. It was there that a kiss of 'thank you' was pressed upon the forehead of one so naïve.

Stephanie looked about the room for the last time. It was with happiness that she went and stood by Sylvie's side. Her hand slipped into one open and waiting.

"Where did Lance and that sweet old man go?" Sylvie asked.

"Mr. Green had to leave by a different door, as for Lance… let's assume he vanished up his own arse," Stephanie said.

Sister Miriam listened and smiled. "It's time to go, dear," she said, turning her head towards Katherine. "Lance is going to need you."

"Is that the truth?" Katherine said.

Sister Miriam nodded. "Yes, Katherine, it's the truth. Lance will always need you."

Katherine got to her feet, and remembering to pick up the Pocket Hammerless, stood with the others. She saw the look of faith upon Sister Miriam's face and felt that her own had almost gone. What little remained, was hanging by a thread.

A signal was received…

A one-second wail pierced air, ear and heart. The large, running man jolted as if he had received an electric shock—resulting in muscular incapacitation—and hit the ground like a legless drunk. The device stopped its flashing.

Eyes flew to the device—the yellow LED was on. It was watched angrily and anxiously—then it went off.

The heap of a man accepted it as a false alarm and that the fool or fools in the room, had left.

Sister Miriam was mentally and physically exhausted, as 'Follow the

Leader' began again. The way stopped inside the old infirmary. The room absorbed them back into its neglect—the stench of death increased.

The bare metal bedsteads gave up clothes for robes. Dividing curtains lost their use as naked bodies—absent of vanity—started putting on attire of familiarity.

Katherine put on her clothes, knowing that Stephanie's eyes were wandering over her curves. She dressed with the exciting manner of teasingly undressing.

Stephanie dressed like Sylvie was her mirror—only she was not looking at her reflection.

When dressed, Stephanie looked at Katherine and silently mouthed: "I'll call you."

Katherine smiled and nodded.

The ghost of the room came and stood by Sister Miriam.

"Miriam," it said, "will you now talk with me?"

"When they have gone," Sister Miriam replied, "and only if you stop vomiting."

The apparition gagged and agreed by not vomiting.

No words were exchanged as Katherine bundled up her husband's clothes and speedily left the room. Sister Miriam let herself smile as she felt a small part of her soul return, removing some of the layers of added age. Katherine was regaining faith.

Stephanie gave Sister Miriam a great big leaving-hug and remembering the instruction to never speak to the apparition, obeyed, as she didn't want to be puked upon.

Sylvie's parting was with a hug and a lip-to-lip kiss. Sister Miriam felt a fleshly desire and repressed it instantly.

A smile and a wink from Stephanie told her that there was no objection.

The smile was returned with a look that spoke of a different time and a different place—Sister Miriam was very much like her Great-grandfather.

The tunnel walls echoed the one-second wail. The sound rebounded towards Lance—it hit him and died. Lance hesitated as his heart missed a beat. It took him several seconds before he was back to speed. Calf muscles had begun hurting the moment he started going uphill. *Pain is only pain,* was his sedative thought. All this running was taking him towards a shape in the distance.

Lance peered into the bleached space ahead of him; he saw what looked to be a giant pink marshmallow. He passed it warily—his thoughts had no comprehension.

The heap of a man's eyes followed what was thought to be a ghost, wearing a dark-green robe, and who looked to be in a hurry. He let it go without saying a word. He was thankful it hadn't spoken to him. He knew it saw him, because its eyes looked right at him.

An odd thought struck him: *What if it is me who is the ghost down here?* His thought made him shake his head of all such nonsense. The huff he provided was his final dismissal of such ridiculousness. He decided to wait five minutes and allow time to let ships in the night navigate their own passage.

Sister Miriam was the only remaining living person in the infirmary. She sat on the bed—the stench of the room was as foul-smelling to her as it was to her companion. A perfume with a head note of fresh corpse, a heart note of liquid tissue, and a base note of rotting dead was indeed a reason to feel nauseated and she almost vomited.

"I thought it was only me and the old man who could smell the stink," the ghost said.

Sister Miriam gagged and said nothing—her face had reclaimed its under-the-desk hue as her cheeks puffed out to make a downward-turned mouth that salivated.

"It's far easier to be sick," the ghost said. "Let it out girl, go with the flow. It's better out than in."

"No! I can control this."

The ghost sat beside a stomach-lurching nun and said matter-of-factly: "It didn't go quite to plan, did it?"

"Not exactly to plan," Sister Miriam said, "but it did make results."

"Will you always have wings?" the ghost asked, like a child.

"That all depends on the good Lord."

The ghost thought about such a declaration and sat in wishful silence.

CHAPTER THIRTY-FIVE

The quicker you run the quicker you get there, Lance thought. And he was right. There came rushing towards him an end. It was not at all what he expected—the tunnel had been bricked up. Crudely placed bricks—as if done in a hurry or by someone other than a bricklayer—filled his vision, and going by the state of the pointing, had been laid from the other side.

Lance put his shoulder to rough brick—it was solid and possibly more than one brick thick, and wasn't going anywhere. He tore at his hair in panic of the same.

In his sheer loss of positivity, that was making his skin writhe, he sat like the giant pink marshmallow he had recently passed, and fell backwards through the wall. To his astonishment he had fallen behind a wall canvas, that was a photographed replica of the tunnel's wall itself. It was over a door's width. *How come I didn't see that? Was I blind?*

Negativity, in its snake-like form, slithered from his pores as he now stood at the foot of someone's stairs. He moved up them like he was playing snakes and ladders, leaving the serpents of hell slithering far below. At the top, he stood in shadowy darkness and amongst a mass of winter coats on hangers. His wits were about him as he manoeuvred his way through them, only to find himself stepping from a wardrobe into a pink bedroom and feeling somewhat surprised. He now knew where the pink marshmallow came from. He closed the doors behind him, not realising how appreciative he should be, that they didn't have mirrors.

He scanned the room for a door—there it was by the bed. He moved towards it. He was in a hurry to leave. The bedside table ignited in the corner of his eye or more likely, it was the book on it that caught his attention. It was the bright red 12:07 of a digital clock that burnt from the book's cover and imprinted itself onto his retina. He rubbed at his eyes as if they were full of smoke. Then it was through watering eyes that he saw the rest of the cover—the Angel boy with its uncanny resemblance to him as a child, was unnerving. The title's black words 'THE SLEEPING' made the hairs on the back of his neck stiffen.

He grabbed the book with anger and flicked along its pages. There was nothing… it was empty of words. Wait! Towards the end pages was written:

At the top he stood in shadowy darkness and amongst a mass of winter coats on hangers. His wits were about him as he manoeuvred his way through them, only to find himself stepping from a wardrobe into a pink bedroom and feeling somewhat surprised. He now knew where the pink marshmallow came from. He closed the doors behind him, not realising how appreciative he should be, that they didn't have mirrors.

Lance couldn't make his watery eyes any wider if he tried. His eyes stung as they searched the walls for a mirror—there wasn't one. His finger was trying to turn the page but something was refusing it. *But what if I can read my own future?* He tried harder to turn the page…

"Now, Lance, you wouldn't want to do that," Mr. Green said. "You have to believe that your future is not yet written. The fight is still on."

The book slammed closed and flew towards the wardrobe. It flapped in the air like a pigeon being hit by a stone and burst into flame. Ash fell in place of feathers and disappeared. Mr. Green's fleeting presence was an eerie comfort.

Lance left the bedroom. He was standing at the top of more stairs. He was unsure whether to go down them. The gloom seemed consuming as he stood there in what little light there was. He looked for another door— one appeared opposite…

He now entered into another bedroom—this one was void of all possessions. The walls had damp in the corners. Wallpaper showed squares where pictures once hung. The light coming in from the window cast a cold whiteness over the walls' loneliness. Lance looked down at his bare feet. He had disturbed the floor's dusty surface. The dust moved in the air and glittered.

The room had another way out—the window. *Sod that!*

Lance turned to leave by the stairs; he noticed that the wall to the left of the door showed that some large piece of furniture had once stood there. The hairs on his neck stiffened again—it was time to go. He left this empty space, closing the door behind him.

Looking down the stairs, Lance could see red and white diagonal tiles. His eyes drew to the church effect of light coming in through a stained-glass door window. He did something he hadn't done since he was a child, when frightened of the shadows in the bedroom. He jumped the stairs in one leap. He needed out of this house.

"The Unwanted is at the house at the tunnel's end," the ghost said.

"Yes, at St. Thomas'," Sister Miriam said. Her face was smiling radiantly.

"No, he's not at St. Thomas'. I told you 'he's at the house at the tunnel's end'."

Sister Miriam's smile fell. She stared at the ghost. "But the tunnel goes to St. Thomas'."

"But he's at No. 7 Chestnut Avenue."

"Who told you this?"

The ghost smiled. "The old man did."

Sister Miriam ran to her room. The ghost countered by vomiting, not with wanting, but with needing. It was better out than in.

A mobile phone was held and a message made—every press upon the keys resulted in the burning of a fingerprint. Back pain was suffered, pain was accepted, defiance felt good.

Message sent:

Lance is at No. 7 Chestnut Avenue. God be with you.

Katherine was running along the snowy streets, when her mobile buzzed and vibrated—she heard it because it was the only thing making a sound. She slid to a halt and withdrew it from her bag. It was flagging up, '1 new message'. She anxiously read it. Within seconds her mobile was displaying a map.

Lance was outside. The streetlights lit house windows, reflecting back over snow-topped sills. The blackness behind glass showed a closed barrier to the cold, stark light as people slept in their own peaceful darkness—it was either that or he was alone in the dark world. He welcomed such brightness and stood under a lamp, bathing in its charitable light. He didn't care that he was ankle deep in snow and that his feet were beginning to freeze.

He looked towards the house from where he had fled. It was like everywhere else—the pink bedroom was evidently at the back of the house. He took to his heels and staying in the light, ran down the street. He needed a bearing—something or someone to guide him to the Sisters of

Hope Convent, and to Katherine. *Why the hell didn't I keep my phone on me?*

He must have been running for 10 minutes, when he suddenly stopped. He didn't know why he had stopped other than something felt extremely odd. He was back where he started—the charitable light above his head flickered. *I took a wrong turn, that's all.*

He set off again… This time when he came to the end of the street, he didn't turn left or right, as he might have done. He deliberately sought the same direction and crossed to the street opposite. He ran with greater speed and purpose. But it was all to no avail—he was soon back outside the house he'd fled and where a charitable overhead light bid him welcome, by flickering once again. Angrily he looked at the house. *Are you pulling me back? This is stupid! I'm leaving...*

Running at least warmed his feet, and the blood that pumped from his heart was comparable to a central heating boiler supplying radiator-like limbs. A sudden crazy thought about being dead and stuck in this getting-nowhere-place, struck him. He was thinking ridiculously—he was sure he wasn't dead. *I can't recall dying. What if I didn't jump the stairs but fell… am I dead at the bottom? But what if I'm not dead, but positioned in some hideous broken heap, dying? And is it because I'm not dead that I can't leave?* He now had the feeling that it was he who was pulling himself back. *I'll go see!*

Lance warily opened the door and went in. He stood in a pool of coloured light and felt a proper fool. *What was I thinking?*

"Hello! Is there anybody there?" he called. He was hoping the person who liked pink would come and tell him how to get away from this place. His mind was whizzing—he knew the pink marshmallow wasn't The Sleeping; they wore black and wouldn't be seen dead in pink. That particular thought made him laugh out loud. His laughter echoed about the hallway and died with his question.

He climbed the stairs—his hand gripped the dark wood banister for comfort. Halfway up he stepped on the hem of his robe and stumbled. His balance was lost—his grip from the banister gone—he was leaning backwards. Seconds ago, his thoughts had foretold he'd fallen. He didn't call for help—he might need his last breath.

"I won't let you fall." The voice was clear. The holding hand was strong. The voice and hand belonged to none other than Mr. Green.

Lance was drawn upright and helped to the top of the stairs. He stood trembling as he looked at the old man—it was different somehow, looking into the face of a ghost, rather than a living dead—and warily smiled his thanks.

"You're not fighting at your best, Lance," Mr. Green said. "Keep fighting. Your Protector is on her way."

"Who's keeping me here?" Lance asked.

"What a stupid question," Mr. Green said. "The light will soon come and dissolve those that belong in the dark. The end of the solstice marks the end of your waking seeing. Soon you will be fighting as you always did, in nightmares. Make a friend of Miriam. Keep your enemy close."

Mr. Green smiled approvingly and began to walk away, down a bright corridor that wasn't supposed to be there.

"Ambrose…" Lance called.

A girl came running to Mr. Green and said quite sweetly: "Will Daddy be safe now?"

Mr. Green said with honesty: "We think we walk our own path, my dear, but often it's been walked on before." He took the girl's hand, said no more, and continued walking.

Lance could do nothing but watch both walk away, 'til the corridor that wasn't supposed to be there darkened and faded from his sight…

It was from behind one of the bedroom doors that Lance could hear movement.

He put his ear to it and listened. He was aware that he could distinctly hear a radio. The frequency was shifting from station to station, just like the old radio sets when you spin the big control. Fine-tuning brought easy-listening to the pink marshmallow in his bedroom fortress.

Lance took hold of the door handle. He turned it in silence. The door refused to open. He rapped his knuckles hard upon it. The music got louder. His bare foot struck just below the handle—nothing came of it but a dull thud.

The landing recalled its silence. The music softened and Lance again put his ear to the door. The radio's frequency shifted through old-time music hall songs to a church choir, singing full vigorous love for God—a brow creased in intensified listening.

Lance, again, knocked on the door. The radio got louder.

Rage made him hurl himself at the door—either he was weak or the door was strong, but the thud his shoulder gave didn't make any form of impression. The door didn't budge one bit.

It might have been that the door opposite opened by a rebound of force. But Lance knew different—the room was, this time, reintroducing itself.

The room was entered nevertheless; it was as silent as the grave. The door closed all by itself. Lance studied the room more carefully this time. Bare footprints led to the window and he voluntarily stepped into them. A strange feeling that he had somehow made them, gave him an odd relief—he walked his own path.

He was now standing, looking out the window. He had to focus past his ghostly reflection to see the world outside. It had started to snow again. Somehow that made the room feel warmer—maybe the charity from the street lamp gave an extra gift of warmth under blanket of snow.

Coming up the street, raced a lonely figure. It ran towards his charity—feet strode the very path he'd just made.

Breath condensed upon glass. Hand wiped over glass. Knuckles rapped on glass. Heart flamed before glass.

"KATHERINE!" shot hot from Lance's lips, and falling upon the glass as a solitary flame, dampened to a whisper.

Shadows suddenly appeared in his window of light. The Sleeping were many. They pressed their white faces up against the dividing barrier and stared at him. Smoke-like fingers seeped between ill-fitting casements and wrapped themselves about his wrists.

Lance could hear them laugh as they pulled on him. His hands were soon pressed up against the thin, dividing barrier. He felt drawn to their world... to be with them.

I'm about to die.

The scar on his wrist was aggravated by tighter gripping fingers—there was no way he was going to be cut again. He pulled backwards and brought The Sleeping in. They were about him like a thick fog—they were the walls, the ceiling, and the floor.

He could vaguely make out the light from the window. Turning away from it—hoping to reach the door—he ran.

With a bump, he hit the wall. His hands spread out... groping.

"KATHERINE!" he shouted.

His hand found the door frame... he felt a sharp sting to his foot. Light momentarily lit the room—his soul was briefly on open view.

Katherine saw the upstairs window of No. 7 flash bright. *I'm coming, my Darling.*

She stepped into footprints that the falling snow was trying hard to make disappear.

Lance felt an extreme anxiety—warmth slunk along the sole of his right foot—as he slumped against the wall.

The room welcomed back the light from the outside, as all the shadows but one left. A face so white and so close as to kiss, seemed to smile in satisfied excitement. Lance shut his eyes...

When he opened them, he was alone and stood in a pool of blood that soaked up the dust. He balanced on one leg while searching his pained foot... blood spat from a sharp needle-like object embedded within his skin. He pulled it out; a severe pain shot up through his body. Lance dropped to the floor in pain. A splinter of mirror, about two inches long, was held tightly between his fingers. Blood ran freely from his wound, non-stopping.

Lance heard the front door open and close. He heard footfall run upon the stairs. He heard the door handle turn. He then heard no more...

12:07 THE SLEEPING is a novel—it is also a story. Whether it is true or fictional has no bearing whatsoever. But what is true, is that things like THE SLEEPING are all too real, albeit to some people only. Some of you sceptical out there can pull from the story what you like. But whatever you draw or conclude, the fact remains, it is only a story—or is it?

The sensation in which some people, when either falling asleep or waking, briefly experience an inability to move, is commonly known as Sleep Paralysis. It's described as a state of transition between wakefulness and rest, which has the effect of complete loss of muscle strength. It can happen at the onset of sleep or upon awakening, and it often has disturbing visions. For example: The feeling that someone has entered the room and is now sat upon you, to which you are unable to react due to paralysis.

Now if that sounds like a nightmare, then I suppose it is. But that's only in the fact that it is a wakeful nightmare. I use the word 'wakeful' because to the recipient of such a nightmare, they feel they are awake.

Sleep paralysis—known also as hag's syndrome—is real. It is now being described, by some, as a paranormal experience. To those who have this supernatural involvement: "Keep on fighting whoever it is that comes, because fighting may just keep you alive."

I've wondered why this doesn't happen to everyone. My deduction is based only on my own circumstances and that is, for some reason, they want my soul. And do you know what? Those dark shadows aren't going to get it. Well, not yet. I fight on…

I can only describe my visits as punishment, nothing more.

I don't thank you for my punishment, so who and whatever you are, and when, and if ever, we meet, you have got a lot to answer for. Amen.

www.ingramcontent.com/pod-product-compliance
Lightning Source LLC
Chambersburg PA
CBHW032032240626
47154CB00003B/878